Fields of Iron

A steampunk adventure novel
Magnificent Devices Book Eleven

Shelley Adina

Moonshell Books

Copyright © 2016 by Shelley Adina Bates. All rights reserved.

No part of this publication may be reproduced, distributed or transmitted in any form or by any means, including photocopying, recording, or other electronic or mechanical methods, without the prior written permission of the publisher, except in the case of brief quotations embodied in critical reviews and certain other noncommercial uses permitted by copyright law. For permission requests, write to www.moonshellbooks.com.

This is a work of science fiction and fantasy. Names, characters, places, and incidents are a product of the author's imagination. Locales and public names are sometimes used for atmospheric purposes. Any resemblance to actual people, living or dead, or to businesses, companies, events, institutions, or locales is completely coincidental.

Interior layout by BookDesignTemplates.com. Cover art by Claudia McKinney at Phat Puppy Studios, with images from DepositPhotos.com, used under license, and the author's collection. Cover design by Kalen O'Donnell. Author font by Anthony Piraino at OneButtonMouse.com.

Fields of Iron / Shelley Adina—1st ed.
ISBN 978-1-939087-61-4

*For Linda McGinnis
with thanks to Derrik Senft
for the use of his shop*

Praise for the bestselling Magnificent Devices series

"This is the first in a series of well-reviewed books set in the steampunk world. For those who like the melding of Victorian culture with the fantastic fantasy of reality-bending science fiction, this one will be right up their alley."
–READERS' REALM, ON *LADY OF DEVICES*

"An immensely fun book in an immensely fun series with some excellent anti-sexist messages, a wonderful main character (one of my favourites in the genre) and a great sense of Victorian style and language that's both fun and beautiful to read."
–FANGS FOR THE FANTASY, ON *MAGNIFICENT DEVICES*

"Adina manages to lure us into the steampunk era with joy and excitement. Her plotline is strong and the cast of characters well interwoven. It's Adina's vivid descriptions of Victorian London that make you turn the pages."
–NOVEL CHATTER

FIELDS of IRON

1

Somewhere in the Wild West
February 1895

The witches who inhabited the canyons and tributaries of the mighty Rio de Sangre Colorado de Christo had controlled its sandstone fastnesses for fifty years. *La bruja* who went by the name of Mother Mary had been the first child born to a member of the original band of runaways, escapees, and criminals. A former dance-hall girl who had run away from an abusive husband and a worse lover, Mary's mother had accumulated a number of companions on her journey to freedom—whores, Navapai laborers, even a Canton scientist who had been forced to be a laundress by the railroad company. Mary had grown up knowing no father, but many mothers, sisters, and friends. They had found the river and its bewildering series of canyons, tributaries, and caverns, to say nothing of its ancient, abandoned cliff dwellings, to be a more welcoming home than the towns of the Texican Territory, and had taken up residence in a country where no one would find them.

Slowly the word spread among the abused, the dispossessed, and the destitute in the desert reaches of the Wild West, and deep into the southern reaches of the Texican Territory that ended at the azure Caribbean, that if one could only get to the river, one could find safety and food and employment. For the witches did not merely haunt and hide. They built. What they lacked in physical strength they hired or invented. The Canton scientist specialized in steam-powered and hydraulic engines, and was only too delighted to teach any who cared to learn about how to control the flow and speed of the river, how to go up and down the seven-hundred-foot cliff faces with the ease of a house spider, and how to construct the underwater traps with which they inspired terror in the hearts of the invaders from the west. These were the enemy—men from across the mountains who coveted the power and commerce the river could make possible if they could only get their hands on it.

Oh yes, they coveted the river and its power. But the witches had no intention of giving up their fierce independence or their arrangement with the small but cheerful armada of steamships plying the races and reaches of the river. No one outside of those echoing canyons could understand how the steamships could navigate the rapids. Most believed the boats to have been wrecked years ago. Some believed there had to be powers of magic or time travel at work.

And so the stories spread.

But the witches knew, and smiled, and counted the gold that bought more iron and more supplies and seeds for their crops and the occasional pretty gown.

Gloria Meriwether-Astor sat upon a wonderfully carved stool made of silvery driftwood from a faraway ocean and tilted up her face for Ella Balboa, Mother Mary's daughter and the girl who had saved her life the week before. With her fingertips, Ella rubbed white paint into Gloria's skin from hairline to throat, and then picked up the paintbrush with its load of black.

The bristles tickled as she traced whorls and webs and flowers around Gloria's blacked eyes, a pattern that, when it was completed, would look like lace upon Gloria's skin and render her completely unrecognizable. *Una bruja.*

"So what happened to the Canton scientist?" she asked, doing her best not to move her lips.

"Jiao-Lan climbed the starlight stair about fifteen years ago, but before she did, she was able to teach two generations of girls what she knew, including her daughter May Lin. One of her students, Stella, is probably the smartest of all of us. She'll be heading upriver with May Lin soon to add some improvements to the original mechanisms that control the rapids. She's been teaching the younger ones, and they'll take over when the time comes."

Ella blacked Gloria's nose and added a flourish between her eyes, then tilted her head to examine her handiwork. "Blue lips, I think, to set off these roses, and I have a crown of silk roses for you. I think pink and blue go better with your hair, though tradition tells us red, for love and blood. Oh!" Her brown eyes, starred with long lashes, widened with an idea. "We could play brides!"

Gloria laughed, and was surprised to find that the paint did not stiffen or crack. Considering the hour and a half that Ella had taken to create her work of art, she was grateful that a single smile would not spoil it all.

"My dear friend, while I confess to having been the unwilling recipient of a number of proposals, it seems that playing brides will indeed be as close as I ever come to that happy estate."

"Oh, no," Ella said quite seriously as she applied pink paint from a tiny pot to this spot and then its opposite on Gloria's cheeks, where presumably there were roses. "You are so beautiful. I am quite sure that had you not left your former life, you would have been married within the year."

"And I am quite sure that you are sweet to say so."

Gloria could not tell if the other girl's color changed under her own paint, but her gaze dropped in embarrassment at the compliment.

Gloria went on, "Fortunately, there is more to marriage than beauty on one side and wealth on the other. My friend Claire Trevelyan Malvern has found love and companionship with a man who is her equal in intelligence. While my standards in that regard must be set considerably lower, I aspire to such a union, too." She paused, gazing past Ella's shoulder up at the wide ribbon of brilliant blue visible from the stone veranda on which they sat, where the canyon walls admitted a view of the sky above. "I am willing to wait for the right one," she said softly. "And to remember that a man's worth is not measured by social skills or wealth, but by temperament, and generosity, and courage."

"Men aren't the only ones with those qualities." Ella carefully applied blue from another pot to Gloria's lips, and then stood back to admire her handiwork. "Could you not make a home among us? Because you know, there is plenty of generosity and courage and intelligence among our ranks, if that is what you're looking for."

"I have seen that already," she agreed. "May I see what you've done?"

Ella waited a moment, as though she expected Gloria to say more, and then got up to fetch the mirror. It was silver, with a chased handle, and could have held its own on any dressing-table in Philadelphia. Gloria held it up and gazed upon the wraith it reflected.

"My goodness, you're talented. No one would know me—all they can see is your beautiful art, Ella. Now I truly feel like one of you."

The other girl dipped her head. "*Gracias, amiga.* It was my pleasure. Will you have the crown and veil now?"

"Oh, why not? In for a penny, in for a pound."

The much abused canvas pants in which Gloria had spent much of the past two weeks had finally given up the ghost when she had climbed the hidden spiral stair up to the witches' main palace in the cliffs a few days ago, and she had been obliged to raid the coffers in the storage rooms. Nothing would force her to part with her custom-made corset with the gold coins and her mother's ring sewn into the lining, but now she wore a ruffled, bleached cotton skirt with several layers of point lace, and the embroidered blouse Ella had given her on her arrival, cinched at the waist with a corselet of tanned and polished leather. Along with the gray wool blanket and boots she had brought with her, she also now possessed a chemise edged in lace, a linen shirtwaist, and a brocade waistcoat with no fewer than four hidden pockets, as well as a short canvas duster against the night's chill. If she could only come across another pair of pants that fit, she would have nothing left to wish for.

Now, her white blouse and creamy skirt would have to do for playing brides, a thought that made her want to giggle. She had never played brides in her life. But with Ella, who may have been past the age of making her debut but still possessed the innocent joy of childhood, it seemed like just the thing to while away a warm late February afternoon while they waited for Captain Stan and his crew to come back with news of the war brewing in the west.

Ella climbed the stone steps and Gloria heard her opening and closing a chest in one of the rooms above. She came down a moment later bearing two veils over her arm and two crowns of silk roses.

FIELDS OF IRON

"Where did the veils come from?" she asked curiously, dipping her head so that Ella could lay the filmy square upon it, with one long point falling over her face. It was edged six inches deep in the most beautiful embroidery Gloria had seen since— "Why, this looks like Burano lace, from the duchy of Venice."

"I don't know." Ella fitted a crown of pink and blue roses over the veil and handed Gloria the mirror once more. "Things come on Captain Stan's boats and we never know where he gets them. Sometimes I believe it's better not to know. Oh, don't you look like a bride, to be sure!"

Gloria gazed at her reflection. She certainly didn't look like any bride she had ever seen—not like Claire must have looked in the ivory satin Worth gown Gloria had sent as a wedding gift two months before. But all the same, the lace was delicately sumptuous, and the rose crown made her feel rather regal, if one overlooked the face painted to look like a celebratory death's head.

"For we are the dead," Ella had explained to her the other day. "Many of us have grown up on the river, but many have come here from the Fifteen Colonies or the Texican Territories or the seaside temples in the southern jungles, to leave their lives behind and be reborn as the dead. So we celebrate both death and life. Besides, it frightens the stuffing out of the Californios if they get a glimpse of us."

"Your turn." She set a smaller veil on Ella's glossy brown curls, and crowned her with red and white silk roses and trailing black ribbon. "I think we make a beautiful pair of brides, don't you?"

Ella turned this way and that, then brought the mirror over so they could look into it together.

"Dearly beloved," Gloria said, laughing, "we are gathered here today in the presence of this lizard and that pair of eagles to witness the union of ... whom? Ella Balboa and ..."

Gloria couldn't see Ella's eyes very well behind the embroidered mist of her veil, but she could see a glimmer of a white smile.

"Never you mind. It's a secret."

"Ah, a proxy wedding," Gloria said. "Very well, let us proceed. Ella Balboa and Meredith Aster, standing as proxy for a person unknown. Do you, Ella, take this—" A chugging sound echoed up the canyon and Gloria stopped. "Is that the boat?"

"I think it is. Finally! Come, let's go meet them." Ella pulled off her crown and veil, and headed up the steps at a run, Gloria right behind her. "We may keep the crowns, but we mustn't let Mother Mary catch us soiling these veils. She's saving them in case there's ever a real wedding here one day."

Gloria contained her impatience as Ella carefully folded the lacy squares into their trunk, then smoothed her hair and set the rose crown back on it as they ran down the passage.

The others had clearly heard the *Colorado Queen*'s engine, which had a distinctive wheeze Gloria suspected needed a mechanic's attention. She and Ella were joined by several others streaming out onto the lowest of the terraces, where the dock was. A few yards upriver was a stone building containing the engine that controlled the great underwater chain that ran from here to the opposite bank. The wreckage of a number of the Californios' attempts at invasion lay along the banks and submerged in the deep waters of this section of the river. Ella had told her that in the late summer, when the river was lower, you could see the hulls and the pale shapes of skeletons.

Captain Stan leaped across the gap between deck and stone dock without waiting for a gangplank, and waved his shabby bowler hat at the witches waiting on the terrace. "I have news!" he shouted, pushing his navigation goggles up on top of his head. "We'll just tie her off and be up shortly. How about something to drink? Spying is dry work."

Sister Clara, who was Mother Mary's second in command and the chief provider of food, snorted and turned away to chivvy her usual helpers into setting up tables and bringing out a welcoming feast. It wasn't until everyone had helped him or herself to flatbread, spiced meat, and vegetables, and had a tin mug to hand containing anything from cactus juice to lemonade to whiskey, that Mother Mary finally said, "Well, lad? You've kept us on tenterhooks long enough. What is the situation downriver?"

Captain Stan swallowed his whiskey with the air of a man who believes that mouthful to be his last. "It isn't good, Mother, to be blunt. What Miss Aster tells us seems to be true." He glanced at her, and Gloria primmed up her mouth.

Of course it was true, for heaven's sake. If he had been so foolish as to think she was making it all up, and had wasted precious days going downriver with the intention of proving her wrong, that was on his head. She had never misled them in any way ... except perhaps in the matter of her real name. That she was not prepared to divulge to anyone.

"The Royal Kingdom of Spain and the Californias has somehow got hold of a massive piece of machinery they call *el Gigante*," the captain went on. "We had not been in the water meadows an hour before we saw it stumping along in the distance. The entire town is talking of it."

"What is that?" Mother Mary asked. "The Giant? Is it a train?"

"No, far from it. In shape it looks like a man as tall as a building, and in purpose it is a weapon."

Gloria sat bolt upright, as though lightning had passed through her. "Yes, it possesses a cannon in one arm and one of Mr. Gatling's rotating guns in the other. I told you about it before. It has a pilot's chair in front of a viewing port in its chest, room for a crew of two, and great hydraulic legs."

Captain Stan gazed at her with a mixture of astonishment and annoyance, his mug dangling empty from slack fingers. "What else do you know of it?"

"I did not know its present location," she said. "If it is the same one, the Californio ambassador to the Fifteen Colonies brought it out here on his train, having purchased it and all the other armaments and munitions I told you about from the Meriwether-Astor Munitions Works in Philadelphia. I last saw it firing at me, moments before I was blasted off the top of a hill near a town called Resolution, in the Texican Territory."

Eyes wide, Ella covered her mouth with her fingers, and Clara and Mother Mary exchanged a glance.

"The soldiers called it *el Gigante*, but in practice it is a steam-powered mechanical behemoth, operated from within by its crew. But—" She fell silent as a new thought struck her. Who could the operator be, if the man who had had that responsibility had been drowned in the same flash flood that had nearly taken her own life? How had it covered all those miles between Resolution and the water meadows known as Las Vegas? It had been on the battlefield when she was taken from Resolution by the Californios as a prisoner on *Silver Wind*, so how had something so enormous been conveyed here without that great locomotive?

Frankly, it was impossible.

"There must be two of them," she murmured. "This must be the first, sent out in a previous shipment."

Then why had it not been among the manifests she had read before embarking on this godforsaken journey?

"Anything else you can tell us, Miss Aster?" Captain Stan inquired with silky civility.

"It cost ten thousand pounds to build," she snapped and, too late, realized her mistake.

"My, my, what a lot of unusual knowledge our drowned kitten possesses. I wonder what else she knows?"

Now Mother Mary and Clara and half the women in earshot were staring at her. Oh, if only she could wind back the last thirty seconds and take a single moment to control her temper!

"That is all I know," she said stiffly, controlling the urge to leap to her feet and run up the steps to the room she shared with Ella. "With the behemoth and the cavalry of mechanical horses, the Ambassador's troops will be difficult to fight, indeed. That is why I have been encouraging you all to ally yourselves with the Texicans. They possess airships—and bombs—that are our only hope of overcoming these mechanical menaces."

A moment passed in which the only sounds Gloria heard were the gulps of a riverman slugging down his whiskey, and the rush and gurgle of the torrent below.

At last Mother Mary turned back to the captain. "What other news have you?"

"Miss Aster's previous information about the war has proven correct. The Royal Kingdom is mobilizing, and not everyone is happy about it. There are acres of tents pitched between the town and the river as each rancho sends its conscripts. But many are not there willingly. While some share the late Viceroy's dream of regaining the Texican Territory and its supposed caches of gold, others have no interest and are content to raise their families on their farms in peace."

"On the backs of their tenants' labor," Clara said grimly. "And that of their captives."

Gloria had learned that Clara's daughter Honoria had been captured during a raid, and was now somewhere on one of the massive ranchos, forced into servitude until she escaped … or died. Captain Stan acknowledged the lost member of their company with a lift of his tin mug, and someone obligingly filled it.

"What of the present Viceroy?" Mother Mary asked, gripping Clara's hand in support. "Does he share his father's dream? Word has it that he's barely out of the schoolroom, and the studious sort. He would have gone to university in the old country had his father not died and left him to inherit the throne."

"All true, from what I hear. One wonders how a bookish boy could be convinced to go to war."

"It is part of their culture," Gloria said bitterly, still stinging from the experience of her own capture. "The boys are trained to war from infancy—though from what I understand, no one has actually fought in two hundred years."

"Remember what she told us—they bought these mechanicals to do the fighting for them," one of the rivermen said. He was the mechanic who ought to be looking after the boat's engine, but what was he doing? Drinking. If a captain cared about his boat and its crew, Gloria thought sourly, he ought to have words with the man.

"Would that we had one of the Texicans' airships, and could travel to San Francisco de Asis in a matter of hours to ask him," Captain Stan said with a laugh.

To Gloria's knowledge, the only airship within five hundred miles was Alice Chalmers's *Swan*, and she and Jake and Captain Hollys were probably back in England by now. Evan had to be dead. A hollow feeling opened up in the region of her heart. Another missed opportunity. Another reminder that she was achingly alone, with a monumental task ahead.

A task to which she had best set her mind before too many more days passed. Sound business practice dictated that when one needed something—such as the cessation of a war—one began at the top. And in the Royal Kingdom, the top meant the Viceroy.

"How far is San Francisco de Asis from here?" she asked.

"It must be six hundred miles of mountains and desert and wildcats and well-armed horsemen," Mother Mary said. "Why? Are you going to see the Viceroy? Shall you ask him to abandon his war?"

"Someone must," Gloria said, pleased at her quick understanding. "Why should it not be me?"

A merry laugh rang out, and to her enormous chagrin, the entire company joined in.

*

Gloria slipped away from the gathering and climbed to one of the southwest terraces, where one could see the sun set. The long, low rays of winter turned the canyon walls to a deep golden red, and the river reflected both the rosy tints of the cliffs and the cold blue of the evening sky. She breathed deeply of air that smelled of dust and pine and the smoke from the cooking coals, and under it all the fresh, cool scent of lifegiving water.

And now, here came another scent—clean sweat, warm cotton, and engine grease. Over her shoulder, she saw Captain Stan take the last stair and emerge onto the small terrace. Gloria lifted her chin and regarded the sunset once more, concentrating on its transient beauty since it was clear she was not going to be permitted to enjoy it in peace.

His boot heels clunked on the stone as he joined her, leaning on the stone parapet a little distance away. "It's never the same twice, is it?"

She did not deign to reply. Perhaps if she gave a good impression of stone herself, he would lose interest and go back to his crew. He could have a wonderful time laughing with them. Or at them. She felt his gaze upon her, and tilted her chin another notch.

"I apologize for laughing earlier. I should have realized that you were serious about going to speak to the Viceroy, and would take offense."

Hmph. Of course she was serious. Did she look as though she were here on a grand tour? Did the women of his acquaintance enjoy being the recipients of his laughter, his disbelief, his derision? Someone had to convince the young Viceroy that going to war was not a practical plan. Was it so very hard to imagine that an intelligent, capable woman should be that someone? If at present she did not have the resources she needed, that was certainly no excuse for hilarity. A gentleman would at least have offered to help.

"You are silent," he observed. "Will you not accept my apology?"

She might have, if the sting of that laughter had faded. Which it had not. "I hesitate to expend the effort when your rudeness will no doubt be repeated in future."

"Come now, Miss Aster. We have been friends until now. Surely you won't hold a laugh against a man? There are few enough to be enjoyed in this hard country."

"I am not accustomed to being the object of ridicule," she said stiffly.

"I imagine not."

"And what do you mean by that, pray?"

"Only that you strike me as a woman who has been used to giving orders. To servants, perhaps, or to those over whom you have some authority."

"As a man who also enjoys some authority himself, it surprises me that you would find it so amusing in others."

"I don't find authority amusing—only hubris."

So thoughtful and yet so impudent! "I am not a victim of hubris."

"Then perhaps you are deceived, for that is the only explanation for your courageous but utterly impractical suggestion."

It was not in the least impractical. It was simply difficult to execute.

"Someone must convince the Viceroy that going to war for gold that does not exist and lands that have long been called home by others will only result in death and disaster for his men, to say nothing of the innocent on the other side of the border."

"Why do you care so much, Miss Aster?" he asked after a moment, moving a step closer. "What in a gently bred young lady's past could compel her into the desert to take on an army all by herself?"

"I have no intention of taking on the army," she responded crisply, sidestepping his question as easily as one twitched one's skirts out of the path of tramping boots. "Only the Viceroy."

She could swear he chuckled, and she came *this close* to marching back across the terrace and leaving him with only his amusement for company. But when he spoke, there was no trace of a smile in his tone. "Tell me, how would you do it? How would you reach him?"

She had given it quite a lot of thought during the long nights when she could not sleep for worry. And fear. And regret.

"I should find a guide, and go disguised as a man," she said with firmness. "Surely the Californios do not prevent ordinary travelers from boarding a train and taking it to San Francisco de Asis?"

"They do not, but I'm afraid I cannot imagine you as a man. I'm having a difficult enough time imagining you as a witch, and yet here you are before me, roses and all."

She resisted the temptation to advise him to read more, thus nourishing his poor powers of imagination.

"Ella painted my face," she said instead. "She is very good—I cannot even recognize myself. I have every confidence she could turn me into a boy if she put her mind to it."

"That would be a waste," he murmured to no one in particular. "But it will not do, you know. You would be discovered within days, and a woman traveling alone in these parts is in grave danger. The rancho families produce gentlemen, but there are soldiers and horsemen and workmen and craftsmen by the thousands who are not so well bred."

A rancho family had produced Ambassador de Aragon, the warmongering megalomaniac behind this disaster, and look how *he* had turned out.

"Why should I be discovered? No one will be so inquisitive about an ordinary traveler."

Now he did chuckle, right out loud. Ooh, if she had been a boy what pleasure she would take in giving him a good hard poke in the nose!

"With that grace, and that posture, and those cheekbones? You cannot help being a woman, and a woman cannot travel alone in the Royal Kingdom, both for reasons of safety and because of the culture."

"Speak in specifics, sir, not generalities."

"A gentlewoman never travels alone. She has an escort, usually consisting of servants and a brother or other male member of her family, or her husband."

"Then I shall not travel as a gentlewoman."

"Then you risk being set upon, raped, and killed."

The bluntness of those specifics stopped her breath, his words thrown as quietly and accurately as a knife. When her lungs would expand again, she said, "There are many women in the Royal Kingdom, I am sure, who are neither gently bred nor dead."

"There are. If they are not under the protection of a rancho or in the care of a shopkeeper or school, then they are working girls in the whorehouses or begging in the streets."

"Cannot a woman set up a business and support herself as an independent being?"

"Not in the Royal Kingdom, no. Women are under the protection of their fathers until they marry, and under that of their husbands afterward."

Her heart sank. She had hoped it was the sort of custom that men spoke of proudly, but that women did not take very seriously. Clearly her hopes were in vain. "How positively medieval."

"I quite agree. So you see how exponentially difficult your task becomes."

But now she had thought of a solution. "Then I shall hire the aforesaid guide, and pretend to be married to *him*."

One winged eyebrow rose under the brim of his disreputable bowler hat. "You would sleep in the same room as a stranger? I don't know whether to be shocked at the damage to your reputation, or dismayed at the damage to your person once you closed your eyes."

"I should, of course, hire someone trustworthy," she said through gritted teeth. Was there no end to the rocks he must kick into her path?

"I wish you luck. The only men you know out here are my crew, and much as I like them, I wouldn't share a room with a single one of them."

Now she did face him, her frustration mounting with every word out of his mouth. "Can you not give me a helpful suggestion? It is very difficult to stop a war when one hears nothing but negativity and pooh-poohing. I expected better of a man as well traveled and resourceful as you appear to be."

Her attempt at a scolding ran off him like the water purling off the rocks below. "You are determined to do this, Miss Aster? Will you tell me why confounding the Californios is so important to you when most women would have fled back to where they came from long before now?"

That was no answer. She bit back the angry words that crowded her tongue and hauled on the reins of her temper. "I will tell you once I have achieved my objective, and not before."

"So there is a reason." His dark eyes searched her face, making her grateful that he could not see her true expression through the face paint of a flowery skull. "It must be a very powerful one for you to risk your life to see it through."

She owed him nothing, particularly not an answer as complicated as hers must be.

"There must be a man in the equation somewhere," he mused at last, when the silence had gone on too long. "A woman may be driven to great things for love."

"Oh, what utter nonsense!" she exploded. "A woman may be driven to great things simply because she has the sense to act and the means to do so! And while I do not at present possess the latter, I *certainly* possess the former."

His eyes widened at her vehemence, and she would have congratulated herself at finally getting past the shell of his humor if she hadn't been so infuriated.

"You are not doing this for love?"

"Certainly not! Cannot a woman act simply because it is the right thing to do? Can she not possess the heroism and courage to attempt what seems impossible, what seems laughable to others?"

"Of course she—that is, I suppose—"

"I will thank you to keep your remarks to yourself, sir. And now I must bid you good night. I have plans to make."

"Miss Aster. Meredith." He put a hand on her arm as she whirled to march across the terrace in the most dignified of exits. "Please. Don't go."

"I shall go where I please, thank you."

"I have no doubt of that. But listen to me for just one moment. No, don't be angry again. I have a suggestion. A concrete suggestion that just might work to help you accomplish your goal."

She must breathe calmly, and think rationally. And his hand was far too warm on her wrist—as it had been under her hand when they had danced together several nights ago. She removed it from his grip rather pointedly. "What do you propose, sir?"

"I propose—" He stopped. Swallowed. Then held her astonished gaze as he went down upon one knee. "Why ... I propose. Miss Meredith Aster, will you do me the honor of becoming my wife, so that I may accompany you to San Francisco de Asis and help you stop this war?"

2

The citizens of the Royal Kingdom of Spain and the Californias were skilled at a number of things---building churches and cathedrals of extraordinary beauty, extracting gold out of the kingdoms they had conquered in their explorations in centuries past, and contriving a network of vast ranchos controlled by rich nobles who educated their sons in the mother country and educated their daughters at home in the useful skills of embroidery, music, and hospitality.

They were also far better at building gaols than a nation had a right to be.

Evan Douglas squirmed in the thousandth unsuccessful attempt to find comfort on the thin pallet he had been given to sleep on, which was all that separated his bruised and exhausted body from the stone floor of his cell. He supposed he ought to be grateful. The Ambassador to the Fifteen Colonies, Augusto de Aragon y Villarreal, needed him to operate the massive mechanical behemoth in which he had so naively come to Gloria Meriwether-Astor's rescue ten days before, and for that reason he was housed in relative comfort.

The groans and cries that issued from the cells farther down the passage, and from the underground pits below, told him that not all the prisoners were so lucky. And, of course, the moment someone else was found to do the job—someone who owed his allegiance to the Viceroy and not Her Majesty the Queen of England— Evan had no doubt he would find himself out on his ear and begging for a bowl of gruel in the common pit with the others.

As it was, he shared this cell with three men, lying in varying attitudes of discomfort about him. The sun would rise soon, so he reached up and made a vertical mark in the mud wall with one torn fingernail to mark the beginning of the eleventh day.

"I don't know why you bother," said Joe, the young man who lay next to him, and turned over in disgust.

Evan ignored him. Joe was young and prone to secretive habits, and had proven most unlikeable. But he'd grown up on the river and so had been assigned to the work team for the dam that was under construction. He had had an education at some point in his past, which put him in this block of cells and not in the pit, where he might be hitched to one of the work gangs. Should that happen, Evan supposed, it would be difficult for his overseers to find him when his knowledge was required.

Barney, on the opposite wall, had been tossed in here sometime after Joe's imprisonment and before that of Evan. He had been beaten twice since Evan had been here and still would not reveal who he was or why he had been in San Francisco de Asis without identity papers, but he was a cheerful sort despite his injuries. It was clear from his diction that he was a gentleman, and clear from his knowledge of steam and hydraulics that he had been educated, perhaps even as well as Evan. But more than that, Evan did not know, and neither did their captors.

The fourth man had arrived only yesterday, and had not said one word in response to the overtures of his cellmates. Evan was not convinced he could speak English. Even now, he cried out in his sleep, and said something in trembling tones in a foreign tongue. He too must be useful in some way, or he would not have been shanghaied, but until they saw him on a work detail, they would probably not discover what it was.

The light strengthened, and Evan saw that Barney was awake too, his gaze on the silvery sky framed by the barred opening of the window. No isinglass. They were subject to whatever weather or vermin that happened to find its way through the foot-square opening, which was why they all slept closer to the other walls. Given a choice, Evan would take weather over vermin. But he had not been given a choice.

"Another cloudless day," Barney said. "Shall we go hunting, or simply mount up for a ride along the river before it gets too hot?"

Joe said something vicious in the Californio tongue and hunched a shoulder, while their newest companion gasped and sat up, terror exposing the whites of his eyes.

Evan reached out and laid a calming hand on his arm, and the man backed up against the wall as though Evan had been a snake. His chest heaving, he stared at them with an uncomprehending gaze.

"It's all right, friend," Barney told him with some compassion. "No one here is going to hurt you. Calm yourself."

No response but the drag of breath into constricted lungs.

Barney repeated himself in French, and then Italian, which did nothing for their frightened companion, but told Evan quite a lot more about Barney's education than he probably wanted.

Evan tried the same phrases in Prussian, the only foreign language he knew, and the man's eyes widened even further.

"Thanks be to God," the man said in that tongue. "Who are you and how came I here?"

"I am called Evan Douglas, and this man here is called Barney. The cross one by the door is Joe. We are prisoners of the Viceroy of the Royal Kingdom of Spain and the Californias. What of you?"

The man looked from one to another, Evan's introductions not seeming to lessen his confusion in the least. "The Viceroy?"

"Do you know where you are?" Evan asked him after a moment. "What is the last thing you remember?"

"I—I—" He passed a shaking hand over his face. "I boarded a train in Reno with my family, I do not know when. It is all a blank."

"Do you know your name?"

But instead of replying, he looked around wildly. "Where is my wife? My children?"

Evan exchanged a glance with Barney, and translated rapidly. Even Joe had become interested enough to push himself up against the wall and sit with his skinny arms wrapped around his knees, his dark eyes on the distraught man's face.

"You are in a Californio gaol in the water meadows known as Las Vegas," Barney said gently. "Reno is a long way north of here, on the far side of the mountains. Have you no memory of the journey?"

The man shook his head as Evan began to translate. "English. You are English. I am English, though my use of the Prussian tongue seems much more familiar. But ... A gaol? Why am I in gaol? *Mein Gott*, what crime have I committed?"

"As far as we can tell, the only crimes we share in common are being on the wrong side of the border and having knowledge that the Californios need," Barney told him wryly.

"For what purpose?"

"For building a dam across the last canyon in the mountains before the river enters the flatlands and loses its velocity," Evan said. "The Californios wish to control the water and thus commerce for the length of the river, which is hundreds of miles long."

"Which river?"

"The Rio de la Sangre Colorado de Christos."

"Ah." The man seemed to sink in upon himself. "I cannot remember my own name. Yet that one is familiar to me. In fact—" He flushed and fell silent.

"In fact?" Barnaby echoed. "Any facts would be helpful if we are to help you remember your identity, sir."

"You will find it amusing, but so be it. It was the river I was dreaming of just now, before I woke."

"Dreaming?" Joe, who hardly ever spoke, snorted. "More of a nightmare. Whimpering and crying out like a child, you were."

"It terrifies me," he whispered, turning his face away. "Deep water. I cannot bear the thought of it."

Evan had not written eight monographs and been hailed as a pioneer for his invention of the mnemosomniograph for nothing. The poor man had been debilitated by his dream, and if they were to have any hope of escape, they needed to be able to trust every man in this cell as an ally—one as whole and healthy as possible.

"Aside from your dreams, have you been injured in any way, sir?" Evan turned the subject slightly out of sheer compassion.

The man was quite a bit older than he and Barney—in his late forties, perhaps. His hair was beginning to turn gray, and his beard had been neatly clipped at one time, though it was streaked with mud and blood now. His trousers and shirt were well made, though he wore no hat or jacket. Lost during the fight that had cost him his memory and landed him here, perhaps?

The man struggled to his feet, testing his weight, bending his knees, examining his arms. He wore boots that seemed to be custom made, but not by any Texican boot maker, who favored flat heels and chased sides. They appeared to be straight out of Bond Street, which confirmed he must have been in England before his journey here. Perhaps he spoke Prussian so fluently because he had lived there? Or taught the language in England?

"I am bruised, and my ankle is tender, but nothing seems to be broken."

"Just your head," muttered Joe into his arms.

Evan rose from his mat to indicate the man's temple. "It seems you might have been struck. There is a quantity of dried blood here, and in your beard, which might account for the loss of memory." Gently, he touched the man's head, and the latter flinched. "I apologize. But this area of the brain is said to control short-term memory. It may be that once the organ recovers from the blow, your memory will return. It may also account for your unpleasant dreams, which might fade as the brain regains its health."

"You a doctor?" Joe squinted up from the floor. "Or just a regular know-it-all?"

"I possess a medical degree, yes," Evan said somewhat stiffly. "But my research subsequently has all been in the field of dreams and visions."

Joe snorted and got up, dusting off his pants. "That's useful."

But the stranger stood beside him at the barred window, breathing the morning air as dust from horses passing on the road outside sifted in on them. "And what do you think of my dream?" he asked, his chin held high as though Evan might think him weak. "Of a river I cannot cross, no matter how furiously I swim. It is so deep, so cold that the more I attempt to ford it, the faster I sink, until at last the water closes over my face and I know I am drowning."

It sounded dreadful, but Evan had heard its like in his interviews ... in a life that seemed to have belonged to someone else, long ago.

"When you are swimming, is it away from something or toward something?"

The Englishman who spoke Prussian frowned. "I do not know. Wait, that is not true. I am swimming toward something."

"There is nothing that has chased you into the water, nothing pursuing you?"

"*Nein.* At least, I have no memory of it. But it is urgent that I cross."

"As though you will lose something important if you do not?"

"*Ja.*" The man nodded thoughtfully. "But what?"

"Perhaps the thing that brought you out here to the Wild West. Were you offered a position of some kind?

Or were you to deliver something important to someone?"

The man's lips parted, as though he was on the brink of speaking—of remembering—

Down the corridor, the doors crashed open and they heard the clank of the tin cup against the porridge pot. Each morning's meal was the same—a tin cup of porridge, an orange, and water. Afterward came review in the parade ground formed by the gaol's quadrangle, and then the men were divided into work crews. Discipline was strict. Evan had never been whipped—for the most part because he was not a troublesome prisoner—but many had, in full view of the others.

The stranger sighed. "It is gone. I thought for a moment you might be right, that—"

The key clattered in the lock and the door was pushed open. "No talking. Stand back!"

"I demand to know why I am here," their companion said bravely, facing the four guards in the middle of the floor while Evan and the others did as they were told.

"Silence!"

"This man has interpreted my dream and I believe I may have come here to take up a position. My employer will be looking for me and I must—"

"I said, silence!"

Their fellow prisoner got an elbow in the stomach that sent him reeling against the wall. Their filled bowls clanged on the stone floor, and Evan dodged to catch an escaping orange. Why such a luxury should be treated so cavalierly in this place was a mystery, but he was not about to let the precious thing be kicked or worse, taken away.

The door slammed shut behind the guards and there was no more talk. Eating and guzzling water was far more important. They had barely finished licking their bowls when Evan, Barney, and the stranger were hauled out and, instead of being forced into lines in the hot sun, were marched together to the fortified yard where the behemoth spent its nights.

A crew boss was waiting for them. "You will repair the arm of *el Gigante* today, but not for use as a cannon. We require a holding and gripping assembly so that he may be used more precisely in building the dam. You have two days for this task."

"Two days?" Evan repeated incredulously. "Even had we any real engineering experience among us, a week would not be enough time."

The crew boss jerked his cleanshaven chin at their new companion. "The Dutch man has plenty of experience. You will begin now."

"Who is this Dutch?" the older man demanded. "Why do you call me that? What do you know of me? Where is my family?"

But he got no reply save a face full of dust as the crew boss wheeled his horse around and spurred it to the gate. The yard was locked and watched by a pair of soldiers who patrolled outside the sturdy palisade. As the gate clanged shut behind the horse, their companion gave a sigh. "How is it these men know more about me than I do myself? I must know what has become of my family."

"I wish he'd taken a moment to tell us your proper name, at least," Barney said. "It is most inconvenient to refer to you as *the Englishman who speaks Prussian* all the time. Or even Dutch."

"Who or what is Dutch?"

"I have no idea. Perhaps they have never met someone who speaks Prussian, and are not fussy about which Teutonic language is which. But it is all we know at present. If it suits you, though, Evan and I have no objection to using it."

The man chewed his lip in frustration and anxiety, but in the end, nodded agreement. They had no option but to do as they were told and make their way over to the shop, which was not a shop at all, but a heap of parts and tools that might have been manufactured in the previous decade and not used since.

Evan climbed up into the behemoth and began its ignition sequence, and once it was operational, caused it to kneel. This brought the arm low enough that Dutch and Barney could tilt a ladder up against it and begin removing the bolts that held the damaged assembly together. It took them the whole morning to get it off and disassembled, and the whole of the next day to fashion a set of ungainly pincers that would operate harmoniously with the hydraulic system of the arm.

"It is clear that, among other things, you are an engineer," Evan observed to Dutch in the pilot's chamber of the behemoth, wiping the sweat from his temple with one dirty sleeve. "There has been no damage to your long-term memory, nor to your motor skills, for which we can be grateful. I would not like to be facing the lash this evening had we not been successful."

Below, Barney was foreshortened and small, his hands on his hips as he gazed upward, ready to supervise the exercises to which Evan would subject the new arm. Dutch gripped a hanging strap as Evan raised the behemoth to a stand. "Do you wish me to work the arms now?"

"You will have to—I cannot do both. It was designed for a pilot and a gunner, one above the other."

With surprising agility, Dutch climbed into the gunner's chair and raised the behemoth's arm. They had modified the trigger so that the pincers would open and shut. The sound of clanking metal came clearly through the air vents as Dutch moved the arm this way and that, testing its range of motion.

"How far is the dam from this place?" he asked.

"About five miles. It takes us about half an hour to walk it in the behemoth, who is faster than the steam drays that convey the crews there."

Dutch swung himself down into the main chamber. "Has it never occurred to you simply to walk away to freedom? What self-respecting man can tolerate this treatment? How long have you been here?"

"It has occurred to me every single day of the twelve I have been here, many times a day," Evan informed him, his frustration with his situation leaking into his voice and giving it an edge. "But I am never left alone. When we walk to the dam, I am always accompanied by an armed guard in this chamber, who stays at my side, pistol cocked, in case I should attempt exactly what you suggest." With a glance at the sun on the horizon, he began to shut down the boilers. "Do not imagine we tolerate our situation. We are prisoners. It is only because they need our knowledge that we are treated as well as we are."

"Have they no engineers of their own?"

"It seems not." Evan led the way out of the chamber, and climbed down the series of iron rungs on one of the behemoth's legs. "They are educated in the mother country, but it seems that extends only to classics, languages, mathematics, and the arts of war. Not to practical pursuits such as engineering and mechanics. Apparently, the Royal Kingdom is the greatest market for railroads and trains on this side of the world."

Dutch hopped to the ground. "But not airships."

"Those would be illegal," Barney told him. "Flying in the face of God and all that. No airships are permitted in these skies, which is likely why you were on the ground in Reno. That is the main transfer point from points east to the Royal Kingdom's rail system."

Dutch shook his head. "I do not understand why they do not simply hire the engineers they need, rather than kidnapping and imprisoning them. But how did you come to be here, you healthy and intelligent young men?"

When Barney did not reply, instead gazing upward as though checking the behemoth's arm at rest, Evan said, "I came in search of a girl."

For the first time since he had been shoved into their cell, Dutch's mouth curved in a rueful smile. "I hope that the young lady was worth the price you are paying."

"She is," Evan said. "Or was. They told me she was dead, but even yet I cannot believe it. One moment Gloria was their prisoner, and the next she had disappeared. But until I see her with my own eyes, I cherish hope that she still lives."

Barney was no longer looking up, but at Evan. "They took a woman prisoner? What had she done?"

Evan smiled with the memory. "Besides have their shipment of mechanical war machines derailed by air pirates before they could reach the border, in an attempt to stop this war? Nothing of significance."

"War machines," Barney repeated. "Gloria."

"Yes. Her name was—is—Gloria Meriwether-Astor. And she is as beautiful as an angel."

"Blond," Barney said, and held out a hand at his shoulder. "About this tall. Blue eyes."

Evan stared. "Yes, in fact."

"Cantankerous and opinionated. The daughter of Gerald Meriwether-Astor, may God damn his warmongering soul."

Through his utter astonishment, Evan managed to close his mouth with some difficulty. "How in heaven's name do you know that?"

Barney laughed and spun away. "That girl makes a habit of being kidnapped, it seems."

"Have you seen her?" Evan demanded. "Is she alive?"

"I have not. Though it seems her propensity for being kidnapped has helped her develop a particular talent for escape, if what you say is true."

"What on earth do you mean? I must know if—"

With a shout, the gate behind them opened, and a squad of four soldiers marched in. And in the chaos of being herded through the streets and back into the quadrangle, reviewed and counted, and watching that evening's whipping of a man who had tried to escape by diving off the dam's scaffold and swimming upriver, there was no opportunity for Evan to shake any information out of him. Not until they had been given that evening's portion of rusty meat, beans, and rice, and had settled on their pallets once again, could Evan speak.

"Where did you meet Gloria?" he asked in a low tone that he hoped would not reach the ears of the soldiers at the end of the corridor. "How is it possible that you know her?"

With a sigh, Barney tilted his head back against the wall plastered in a substance the inhabitants called *adobe*. "I hardly know where to begin."

"The beginning is usually a good place," Dutch suggested.

"I am afraid that in this recital, there is no good place. In the autumn of last year, I was the captain of an undersea dirigible called *Neptune's Fancy*, belonging to the fleet of Gerald Meriwether-Astor. We were massed in the Adriatic Sea for reasons I will not go into, and I was given orders to proceed to Venice to allow Miss Meriwether-Astor and a party of friends to board for some sightseeing. I followed my orders, and in the course of time she became my guest at my home in England."

"In England?" Evan repeated. "You've missed a bit in the middle, I think. 'In the course of time'? How did you get from Venice to England?"

"I am not permitted to say," Barney told him. "Are you familiar with friends of the young lady that include Captain Ian Hollys and Lady Claire Trevelyan?"

"I certainly am," Evan said. "Lady Claire's wards, Elizabeth and Marguerite, are my cousins. Our grandmothers were sisters. And incidentally, Lady Claire is now Mrs. Andrew Malvern."

"I only met the lady briefly," Barney said.

"Lady Claire is one of the most intelligent and resourceful women I have ever known," Evan said. "If not for her, for an airship captain called Alice Chalmers, and for my young cousins, I might not have survived a very dark period in my life."

"Then perhaps she has shared her resourcefulness with Gloria, for the latter lost no time in leaving my house and making her way back to Philadelphia."

Evan made up his mind. While he knew from Maggie and Lizzie that they had suffered some dreadful experiences in Venice, Barney did not seem inclined to expand upon them. Perhaps if he shared a little of what he knew, he might receive some information in return.

"I had the privilege of flying here with Gloria from Philadelphia on Captain Chalmers's ship, *Swan*," he said. "She knew that her father had been selling arms to the Californios and she was determined to stop the final shipment and the war that is brewing. We enlisted the help of air pirates in Resolution, in the Texican Territory. However, in the course of the battle that ensued between the pirates and the Californio mercenaries, I was knocked unconscious. When I regained my senses, Gloria, the Californios, and their steam train *Silver Wind* were all gone. I pursued her in the behemoth and had just caught up to the train when we were surprised by a flash flood. The Californios assured me she had been swept away alive by the river, but despite my searching the banks for days, I could not find her. Then, once I was over the border with the behemoth, they informed me I was a prisoner of war and that Gloria was dead. They had simply been stringing me along in order to get the behemoth into the country."

Joe had been listening with interest, his chin resting upon his folded arms. Now he shook his head. "Sneaks," he said contemptuously. "Always talking about honor and showing none."

"Quite so," Evan agreed. Joe was not in the habit of conversing voluntarily, so perhaps this little victory would encourage Barney to talk, too.

"Now I see." Barney nodded, as though to himself. "You have no proof that she is dead, nor any that she is alive. But what can a man do under circumstances such as these?"

"Why, that is obvious." Dutch smiled a real smile now. "You must escape in the behemoth and try to find a sign of her. As I shall do for my wife and children. As any man of honor and compassion would do."

With a snort of derision, Joe shook his head. "If it were that easy, old man, would they be sitting here still?"

"We cannot merely escape," Evan told them. "Whether she is alive or dead, we need a plan that will also aid her in her efforts to stop this war."

"We might destroy something on our way out," Barney suggested.

"Start with the dam." Joe's eyes glittered with hatred. "It's going to raise the level of the river and kill everything that lives in the canyons."

"The only things living out there are desert creatures and witches," Evan said.

"Meaning no great loss if they all die?" Joe snapped.

Evan braced himself. Joe might be slender, but he would not put it past the man to leap upon him and beat him unconscious with his fists alone. "Of course not." Were those tears swimming in Joe's eyes? "Is there someone among them who means something to you?"

"None of your nevermind."

"Getting back to the plan," Barney said, waving the young man into his place against the wall, "how might we do this?"

"No matter in what way we choose to do it," Evan said, "one thing is necessary. The behemoth goes with us."

Joe made a sound of derision into his folded arms. "It's not like stealing a rifle. Hard to hide it when you're on the run—and you have to keep it powered. What if we run out of coal or water in the desert?"

"We will be following the river, you ninny," Evan snapped. He very much disliked having facts pointed out to him that a child could perceive. "I will not leave it here to be used against the innocent. Whether or not we destroy the dam, the war will still proceed."

"No. The war cannot proceed without the dam," Dutch told them thoughtfully. "How else can they penetrate so deeply into the Texican Territory with the greatest ease and the least expense?"

"Trains," Joe said.

"They are too easy to stop. One stick of Canton explosive and an entire line is rendered useless. No, they need the river. They have been building that dam for some months before we all arrived. Clearly it is for a larger purpose than merely flooding out a small number of inhabitants."

"Then we use the behemoth as the instrument of its destruction," Barney said. "We fill it with explosives and set it walking toward the building site, where it destroys both itself and the dam."

Evan wanted to shout his disagreement, but he pushed the urge down until he had marshaled his thoughts. He was not used to basing his decisions on emotion—on this ball of resistance in his gut that absolutely refused to allow the behemoth's destruction. But it was as though they were discussing taking a part of him—of his skill or accomplishment—his very being—and lobbing it at the problem with no more thought than if it had been a stick of Canton gunpowder.

"And what if we fail?" he asked when he had himself under control. "What if we send the behemoth walking at the dam and it doesn't blow it up?"

"It will put a nice hole in it." Joe seemed quite cheered by the prospect.

FIELDS OF IRON

"I don't think so. How much dynamite and gunpowder would be required for such a task? Is filling the pilot's chamber going to be enough?"

Dutch pinched his lower lip between his fingers as he considered the question. "I do not believe so. An entire train car ought to do it, but it is not likely that we might be able to help ourselves to one of those."

"There's the crane," Barney pointed out.

"The spur runs up to the building site." Clearly, Joe had caught his drift, but Evan was still all at sea.

"Please explain." He would much rather they left the subject of the behemoth behind, so he was quite prepared to play the simpleton.

"The crane can move tremendous weight. With only one of its four arms, it can pick up a rail car from one track and move it to another," Joe explained. "I'll wager that if you gave it enough steam, it would chuck a car quite a distance. And explosives are fairly light."

Evan had seen the multi-armed cranes working near the rail spur in the course of his labors, but it had never occurred to him that they could be made to throw their cargo as well as pick it up.

"So we steal the explosives, fill a car with them, pick it up with the crane, and fling it at the dam, where it blows up." Barney stretched out on his pallet. "Child's play ... if you're a giant."

Dutch gazed at him, and then up at Evan. "The services of a giant, it seems, are the only thing we do in fact possess."

3

Gloria stared at Captain Stan with something akin to horror. "Do get up," she said, her cheeks burning with embarrassment and irritation. "You look ridiculous, to say nothing of uncomfortable."

"I'm quite serious."

"Get up, I beg of you, before someone sees you."

He rose, and she took a step back lest he make things look worse by taking her hand. "You don't believe my proposal to be sincere."

"Certainly not." She turned to gaze at the deepening sky, thankful both for the fading light and her skull paint. "You are the next thing to a pirate, making a living by who knows what nefarious means. Only a madwoman would believe a word."

"And yet I have never lied to you."

"While we have only been in one another's company for a matter of hours, that is enough time for a man's true colors to show."

"I feel as though you mean to hurt me, Miss Aster. But surely not. Not a young lady of your breeding and aspirations to the betterment of the world."

She would not look at him. She would not acknowledge by the slightest softening that his proposal had taken her utterly by surprise, and that defensive words were falling out of her mouth in a torrent with no thought behind them except that they might push him away from her.

It did not help that he was right.

"You hurt me when you laughed earlier."

Oh dear. Now she sounded like a sulky child. There were reasons that occasions like this called for certain polite expressions. She just wished she might have recalled them a few moments sooner.

It took all her courage to face him once again. "I am grateful for the honor you have done me in—"

"Are you? A moment ago you called me ridiculous."

If he did not stop provoking her, she would never be able to remember the polite things to say. "—asking me to be your wife, but I am sure you will not be surprised when I must decline."

He gazed at her a moment in a way that left her unable to look away. No words stabbed the air between them, only an unhappy honesty in which she saw herself clearly for the idiot she was.

She did not want him to think her an idiot. Was it surprising that she wanted a man to look at her as Andrew looked at Claire—as a heroine, as the only treasure worth possessing in an uncertain world?

What nonsense was this?

She cared nothing for his opinion, and he clearly cared nothing for hers if he could laugh at her, publicly shame her, and then toy with her sensibilities in this manner.

Just as you have now privately shamed him.

She was not obligated to accept a man's proposal just because he offered it. If that were the case, she would have been Mrs. Winston Humphrey and no doubt be expecting Winston Humphrey Junior by now, back in Philadelphia.

"I'll be ashore until the day after tomorrow," he said. "We are doing repairs on the *Queen* to give her a little more speed, and adding some defensive mechanisms in case they're needed in the next few months. If you change your mind, I'll be about."

"It is impossible, regardless of my state of mind," she said past the constriction in her throat. "There is neither church nor registry nor minister within a hundred miles."

"There you are wrong," he told her with no small satisfaction. "Padre Emilio is in Santa Croce, the crossing about ten miles downriver from here. He travels around to all the churches in these parts on an annual circuit, hearing people's vows and a year later baptizing their babies. He performs last rites and funerals, too, but that is outside the purview of this discussion."

"Don't be so sure," she muttered.

But he had heard her. "That's a thought," he said, a sardonic tilt to his lips. "You can murder me on our wedding night and proceed with his party as a widow. That ought to get you at least halfway to San Francisco de Asis, if you're lucky."

If he had thought to make her laugh, he was unsuccessful. "There has been enough death in my life thus far, sir," she whispered, "that I have no desire to be responsible for more."

"Of course not." Now he did capture her hand, and for one shocked moment she did not remove it. "I spoke carelessly. Forgive me."

She pulled it from his grasp and at last had the sense to cross the empty terrace herself, since he showed no signs of leaving.

"I hope you will reconsider," he called as she reached the stairs. "I have never been any woman's only hope of success, but they tell me there is always a first time."

Gloria did not dignify that with a reply.

It cannot be said that she spent a comfortable night in her hammock bed, watching the moon move past the window in remote majesty and wondering how she, who had been the toast of Philadelphia society, could have been reduced to fielding proposals from disreputable outlaws in the wilderness.

Then again, she herself was a disreputable outlaw in the wilderness.

As for his character, there again this pot could hardly call that kettle black. She suspected him to have been a gentleman at one time, educated in the ways of society as well as academics, and he had made it plain he'd observed the same of her. So perhaps their backgrounds might be similar. She could only assume there was no Mrs. Captain Stan, though no doubt he kept a mistress in every river crossing from here to Denver.

Well, what was that to her? He had proposed a union of convenience—though if the truth were told, the benefit lay all on her side. Traveling as his wife, she had at least a slender chance of reaching San Francisco de Asis and requesting an audience with the Viceroy. But what would a marriage to her net him other than a companion whose ambitions and opinions bore no resemblance to his own? Or did they? No, that could not be so. He was a riverboat captain and a gambler, not a crusader.

Was he some kind of knight-errant, coming to the aid of a damsel in distress, or simply a world-weary man who had seen too much and was ready for a new diversion of the most outrageous kind? An adventurer who would saddle himself with a wife, just for a lark?

She didn't want to be a lark. She wanted to be a heroine—or at the very least, a woman who could set out to make things right and succeed. There simply had to be a way to achieve that without becoming Mrs. Captain Stan. And what was the man's last name, for goodness sake? She couldn't imagine any woman waiting until she was standing at the altar to find out.

There were simply no answers to these questions. She must talk with someone who knew him and had more familiarity with this strange and uncooperative world.

FIELDS OF IRON

She must talk with Mother Mary.

With one decision made of the many that lay before her, Gloria fell into a restless doze that left her slightly the worse for wear in the morning.

Gloria found Mother Mary shortly after breakfast in one of the storage rooms, spreading corn with an odd short-tined rake. She looked up as Gloria hesitated in the doorway, then jerked her chin toward a similar rake standing against the wall. "Make yourself useful."

"Do you have a moment to talk?"

"I always have time to talk. But that don't mean we can't work while we do it. What's the trouble?"

"No trouble," Gloria hastened to assure her. She picked up the rake and imitated the other woman's smooth strokes, leveling out a pile of corn all over the clean stone floor, where presumably it was to dry. "But I seem to have a problem that only has one solution, and I hoped that between us, we might come up with another that is more palatable."

"More problems, or more solutions?"

"The truth is, the solution that has just been suggested to me is the last one I want to take. I know there must be others."

"Oh?"

Gloria got into the swing of the rake, scattering corn across the floor in fans. "Captain Stan proposed to me last evening."

With a clatter, Mother Mary lost her grip on her rake. When she picked it up, her eyes were snapping in their dark painted hollows. "What are you saying, child? Are you funning me?"

"Indeed, I am not. After laughing at me so rudely over the suggestion that I should approach the Viceroy about stopping this war, he had the temerity to propose marriage. He says that going to San Francisco de Asis as his wife is the only way that I will reach that city without being assaulted or murdered."

"Them Californios do have their odd ideas about women traveling and living alone," Mother Mary conceded, still sounding a little winded.

"Well, yes, but surely there must be a way to travel in their country if one is not a citizen. Surely they do not set upon ordinary folk from other places merely as a matter of course. Why, I understand Madame Tetrazzini herself has sung at the opera house in San Francisco de Asis, and presumably she was not accosted."

"Don't know who that is, but there ain't many travelers crossing these borders anymore, especially since they began to build that dam and people started going missing."

"Missing?"

The older woman resumed her raking. "Mm. I've heard a story or two. Seems even if you take the case to the authorities, nothing gets done other then a lot of paperwork and prevarication."

The addition of problems to the teetering pile that already confronted her was not what Gloria had come for. "So are you saying that Captain Stan is in the right? That if I am to attempt to reach the Viceroy, the only way that I can do it is with a wedding ring on my finger? Why can we not simply pretend to be married?"

"You could," Mother Mary allowed. "But when they ask to see your papers, what will you do then? The marriage lines in these parts are a serious business, probably because the missions have made it so, marriage being a holy ordinance and all." The strokes of her rake scratched to a halt. "Seems to me you have two choices. Either you abandon your brave plan, or you take the captain up on his offer. He is an honorable man, and goodness knows plenty of the girls along the river will vouch for his skill between the sheets."

An epithet that had never before escaped Gloria's lips escaped them now. "That is hardly relevant to the current situation!"

Mother Mary shrugged. "You'd be surprised how soon it might become, as you say, relevant. He's a healthy man, and there don't seem to be much wrong with you. You might see it differently sooner or later."

"Certainly not!"

But the older woman only shrugged. "Suit yourself. That's a little talk you'll have to have with him."

It was becoming increasingly obvious that Mother Mary saw no problem whatever in her marrying a perfect stranger, if she was so intent on achieving her goal. It was also increasingly clear that Gloria's options were even more limited than she had feared.

"Thank you for your honesty," she said. "I suppose that in the end, I am simply going to have to decide how important it is to me to stop this war."

She had underestimated Mother Mary, if the dark, furious gaze that met hers was any indication.

"I'd say it was pretty darned important. You've seen the water rising. You've heard what Captain Stan has to say. We witches can do what we must from here, but the truth of the matter is that if something don't happen soon, the water will wash us right out of our homes. We're pretty powerful, but we're no match for the mighty Sangre Colorado de Christo." She gazed at her hands for a moment, clenched on the rake handle, and Gloria was sure she saw the glimmer of tears on her lashes before she blinked them away. "If you're the only woman in this entire country who's brave enough to try, then me and the girls will do everything possible to give you what assistance we can. Even if that means sending my own daughter with you to play maid-and-mistress."

Gloria drew in a long breath. "Mother, no."

Ella's mother now gripped the rake as though she might use it as a weapon. "She speaks the lingo even better than Captain Stan, and she knows enough of reading and writing to make it practical to send or forge a message if you need to. You can't pass for a poor woman, that's certain, so you may as well pass for a well-to-do one. For that, you'll need servants and a wardrobe something better than what you got. We might be able to find a dress or two in the storeroom, and hats and laces and such. They won't be in the pink of fashion, but they'll do to fool a soldier—or a priest."

Gloria's corset was beginning to feel altogether too tight. This storeroom was too small, its walls closing in on her. But she could not bolt and lose the witch's respect. She must stand her ground.

"You sound as though you have been thinking about this for as long as I."

"Fact is, I have. I know your options as well as you, though I for sure and certain don't like them any better."

"I cannot ask this of Ella. She is your daughter. What if she—what if we were—"

"If she stays, she risks the flooding. And the battle. At least if she's with Stan she has some hope of survival. The Californios in these parts know him, and you two won't be painted dead, so they won't know she's had a hand in putting paid to any number of 'em." Mother Mary's eyes turned bleak. "I won't ask you to promise to bring her back to me, but I will ask you to treat her as your own sister. To value her life as much as your own."

Hot tears flooded Gloria's eyes. "How can you ask that of me?"

"She ain't no servant," Mother Mary said with a dangerous quiet. "She's a woman with smarts and skill and she deserves respect."

"That is *not* what I meant." Gloria's voice cracked. "I owe Ella my life. I value her as much and more as any of my dearest friends—because believe me, I do not have so many that I can treat them lightly. Every one matters to me." She dragged in a breath so that she would not weep. "If indeed this is the path that I must take, there will be no one more grateful for Ella's company than I. And no one who will care more for her safety."

After a moment, Mother Mary nodded, and lowered the rake to an angle more suited to work than assault. "Can't ask for more than that."

"But this may all be moot, if I can find another way." She struggled to master her emotions, leaning on her own rake and pressing a fist to her heart.

"I can't see another way, to be honest. If you're certain and he's willing, best not to waste too much time. The river rises a little more every day."

"We must stop it, then."

"You leave that to us. Fixing that problem is all very well for us folks here, but it won't fix the bigger problem of the war and the invasion. That's between you and the Viceroy."

"*If* I can get to San Francisco de Asis and make him see sense."

"Stan will get you there. I got no worries on that score. And you're a fetching little thing. You've got as good a chance as anyone of talking a prince out of something he's set on, I suppose. Much as I love my Ella, I don't know as she could pull it off, if the two of you traded places."

"I would not put Ella in that position." Gloria shook her head. "My father got us all into this—it is I who must get us out. As long as the Ambassador stays away. It seems quite clear to me that he is the moving force behind all this. It would not surprise me if he means the Viceroy to be merely a figurehead, rubber-stamping all his wretched plans without a thought for what it is doing to his people."

"Even a figurehead can be useful if you throw it in the road at the right time."

Gloria smiled at the picture this painted in her imagination.

They finished spreading the corn in a companionable silence, and when Mother Mary went on to her next task, Gloria went in search of Ella.

"Meredith! I wondered where you'd gone." The girl's brown eyes were warm with welcome.

"I was helping your mother with the corn. She mentioned—that is—Ella, would you mind showing me which of the rooms might have a trunk or two with bodices and skirts in them? Not that I need a dress immediately, or at all, really, but—"

Ella clapped her hands in delight. "Dresses! Shall we play dress-up? Oh, what fun!" She danced along the terrace and sprang up on the first rung of one of the stout ladders that did duty as stairs between levels. "Come with me—I know just the one."

Ella must have an inventory in her head of every trunk in the village, for she led Gloria straight to a storeroom set deeply in the cliff. She dragged one of the old trunks away from the wall and flung open its lid. "Here we are. We've had these for some time, but they're so awfully pretty that none of us has the heart to tear them up for rags or make them over into more practical skirts."

She held up a dark blue silk trimmed in black velvet ribbon that Gloria recognized instantly as the height of fashion from ten years before. Ella pulled on the strings within and the rear half of the dress pulled itself up into a poufy bustle.

"Isn't it clever? Though what a girl would want with all that fabric behind I never could fathom."

"That's called a bustle, and they were madly fashionable for years," Gloria told her. "I never could fathom it, either, though some women carry them off beautifully. Is there a bodice as well?"

There was, and even a black shawl made of taffeta with black crocheted lace all around the edges.

"These are awfully dark," Ella said doubtfully. "What do you want with them?"

"You must promise me you won't laugh," Gloria said.

"I promise." Ella's eyes were wide and questioning. "Is it for a party?"

"No, darling, though I suppose a form of one might follow." Gloria folded the silk skirt over one arm. "I'm very much afraid it is for a wedding."

Ella gasped. "A wedding! A real one? Who is getting married?"

Gloria gulped. If she had been standing at the top of a cliff preparing to dive into the river far below, she could not have felt more ill and afraid. For once she told Ella, she must forthwith seek out Captain Stan and tell him that his proposal was accepted.

"I—I believe I am."

To her surprise, instead of another gasp or some expression of disbelief, Ella laughed, the sound bouncing off the sandstone walls to cause a merry echo in the passage. "Oh goodness, I thought you were being serious. I think we can find something more cheerful to play brides in than this dull old blue," she said. "There is a yellow cotton buried in here somewhere—or is it in the other trunk?"

"I am perfectly serious," Gloria said, laying a gentle hand on her arm to stop her fruitless digging in the welter of clothes. "Captain Stan proposed to me last night, and I fear I have no choice but to accept him."

Still kneeling, the girl searched her face as though looking for confirmation of anything but this news. "Actually proposed, not playing?"

"While I doubt that Captain Stan is serious about very much, he appears to be so about this. Your mother agrees with him that it is the only way that I will reach San Francisco de Asis safely. If I am to have any chance at all of stopping this war, I must become Mrs. Captain Stan and travel there as his wife." She paused. "You don't happen to know his surname, do you?"

Ella did not seem to hear. She was staring at Gloria as though she had just been informed she was about to be executed. "No," she said softly. "No, you can't."

"My sentiments exactly. But it seems I must."

"No, please don't. Don't go." Tears welled in Ella's eyes and her lips trembled as she got to her feet. "Abandon this mad plan and go back to Philadelphia. Please, Meredith." She took Gloria's hand in both of her own, and Gloria could actually feel them trembling.

"I confess that I gave it all the consideration you could wish, last night when I couldn't sleep," she said softly. "I do not want to be married yet—and certainly not to a stranger."

"Then don't! Let's take food and one of the smaller boats and go to Denver," Ella said eagerly. "You can find passage from there to Philadelphia, can't you?"

"I'm sure I could." The gold pieces in her corset would see to that. "But what would happen to your mother? To Clara, and all your friends and sisters here? Would you stay in Denver and leave them to the Californios?"

At this, Ella released her hand and turned away, her fingers pressed to her lips.

And watching her, a crazy thought darted through Gloria's brain, wheeled like a swallow, and came to rest in a conviction. Ella was not encouraging her to abandon everyone because she feared for her safety. She wanted Gloria to go so that she would not marry the captain.

Ella was in love with Stan herself.

Oh, dear. It was clear that Mother Mary had no idea, otherwise she would never have broached the plan best guaranteed to break her daughter's heart and make her miserable. But Gloria had no choice but to tell her. Perhaps between them, they could convince Mother Mary that another young woman should go as Gloria's maid. There was no compelling reason for Ella to place herself in such an untenable position.

"You see how convincing are the arguments I made to myself last night. But there is more."

"How much more could there be?"

"Your mother suggests that the illusion would be complete if you were to go with us as my maid. And presumably one or more of the captain's crew would act in a similar capacity for him. At the very least, I suppose we must have bodyguards."

"*I* go with you?" Blindly, Ella reached out and fumbled the lid of the trunk closed, with skirts and sleeves still half in and half out. Then she sat on it as suddenly as if her knees had buckled. "Oh, no. I couldn't."

"I wouldn't blame you in the least." Gloria's heart ached for the poor girl. Could there be any form of torture more dreadful than to be forced to watch the man you loved begin his life with someone else, with no ability to leave, no space in which to learn to forget? "Surely there must be some other capable young lady here who would do as well—who can speak the language, and read and write?"

"You do not want me to come?" Ella's face crumpled, and the pain in her eyes as the tears brimmed over was more than Gloria—the author and finisher of that pain—could stand.

Coward that she was, she flung down the blue dress and fled.

4

"You there!" Evan's stomach plunged as a guard banged the stock of his rifle on the iron bars of the aperture in the door of their cell. "Stop talking unless you want a few extra hours added to your work detail."

Evan and Barney exchanged glances and settled onto their pallets for the night. It was all idle talk they'd been indulging in anyway, the far-fetched plans of imprisoned men. No one in his right mind would fling a train car at a dam and hope to accomplish anything greater than the construction of a pile of bent iron and broken planks.

Still, he could not sleep despite the exhaustion of both body and brain. His mind toyed with the idea despite himself. Toyed, then tussled, then gave it up as a bad job.

He was no engineer, though he had acquitted himself pretty well following Dutch's instructions in adapting the behemoth's arm. His training was not in the mechanical, but in the mental. The human mind was an even more difficult and convoluted conundrum than the destruction of a dam. What a pity his own mind was so tired and useless in his present situation.

Evan fell into an uneasy sleep as the moon rose over the razor-edged mountains to the east. It had passed its meridian when he was startled out of sleep by a terrible cry that echoed across the parade ground.

"What's that?" Dutch mumbled, struggling to his elbows. "Are we under attack?"

Evan pushed himself to his feet and looked out the window. The guards patrolling outside had set off at a run for the low adobe buildings that housed the officers' quarters on the far side of the square, guns at the ready even as they formed an attack phalanx. They spoke in agitated tones as a lamp was lit within.

In a moment, a male shape appeared in the loggia and conferred with them. Voices rose. What was going on? Had someone been assassinated? Perhaps even the Ambassador? Aside from the young Viceroy, de Aragon was the person whose death would best bring the war to a grinding halt, if not stop it altogether.

Now the guards reformed and set off back toward the prison block. Evan sighed and turned away from the window. "It's nothing. It seems to be over."

But oddly, the beat of marching boots came closer, and two men detached themselves from the main body of guards. Tramping steps came down the stone corridor. As if they had signaled one another, all four men in Evan's cell rolled over and pretended to be asleep.

Once more, a rifle barrel crashed against the bars of the door. "Douglas!" When Evan did not move, the guard shouted again. "Douglas! Get up! Your services are wanted."

Evan pushed himself to his feet. "What is it?" He sounded as bemused as he felt. They could not want him for a work detail, for it was the middle of the night. Perhaps the four of them had been overheard. Perhaps he was about to be tossed into the pit below. Cold fear seeped into his stomach as he prepared to take the first opportunity to flee.

The keys clinked against one another as one guard unlocked the door and the other grabbed Evan by the elbow.

"Where are we—"

"Silence!"

The man twisted up his arm behind his back and frog-marched him across the parade ground to the officers' quarters. Evan did not know whether to be relieved or to say his final prayers. Perhaps he was about to be executed. The adobe building felt cool inside, and smelled of lemon and dust. A candle burned in a niche below an icon of the Madonna. He was marched down the corridor to a richly carved door at the end, where they were met by what appeared to be a butler or majordomo.

Thanks to Joe's slightly unwilling tutelage during their imprisonment, Evan now knew enough of the Californio tongue to understand him when he said, "Is this the man?" When the guard nodded, he peered into Evan's face, evidently seeking something beneath the grime. "You are a doctor?"

Evan nodded.

"You have some ability to interpret dreams?"

Another nod. Best to keep things simple.

"Our esteemed Commander de Sola is plagued with nightmares. You will interpret his dream to his satisfaction, so that he may sleep."

"It is not that precise a science," Evan managed. "Dreams can mean many things, and can even be specific to a single person."

"You will interpret this dream, or you will be removed from your privileged position and thrown in the pit. See that you use your abilities well."

His belly quaking and the tips of his fingers going cold with fright, Evan followed the majordomo into the room. The commander of the fort sat on the edge of his bed in his nightshirt and dressing gown, rolling a snifter of brandy between his fingers. A lamp burned on the dresser under a portrait of a young man Evan could only assume was the new Viceroy.

"Here is the man, sir."

De Sola eyed him, his own face drawn and exhausted. "You do not look much like a medical man."

Evan straightened his spine. "I am a medical doctor, with a degree from the University of Edinburgh, and a specialty in the unconscious and dreams. I have written eight monographs on the subject, and my research has been well regarded in academic circles in England."

"Then I am fortunate indeed," the commander said. "Please. Sit. I will tell you ... in a moment." He gulped the remainder of the brandy and appeared to be lost in thought.

Gingerly, Evan settled on the edge of a chair while the two guards took up their posts outside. The majordomo stood inside, his back to the door, watching. Should Evan wish to flee, he would have to fly through the window, and with his luck, he would only land in a walled garden or back on the parade ground.

The commander took a breath. "In my dream, I was walking down a deserted road. It was night, but the moon was bright, and the desert stretched away on every side as far as I could see."

"Where had you come from?" Evan asked. It was the same question he had asked Dutch. He could only pray the results would be as positive.

"Do not speak without permission!" the majordomo snapped.

"I am requested to interpret the dream. I rather thought I *had* permission," Evan said mildly. "Do you want my assistance or not?"

The majordomo flushed, and his hand jerked toward a ceremonial sword buckled to his waist, though it was clear he had pulled it on over his black breeches and his nightshirt without much thought. Perhaps it was the badge of his office, and he could not respond to terrified cries in the night without it.

FIELDS OF IRON

"Peace, Carlos," the commander said. "We will make an exception on this uneasy night."

"As you wish, sir."

De Sola's gaze returned to Evan. "I do not know where I had come from. Nor do I know where I was going. I was merely walking."

"How were you dressed?"

"In my uniform." His brow creased. "I must have been, for I remember looking down and thinking that Carlos would have to polish my boots again when I returned, for the white dust of the road had quite covered them."

"Go on."

He paused. "I was looking for something."

"Something you had lost?"

"No, something I needed to find. That is why I was scanning the sides of the road. I was looking for it—behind rocks, the sage, the ocotillo."

"So you were not here, in this valley of the water meadows?"

"No. Farther east, toward the dam. Yet I could not see it. It was miles away. And then I saw someone ahead of me, on the road. I could not imagine how they came there, for we were both on foot, and neither of us carried water, as we would have if we had come a long distance."

"Perhaps you were looking for water?"

"No, it was something tangible." He frowned. "Something for His Serene Highness the Viceroy. Something he had lost." The commander looked up as

• 63 •

though surprised. "That was it. I had to find something His Highness had lost."

"Ah, now we are getting somewhere." Evan leaned forward. "And then?"

"I approached this person, and as I came closer, I realized she was looking for something, too, searching the waysides and ranging back and forth a little way into the desert, as I had been."

"She?" Evan repeated. "Who was it?"

An expression of disgust creased the other man's face. *"Una bruja.* A witch, with a painted face and a skirt of white. Yet she wore a man's waistcoat and boots and hat. A caricature of a woman, neither one sex nor the other."

"She was looking for what the Viceroy had lost, too?"

"Si. And my urgency increased. I must find it before she did, or there would be disaster. And then I thought—no, this is not a race—I can simply kill her and get on with my search. So I unsheathed my sword and ran at her."

It did not take an expert in dreams to interpret *that.*

"Did she flee?"

"No." The commander got up and poured himself another brandy, waving his majordomo back into his place before the door. The lip of the decanter tinkled on the rim of the glass before he replaced it on the sideboard. "She changed into a dragon, a giant metal dragon, growing and roaring with the fire in her furnace-like belly. Her long snake's neck reared back and flung a great gobbet of fire at me, and though I raised my sword to defend myself, it melted. The fire burned off my hand and raced up my arm, and as it engulfed me, I screamed ... and woke myself up."

Evan sat silently, the image vivid in his mind, while the other man tossed back the brandy and gave a sigh.

"So. What am I to conclude, senor? That I am to die a fiery death, or merely that I must avoid eating the small red chiles with my dinner henceforth?"

"Neither, sir ... though in my mind, it would not hurt to leave those dreadful red vegetables alone. I believe your unconscious mind is sending you a message."

"And?"

"What is it that your forces here and the witches both seek? What belonging to the Viceroy are the two sides most interested in?"

He thought a moment. "The river. The land. Trade."

"To my knowledge, the witches have no interest in land or trade, outside of what they need to live on."

"There you are wrong. They seek to control the river, and he who controls that has power over the other two."

Evan sat back. "You have said it, sir. Power."

"But the Viceroy has not lost his power. If anything, it only increases every day with our work here."

"But who is really in charge of the Royal Kingdom?" He must tread carefully here. He had no idea of the man's loyalties. He could toss Evan into the pit or have him executed as easily as he took his next breath, should Evan make one misstep. But he had been commanded to interpret, and perhaps the truth would set him free. "Is it he, or is it the Ambassador, Senor de Aragon?"

The commander's eyes widened, and he flicked a glance at the majordomo. "You speak treason, senor."

"I do no more than give voice to what your own mind is telling you."

"It is a lie."

"Perhaps. Mine is an uncertain science, and there is not as yet much research into the workings of the brain. But if you believe the Viceroy has lost his power, and both you and the witches are seeking to find it and give it back to him, then I wonder whose loyalties are really illuminated here? For there is no treason in being loyal to one's prince."

"Sir," the majordomo whispered, "you must not let this man speak such things aloud."

The commander cleared his throat. "And what of the dragon? What of this witch who has the power to melt a sword of Damascene steel and burn me to death?"

"I do not know," Evan confessed. "But perhaps it is part and parcel of what we have just said. If the Californios do not make peace with the witches in your prince's name, perhaps it may mean the melting of many swords and death to many men."

The majordomo chuckled. "You place too much importance on the feeble powers of women, sir. *Las brujas* are only beggars and outlaws."

And yet the Ambassador himself was afraid of them. "De Aragon wishes to exterminate them, so they must be some threat to him. He believes they possess magic."

"He believes they possess gold," the commander said bitterly. "And to some, that is all the magic any ruler requires. You have my thanks, senor. I will think upon what you have said."

Evan would have asked him more, but the interview was clearly at an end. So he gave his best society bow, and the majordomo and the guards escorted him along the colonnade and out into the parade ground. When they would have twisted up his arm for the return march, the majordomo shook his head.

"Leave him. He has done the commander a service, and you will no longer treat him like a miscreant."

The guards exchanged a glance, then nodded. Evan was escorted back to his cell in silence, though the taller one couldn't resist giving him a shove in the back when he hesitated on the threshold of the cell.

His three mates were awake, their eyes gleaming in the retreating light of the lantern. "Didn't expect to see you back," Joe whispered as the sound of boots faded. "What happened?"

"They wanted me to interpret a dream." Even to himself, it still felt unreal.

"Whose dream?" Barney said. "And did you?"

He settled onto his pallet, feeling suddenly exhausted. "I did. The fort commander had a nightmare. He met a witch in the road who turned into a dragon and burned him up. That was the scream we heard."

For the first time since he had been imprisoned, Evan was startled to hear Joe laugh. It was a high, unrestrained sound, dancing on the edge of hysteria.

"Shut up!" Barney told him savagely. "Do you want to bring them down on us? Evan, how did you interpret that?"

"The witch and he were both looking for something the Viceroy had lost. His power, I believe." He gazed at them. "Gentlemen, I am convinced that when push comes to shove, the Ambassador may not command the loyalty we thought he did. There seem to be those who see him for what he is—grasping at a kingdom that does not belong to him. Who do not support him in their hearts, despite their building of dams and imprisoning of travellers. And that just might be turned to our advantage."

"If we can stay alive long enough to make it turn," Barney observed.

Yes. There was that.

FIELDS OF IRON

5

Alice, Lady Hollys, had never really understood what compelled her best friend, Lady Claire Malvern, to cross entire continents and set the captains of industry at naught in order to come to the assistance of the people she cared about.

She understood now.

They had had a busy couple of days in Resolution, the dusty riverbed ruin in the Texican Territory in which she had been born and raised (if one could use that word). The town, such as it was, had nearly been destroyed by the battle between the air pirates and the mercenaries guarding the Californio Ambassador's train. Even yet, the funeral pyre of the soldiers who had been killed by the desert flowers prior to their departure still smoked. When the wind was right, well, you simply moved upwind before the smell of charred human remains got to you.

"Captain?"

Alice turned from her dismal contemplation of the bonfire to see her navigator, Jake Fletcher McTavish, leaning against a rock looking filthy and exhausted. Since she was also filthy and exhausted, she belatedly wished she'd laid claim to the rock first.

"We've finished loading the crates of the mechanical horses and hunting cats." Jake wiped his forehead on his shirtsleeve. "Captain Hollys wants to know how much of the other cargo—bullets, rifles, and such—we'll take. He says the Texican army can use them immediately if they find they need to."

"The army doesn't believe in mechanical horses?" she asked rhetorically. Across the rutted field, the tall figure of her husband of only a week hefted long wooden crates of arms onto the last operating vehicle in Resolution—a steamcart they'd found in one of Ned Mose's sheds. "They prefer to send living creatures to their deaths in battle?"

"I have to admit I'd like to see one in action."

"Uncrate one, then, and have at it."

Jake's exhaustion vanished. "For true, Captain?"

Sometimes her cynical, frighteningly competent navigator was just a nineteen-year-old boy who loved to tinker. She smiled in spite of herself. "For true. Take Benny with you. Once you get one going, I'll come and have a look. Might be a valuable thing to know how they work, one of these days."

If the Texican Territories actually went to war with the Royal Kingdom of Spain and the Californias. If Gloria wasn't dead, and she succeeded in her mission to stop it. If Evan and she were together and could help one another.

If. Alice was coming to hate that pallid yet powerful word.

Never mind. She and Ian and Jake and Benny, her newly promoted gunner, had their work cut out for them here. The Texicans didn't believe their neighbors to the west were preparing for war. They could deliver all these armaments to them in Santa Fe as proof, but the odds of Alice being recognized not as Lady Hollys, but as Alice Chalmers, the daughter of air pirate Ned Mose and the woman who had sprung a prisoner from their blasted pinnacle cells, were pretty high. The less she showed her mug there, the better.

With a deep breath, she forced her tired limbs to move down the slope to where Ian was loading the cart.

"Where has Jake gone?" Ian stretched, as though his back had kinks in it. He didn't resemble a baronet in the least. While his face bore the lines at the corners of the eyes that all aeronauts did, from gazing into the clouds, and his face was tanned from years of flying, his body was muscled from hard work and capable of pulling the heavy crates out of the train cars and on to the cart with one heave. No smooth hands and fashionable dancing shoes for her man, no sir.

"I've set him and Benny to firing up one of the horses," she said, coming around the corner of the cart and giving him a kiss just because. Besides, the Hollys sapphire flanked with two diamonds set in gold on the fourth finger of her left hand said she could. "You never know when it might be handy to know how to ride one."

"Are you planning to lead a charge?"

"No, but you know what happens to the best laid plans."

"I do indeed. So when the boys satisfy their curiosity and yours, I still believe we ought to deliver the lot to Santa Fe."

"You'd be on your own, then. I'm confined to quarters when Robert Van Ness is within five miles." The commander in charge of the garrison knew her smiling face all too well. "Besides, how do we know they'd use them to defend the border? They might send them to Mexico City to fend off trouble there."

"That is a concern, I grant you." Ian gazed into her dirty face as though he didn't even see the grease and dust. "But I have a feeling you have already made an alternate plan."

She smiled into his eyes. "As a matter of fact ..."

"Let's have it."

"Alaia's people are scattered across the mesas and canyons from here to the Rio de Sangre Colorado de Christo. If I've heard one tale of caves full of gold, I've heard a dozen, but the caves do exist. What better place to stash a hold full of arms than in the country that will need them, with people who may not get so much as a glance from the army once war is declared?"

He considered this, examining the question from every side. "You have a point."

"I usually do. And these folks aren't savages. They're as capable of using steam and metal as anyone—why, I saw one of Alaia's boys riding a version of a mechanical horse when we left Santa Fe. It was mostly for show, but still."

"I thought you were half unconscious," he said with a laugh. "Trust you to perk up when there's a mechanical device anywhere near."

A whoop drew their attention across the battlefield to *Swan*, who bobbed at her lines with her cargo ramp down to receive the contents of the wrecked train. Jake and Benny had a crate open and its packing material scattered all over the ground, much to the joy of their three hens, Mrs. Morse, Soot, and Rosie the Second, who were already belly-deep in seed heads and dry hay.

With the legs on, the mechanical horse's withers were taller than Jake, who was no shrimp. The way he went through food, he was going to be as tall as Ian soon.

"He's going to need help to get the head on and the guns installed," Alice said, one hand shading her eyes. "Come on. I have to see this."

The boys might have had no trouble with the mechanical's legs, but the rest of it was both heavy and complicated. It took Alice and her crew the rest of the afternoon to put the thing together, and when it was finished, there was no doubt it was a thing of beauty.

A terrifying beauty.

Its bones were pistons, its tendons and muscles plates and hydraulic tubing. When Jake completed its ignition sequence, steam issued from its nostrils. The operator rode behind the head and neck, just over the engine, which was protected by armored plate, and from where he operated a matched set of repeating guns and a rocket launcher mounted in the chest.

Alice set her wrench down on a rock and looked around for the hens, who had deserted their hay when the mechanical had begun to steam.

"Well, Jake, it's ready for you to ride."

"Me?" He looked horrified and elated at the same time.

"This was your idea. It's only fair you should take it for its maiden voyage. Just don't go too far. If something fails, we'll never be able to drag the monster back here."

Jake scrambled up the left side foreleg, where pegs protruded from the plates, and settled into the metal saddle. "For my next order," he said, "I'll ask if these come in a pony model. It's a wee bit big for me."

Truly, he did look like a child mounted on a Clydesdale.

"Where is the acceleration bar?" His hands settled naturally on a pair of levers in front of his knees. "Never mind. I think I found it. The neck seems to act as a shield, and these braces here—" He indicated them by giving them a kick. "—protect my legs."

He pressed the levers forward and the horse began to move—not, as one would expect, like a horse might in the flesh, but as the wheels of a locomotive did, under moving pistons and turning gears. Faster and faster the legs moved, Jake whooping in exhilaration with an edge of alarm, down the length of the field to the riverbed, along it, and then in a wide turn, back again.

He took aim at one of the empty, ruined houses and yanked on a handle. With a whine and a shriek, a rocket sang out of a tube running under the length of the mechanical's stomach. It detonated on the house with a blast that made Alice cover her ears and yell, dropping to the ground in fright with Ian's arms tightly around her, while the three chickens flung themselves up the ramp into *Swan*'s belly in a flapping cacophony of alarm. When Alice clambered to her feet again, it was to see Jake, white as smoke, hauling the machine to a stop near *Swan*'s stern.

The rocket had destroyed not only the house, but the entire cluster of its neighbors—Ned Mose's included—leaving nothing but a smoking crater. Dust and soot spiraled thickly into the air in a cloud like a grave marker.

"Sorry," Jake said hoarsely.

Ian closed his mouth with a snap. "Do not be sorry. We wanted to know its capabilities, and now we do. I must say, I would not wish a weapon like this leading the charge at the head of the wrong army."

"She was right to want to stop this," Jake said, climbing down much more slowly than he'd gone up. "What kind of monster could conceive of such a thing, much less sell it to the highest bidder to use on innocent people?"

By *she*, Alice could only guess he meant Gloria. "The more I think of it, the more I'm convinced these mechanicals don't belong with the Texicans. It's lucky they don't believe us. Can you imagine what would happen if they decided someday to take a war into the Canadas? Or to the Navapai?" It did not bear thinking of. "Maybe we should disassemble everything and melt it all down."

"Once the war is decided one way or another, I think that an excellent plan," Ian said. "Either that, or refit this thing into some kind of cargo conveyance."

"It was built for war," Jake said flatly. "I for one volunteer to send one of its own bombs into the whole lot and then set a course for home once we're finished here."

"Done," Alice said.

"I shall hold you to it, Captain," he warned. Something in his tone told her he was utterly serious—that in fact, he might have Gloria in his mind at that very moment, and the impossible mission she had set out to accomplish.

"I hope you will," she said mildly. "Now, let's get this thing into the bottom-most cargo bay, where the landaus go. It won't fit in any of the others, and I don't fancy wasting the rest of the day taking it apart again when we might have to use it sooner than we think."

Luckily the mechanical had a non-attack mode meant for simple movement, and Jake used the other lever to steer it into the largest bay, where he made it kneel amidships. They tied it down so it would not fall over and send poor *Swan* heeling with the massive shift of weight. The crates where the other members of its herd lay in pieces were arranged about it, to keep the weight distributed evenly and *Swan* in trim.

FIELDS OF IRON

Then at last it was time to pull up ropes and take crew positions. Alice gazed out the viewing port at what was left of Resolution—ruined houses with shabby wood tops and stone bottoms as a safeguard against the flash flooding, a smoking crater, and a broad field pitted with bomb blasts and littered with unusable steam chariots and pieces of rail car.

She was never coming back here again. With a feeling of relief and a glance at her husband, she pushed the lever that sent power from the boilers into the engines. "Vanes full vertical, please. Up ship!"

And they fell into the sky, wallowing a little with the sheer weight of the mechanicals in the hold.

"Course, Captain?" Jake asked formally from the navigation table.

She eyeballed the sun, which hovered in a reddened cloud about an hour above the horizon.

"The Navapai village west of Santa Fe, Mr. McTavish ... via the border. I think we have time for a look-see at the Royal Kingdom before the sun goes down, and we'll have information to share with Alaia's people when we get there."

"The Royal Kingdom's border?" Ian's brows creased in concern. "Are you sure, with so much weight aboard? I can feel already that we're not nearly as nimble in the air as usual."

"Just a look, Ian. We won't fly anywhere near their air space, but we'll be high enough that even twenty miles off, we can get the lie of the land. I want to know if there are troops massing, or suspicious-looking roads being built."

"With respect, dear, I do not think it safe."

"Noted." She touched her husband's cheek and smiled into his worried eyes. "But *Swan* is capable. She was built for this, remember? She's a military transport and the fastest thing in these skies, you know, outside of the Ranger ships in Santa Fe. The Californios will barely have time to register that we're not a cloud before we'll wheel on our propellers and run."

After a moment, he firmed his lips and gave a curt nod. "I shall take the watch, then."

Her heart swelled with love for this man, who would express his opinion and then, when it was acknowledged, not insist on taking the helm from her. He might outrank her in more than one way, but on this deck, the helm was hers and he would not challenge her authority in front of her crew.

"Set a westerly course, Mr. McTavish," she said. "Let's float in, have a look, and then hightail it out of there on a direct course for Alaia's moorage. I have a hankering for some of her cooking tonight."

"Aye, Captain."

Swan flew as though she were heavily pregnant, swimming through the clouds and proving just a bit reluctant to obey her helm. Alice had never burdened her with so much, not even when there were landaus and building materials aboard. No wonder the mechanicals had gone west on a train—even the transatlantic passenger ships would have had a slow voyage with such a cargo.

Still, Alice and her loaded ship adjusted to each other quickly, and it was not long before the great Rio de Sangre Colorado de Christo came into view below, a silver ribbon in a serrated scarlet and umber and gold landscape. Wider she became, and even from a thousand feet above they could see the sheer rush and volume of water she carried to the sea far away.

"That range of mountains is the border, Captain," Jake said, one finger resting on the chart. "No airships may fly beyond it."

"I don't mean to fly beyond it—just up to it. Enough to take a peek over it and see what we can see."

Ian made a noise in his throat that he quickly converted to a cough. He had said his say and wouldn't repeat himself, but she knew what lay on his mind.

"It will be all right," she said to her crew, though no one was arguing outright. "Just one look, and then we'll go. Follow the river, but stay at this altitude. With our weight, I don't want to get caught in an updraft or a sheer."

The automaton intelligence system accordingly adjusted the vanes so that they rose a little higher, and soon the river formed a broad reach through a notch in the mountains.

Ian leaned into the view, as though unaware there was glass between him and the panorama below. "Why, they're damming the river. How is it the Texicans can be unaware of this?"

From the helm, Alice craned to see. No wonder the miles of river backed up behind the dam seemed so wide, so crushingly powerful. She wasn't sure if there were towns and villages along the cliffs, but there were certainly crossings that boasted inns and honkytonks. Were they going to be inundated when the water rose high enough?

But Ian's sharp eyes had seen something more. "Look, out where the country flattens and the river has carved channels. Those are military tents, if I'm not mistaken."

When it came to soldiering, Ian was very rarely mistaken.

"This doesn't look good," she murmured. "I wish the Texicans could see this—they'd be a little less confident about their friends to the west."

"Captain!" Jake said suddenly. "We're over the border. We must make our turn now, without a moment to lose."

Alice spun the helm and *Swan* lumbered into a northerly turn. But whether the winds were against her or she simply took longer to execute, they were already drifting farther into the Royal Kingdom's air space. Its religious government had made it abundantly plain over the last century that dirigibles and airships were the devil's work, and felt no compunction about shooting them out of the sky if only to prove that flying in the face of God was worthy of death.

"Alice, we need more speed," Ian said tersely. "The winds are southerly—I suggest an immediate turn with them, not against them."

"But the mountains curve away here." Alice hauled on the helm, but *Swan* could only give her so much. Each second allowed her to make way a little, but not

FIELDS OF IRON

enough. "We'll be over the border faster, and we're halfway through our turn now."

"They are bringing a great machine to bear," he reported. "Great Caesar's ghost, did that monster Meriwether-Astor make another telescoping cannon for these people?"

"Like the one that nearly brought down the Prince of Wales's ship?" Jake's finger moved with despairing slowness on his chart.

"Exactly. Alice—"

Come on, darling. Just a little bit more. I know we loaded you with more than you're used to, but you can do it.

With a screech like a stooping hawk, a projectile flashed past the gondola, sparks trailing aft.

"A rocket torpedo!" Ian exclaimed. "It is a cannon—and they'll have adjusted their trajectory. Can you not get anything more out of these engines?"

Her beloved Daimlers were the best in the world. "Ian, take the helm!"

Alice flung herself down the corridor to the engine room, where Benny Stringfellow was shoveling coal into the boilers like a man possessed. She snatched up a wrench and had the covers off seconds later, but before she could so much as adjust a single bolt, her beautiful ship shuddered.

The bottom fell out of her stomach.

"Ian!" she shrieked into the trumpet. "Are we hit?"

"Aye," came a tinny shout. "Straight through the fuselage. We're going down."

Alice threw the engine covers back on and bolted them down, then ran back to the navigation gondola. "On which side of the border?" she gasped.

Jake's finger, thank all the angels, rested on the eastern slopes of the mountains. "Best find a security line, Captain," he said grimly. "It's a long slow glide, but in this godforsaken country and with our weight, we're not going to find a soft landing."

FIELDS OF IRON

6

"Dearly beloved, we are gathered together here in the sight of God, and in the face of this congregation, to join together this man and this woman in holy matrimony."

Padre Emilio did not speak very much English, but he read it fairly well, so between them, Gloria and Captain Stan had written out as much of the marriage service as either of them could remember. Gloria's portion had been much larger than that of her fiancé; a consequence, she supposed, of her having actually attended a number of weddings instead of galloping about the landscape being an outlaw. She found herself giving in to the temptation to change just a few details of the vows on the theory that no would know the difference.

So unbeknownst to either the good cleric or her imminent husband, *obey* became *cherish* and was subsequently sworn to upon the thick, illuminated Bible with no one the wiser.

"I, Stanford Fremont the third, take thee, Gloria Diana—" He stopped, her hand in his and a heavy gold ring poised at the end of her finger.

"Senor?" the padre inquired. He was about Gloria's height, and very fit, if the tanned feet and muscular shoulders under the rough brown robe were any indication. He had the hands of a man who traveled hard and worked harder when he was needed by the members of his parish, despite his age. His brown gaze below bushy white brows lay upon the captain expectantly.

Around them, the simple wooden pews in the tiny adobe church of Santa Croce were filled by the witches and the members of the *Colorado Queen*'s crew, none of whom had yet recovered from the news last night that their captain was to be married, nor from the celebration that had followed.

It was very quiet. Somewhere in the rafters, a dove fluttered and cooed, calling its mate.

The captain, meanwhile, stared down at her in some perplexity. "Who am I marrying, exactly?" he whispered over their joined hands.

"That is my real name," she whispered back. "You can't expect me to enter into a legal contract under a false one."

"No," he said after a slight hesitation. "Of course not."

FIELDS OF IRON

For one dreadful moment, she thought he would not go on, that she was to relive the wedding scene in *Jane Eyre*. But no, with a clearing of his throat, he picked up where he left off. "...take thee, Gloria Diana Meriwether-Astor, to have and to hold from this day forward, for better or for worse, for richer or for poorer, in sickness and in health, to love, honor, and cherish, until death us do part."

The heavy, chased ring that had probably been stolen from some Californio grandee slid onto her finger, and then it was her turn.

At least now she knew his name. It sounded vaguely familiar, but she couldn't for the life of her think why. Perhaps she had read it in a book, for it was rather fanciful.

"By the power vested in me by God and His holy kingdom of Spain and the Californias, I now pronounce you husband and wife together." The padre heaved a breath, as though the worst of it was over. He glanced down at the paper that lay on the Bible. "You may now kiss your bride."

Oh, dear. Gloria had hoped he might overlook this part. But it was quite clear that Captain Stan—Stanford—good heavens, she was never going to be able to call him Stanford with a straight face—would not. He was leaning toward her. His face was solemn, but his eyes danced, as though he knew perfectly well that at the ripe old age of twenty-three she had never been kissed. He was quite enjoying the prospect of being her first in front of the whole congregation.

Ella, standing behind her holding her bouquet of hastily gathered bougainvillea, made a sound suspiciously like a sob.

Oh, dear.

Feeling horribly guilty, and overwhelmed, and a little bit angry that she was being forced by her own wretched principles to marry someone she hardly knew, Gloria tilted up her face and allowed the captain to lift her small blue eye veil. He folded it back carefully on the black straw tricorne covered in musty velvet flowers that someone had unearthed from one of the trunks. She had a fleeting moment to regret the loss of the Burano lace veil, when—

Her eyes slid shut as his lips met hers softly. When he straightened, it was only with the greatest presence of mind that she managed to remember to breathe.

The padre said something rapidly in the Californio tongue that ended with *"el Capitan y Senora Fremont."*

With his tug on her hand, Gloria understood what she was to do next. She and her new husband knelt before the simple plank table covered in an altar cloth thickly embroidered in the same patterns the witches favored on their blouses, and received the padre's prayer and blessing. When they rose, he guided them into a tiny niche of an anteroom, where an imposing document lay on a small table with a book.

He indicated that they should sign the latter, clearly the parish register. *Gloria Diana Meriwether-Astor*, she wrote for the last time. Really, it was rather a relief. Such an unwieldy name. *Spinster, of Philadelphia. The twenty-seventh day of February, 1895.*

FIELDS OF IRON

The captain wrote his name and profession, and dated the document. By the time he had done so, the padre had filled in their names on the illuminated certificate, which actually bore gold leaf. The old man signed it, dated it, and then melted a bit of wax under the candle flame. Red drops fell on the bottom next to his signature, and in a moment he pressed his gold ring into the wax.

Marriage was clearly a very serious business in these parts.

Captain Stan spoke with him in rapid sentences, pressing a few silver coins into his hand. With a smile that seemed to warm Gloria from the inside out, the padre cupped her cheek and said something softly. She smiled back, and could not help the tears welling in her eyes.

He was so kind, and she felt as though she was duping him somehow—allowing him to perform this simple, beautiful ceremony because she planned to pull off a political coup.

As he led them back to the altar, she took the captain's arm and whispered, "What did he say to me?"

Into her ear he replied, "He said that you were beautiful, would have beautiful children, and wished you every blessing under heaven."

And so it was that Gloria turned from the altar a married woman on her husband's arm, with tears of guilt and chagrin trickling down her cheeks.

Ella burst into tears, too, and buried her face in the bougainvillea, completely forgetting she was supposed to return the bouquet to the bride.

The recessional had no music save the dove, and as the wedding party and guests spilled out into the dusty square, Gloria saw that a few of the children had gathered near the door to throw pink and purple petals on the happy couple.

For their sake, she smiled and tossed pennies ... and wondered how on earth she would ever explain this to Claire and Alice. If she ever saw either of them again.

There was no wedding breakfast, for there was too much to be done before the noon train departed. Gloria felt nothing but relief. The thought of nodding and smiling and presiding over a table while Ella tried not to cry and the ship's crew became increasingly drunk again was simply not to be borne.

Instead, she and the witches returned to the *Colorado Queen*, which was moored on the edge of the tiny village at a rickety dock, to pack food into Gloria's trunk for the journey.

The fact that she had a trunk seemed miraculous. What had happened to the one she'd brought aboard *Swan* all those weeks ago, when she'd set out so bravely with Alice and Evan and Captain Hollys and Jake? Where were they all now?

"Mother Mary," she said suddenly, straightening, "is it possible to send a letter from here?"

"Depends where you want it to go." The older woman handed her a packet wrapped in oiled paper that must contain dried meat of some kind. Best not to inquire exactly what. "If you're sending a letter to the Viceroy letting him know you're coming, that's simple enough. They'll take it on the train. But if you're writing to anyone east of here, well ..."

"Padre Emilio goes as far as Santa Fe." Ella had scrubbed her face and was bravely carrying on as though they were about to go on a shopping trip and nobody had been to church the hour before. "He takes letters all the time from place to place along his route. Of course, folks who can read and write are pretty much only on the ranchos."

"Santa Fe would be fine," Gloria said. "I expect if I enclose the money for a pigeon, he would see it sent?"

"A pigeon, now?" Mother Mary eyed her. "Has a ways to go, does it?"

It did indeed. Gloria asked directions to the captain's—er, her husband's quarters, and soon found herself in the stern, in a relatively spacious cubicle that looked as though its primary purpose was not sleep, but gambling, if the card table was any indication. But no, here was a desk that folded down out of a cupboard, along with the items she sought.

Dear Alice,

I have no idea if you and our friends are alive or dead, but I am sending this care of Swan in the event she, at least, has survived.

I am well, and this morning I was married to Captain Stanford Fremont III, who pilots a riverboat on the Rio de Sangre Colorado de Christo and appears to be my only means of reaching San Francisco de Asis, the capital. I am determined still to stop this war, and will attempt to speak to the Viceroy himself. I will not bore you with my opinions of a country that treats women like chattel at best, but suffice it to say that if there had been any other way, I would have taken it. I am alone and without means, and the captain at least is willing to help, if only for his own amusement.

I pray that you are alive. I know nothing of Evan, so must only conclude that he died at the Battle of Resolution after so bravely trying to protect me. Please convey my love to Claire if you ever see her again. Her friendship and yours have been the greatest gifts of my life.

Bless you,
Gloria Meriwether-Astor Fremont

It was not a very coherent letter, but then, she did not know if anyone would ever read it. She folded it up and looked fruitlessly for an envelope, but the captain's supplies did not extend that far. In the end she took from her hat a rusty ribbon that might once have been blue, and tied it closed with that.

"They told me I might find you here."

Gloria jumped as though she had been caught doing something she oughtn't, and turned as Captain Stan closed the door behind him. "I hope you don't mind," she said a little breathlessly.

"I have just promised to share all my worldly goods with you." He gazed about and spread his hands as if to indicate the ship. "This, I am afraid, is the extent of it."

"Then I am getting the better end of the bargain by far." She stood, smoothing her musty skirts with one hand, the letter in the other. "For all my worldly goods fill one trunk—and that is mostly food for our journey."

"We'll be glad of it. But I am sure there is more to you than that," he said easily.

What did he mean? Was he remarking upon the resources of her mind and determination? Or ...

For the first time, another of the many consequences of her hasty wedding was borne in upon her. For was it not the law that all she possessed now belonged to her husband? If she ever saw Philadelphia again, would he become the president of the Meriwether-Astor Munitions Works? And the master of the fine house on Washington Avenue? Would he even want to go to Philadelphia?

"Pardon me," she said. "I have just remembered someone else I must write to."

Mr. Elias Pitman must be informed of her whereabouts, and of her marriage, without delay.

"Telling your friends and relations the good news?"

She settled herself at the folding desk once more. "If they do not think me dead, it is only right to let them know of our ... marriage." She began to write as he watched her from the door. "Please, do not let my presence prevent you from packing."

"It doesn't," he said. "I'm still recovering from the sight of a woman at my desk. It's a novel experience. I want to take it in."

She bit back a caustic remark about where else in the room his women were likely to be, and focused on the brief lines toward the end of her letter.

If you can, please make enquiries into my husband's family. He gives me no details, but I am sure he is concealing as much from me as I am from him. His name is familiar to me, and the associations are tragic, but I cannot remember why.

I hope you are well, and that we will see one another again.

She folded up the second letter and addressed it carefully. It could go on one of the colonial airships out of Santa Fe, she was quite sure. What a stroke of luck that Padre Emilio was so useful!

Sadly, her poor hat had no second ribbon to offer. "Do you possess an envelope, or a piece of string with which I might tie this up?"

"Certainly." He fished in a drawer and drew out a red ribbon of a particularly lush and painful shade. "I meant to give this back, but you know how that goes."

"I certainly do not." She took the ribbon from him using the tips of her fingers, and tied up the letter as best she could. "I must find Padre Emilio and give these to him."

"He's probably still at the church. There is quite the line of couples waiting to be married. Lucky we got there first, or we might have missed the train."

Yes. What a very lucky thing.

"Are those for your family?" He nodded toward the letters.

"No. To friends." This was dreadfully awkward. "My mother died several years ago, and my father only recently. In November." His brows rose, and she added hastily, "Please do not judge me for not wearing mourning for him. One hardly needs to in these parts, and our relationship was ... difficult."

"I was not thinking of that at all. Only of similarities of circumstance. My relationship with my father was also ... difficult. And he is likewise passed from this mortal coil. Several years ago, now." He turned to look through the large round porthole that overlooked the great brass wheel-and-gear assembly that propelled the boat. "I have not thought of him in months. I suppose that is progress."

"And your mother?" she asked hesitantly.

"I do not know. I suppose she is well, but I have not seen her in some years. She is an invalid, which I suppose gave my father his license to behave as a single man." His face darkened, and he reached for the latch. "I hope you will treat the *Queen* as your own for the few hours you are aboard her. Try to get some rest, if you can. The train journey may be ... trying. The first leg will take us to Mission Nuestra Señora la Reyna de los Ángeles, and it is a journey of many hours."

"What will we do there? Change trains?"

"I have already registered our party as travelers at the station here, and have been issued traveling papers, but there we must have the certificate of our marriage legally recorded."

"But—" Stan? Stanford? Captain? "I am sorry, you will think me foolish, but I have no idea what to call you."

He opened his mouth to say something, and then appeared to change his mind. "Stan is fine. If you call me Stanford, I can't promise I'll answer."

The boatmen called him Stan, as though he were a pal and not their captain. His women likely did, too. Gloria balked at sharing anything with them, even something as ephemeral as the syllables by which she addressed her husband.

"I shall call you Mr. Fremont," she decided. "That is what the married ladies do in Philadelphia."

One brow rose in mock astonishment. "Why, Mrs. Fremont, is that where you hail from? Can it be that I now know one more concrete detail about my wife other than her real name, the fact that she once had parents, and the alarming amount of her knowledge of arms?"

Nettled, she glared at him. For goodness sake, he saw her write it in the parish register! "It is two more than I know about you."

"Very well, if we are laying down facts like cards and keeping our poker faces on, I will see your city and raise you another. I was born in London, but we returned to New York when I was twelve."

The two facts clinked together, resonating like coins thrown in a pot. She had known he was from New York. But *why* did she know it? Oh, why did her memory choose now to fail her?

"I wondered why I could not place your accent," she said mildly. "Have you been in London since?"

"Once or twice. You?"

"I went to school there. At St. Cecilia's Academy for Young Ladies."

"I am sorry. Sounds appalling."

"For the most part, it was. Though I did learn how to blow up the Chemistry of the Home laboratory one afternoon. The rest of it was a dull procession of mathematics, languages, pouring tea, and walking up and down the corridors with a book upon my head."

He smiled. "To this we owe the demoralization of our youth."

She smiled to herself, and he looked at her curiously. But she was in no mood to explain. "It turned out well in the end. I met one of my closest friends there—though at the time, neither of us could abide the other."

A shout came from up on deck, and the captain opened the door. "Take my advice and rest. I will see you in an hour. If you give me your letters, I'll send one of the boys to the padre with them."

She handed them over with great care not to touch his fingers. "Thank you, Mr. Fremont."

"Gloria."

She held one corner of the little packet, and he the other. "Yes?"

"That is going to get very tiresome by about the eighth hour of our journey, when we are hot and covered in smuts from the train. If there is something preventing you from using my first name, then for heaven's sake let us clear the air about it. I do not care to have my family name bandied about this country. Bad enough the good padre was obliged to say it aloud in church."

"I am glad he did, for otherwise I should not have known it until I saw the parish register," she retorted.

"You might be able to get away with Captain Stan on a daily basis, but I am afraid that my being addressed as Mrs. Fremont is unavoidable."

"Not by me," he said. "Or my crew."

"But—"

"Just do as I ask. I need not add that I am doing much more for you."

When the door closed behind him, she was tempted to kick it. "No, you need not add that," she told the carved and glossy planks. "And I hope you do not intend to cast it up to me every five minutes. If you do, I shall *Mr. Fremont* you to death, sir."

But there was no reply save the creak of the ropes as the *Queen* swayed on the current.

She could not possibly lie down on that bunk, where who knew how many women had preceded her. Thank heaven they were not to spend the wedding night here, for if they were, she should be hard pressed to decide whether she ought to throw him out of his bunk, or herself. Sleeping sitting up on a hard train bench was infinitely preferable.

Instead, she folded the desk into its cupboard and prowled about the room—six steps from bow to stern, seven from port to starboard. A white shirt hung on a peg next to the washstand, where a bowl and ewer and a brush and razor stood in a brass rack designed to keep them from falling over with the movement of waves. A black string tie hung over one of the bars, and a disreputable coat hung from a hook behind the door.

Several small cupboards matching the one that concealed the desk marched under the window. Idly, she opened one after the other to find books, charts, a pair of boots, and a set of china and cutlery. In the fourth cupboard she found more intimate garments, upon which she closed the door hastily. The last one was smaller than the others. Inside it lay a small empty case that had likely once housed the ring upon her finger. Next to it was a picture, lying face down in its frame.

With a glance at the door, she pulled it out and turned it toward the light. It was a daguerreotype, a family portrait, taken some years previously. There was her husband as a young man in his middle teens, standing straight as a poker with a fearsome scowl upon his face. Seated on a fainting couch was a woman dressed in the height of fashion of about the same vintage as the dress Gloria wore now. She wore her hair piled high and a pair of chandelier earrings, and her face was drawn with exhaustion or pain. Next to her on the sofa was a little girl of about five in a frilly dress and an enormous hair ribbon, and on the mother's lap was a baby.

With a jolt of recognition, Gloria realized what this was. A bereavement photograph. For the baby was unmistakably dead, held tightly in its mother's arms as though the next ordeal following the photograph was the funeral, and a tiny white casket.

Oh, how dreadful. And how terribly sad.

At last her gaze moved to the patriarch standing behind the couch, both hands extended along the back of it as if to embrace his family … or to declare his dominance over them. Here was the man whose name her husband was so reluctant to bear. She had never seen him before—his face large, florid, and framed by a mane of light hair and a luxurious moustache. He looked like the kind of man who enjoyed excellent cognac and fine cigars, and women who wore brocade corsets and high-heeled opera slippers.

With a quick movement, Gloria slipped the picture into its cupboard face down and closed the door.

Here was something else she shared in common with the stranger to whom she was now married. It seemed that their fathers were wealthy men married to pale, fearful women whom they put on pedestals as miserable, housebound saints. *The angels of the house*, the popular press used to call them. Ignored while they were alive and sainted once they were gone.

Gloria snorted. Well, history was not about to repeat itself in *her* generation. She was *una bruja*. In the unlikely event that Captain Stan hankered for an angel, he was in for a grave disappointment.

FIELDS OF IRON

7

"Was that an explosion?" Evan froze in the behemoth's piloting harness, the mechanical giant likewise freezing in the act of fitting an iron beam into place on the dam.

The Californio soldier whose duty it was to ride about inside and guard him as he worked said something sharply in his own tongue, and leaned to look out the viewing port. Joe rolled his eyes from where he worked the steam flanges.

"He says they just fired the pressure cannon."

"At what?" Evan dropped the beam into place and swung the behemoth around in order to get a better look. There was only one direction from which any threat to the Royal Kingdom could come, so he brought the behemoth to a standstill facing east.

As the stern of what must have been their target sank out of sight behind the serrated peaks of the mountains, his stomach swung and plunged with a wave of nausea.

"That was a Texican Ranger ship!" exclaimed the guard. "How dare they enter our air space with their floating abominations!"

No. It was not. It could not be.

Evan's head felt as though it would lift off his neck and float up to follow them, and with difficulty he remembered to breathe. That was not a Ranger ship. Not that blue and silver shape, so elegant and long, slicing through the sky with the ease of a fish. A shape that he remembered as well as that of his own face.

Alice Chalmers's ship, *Swan*.

Come to rescue him. Somehow they had found him. It was a miracle, when he had given up all hope.

And the dadburned Californios had shot at her!

"Was it a hit?" he asked as casually as his tight throat would allow.

"Oh, yes," the guard said with satisfaction. "You see?" He pointed at the cannon's crew below, on the turret that guarded the digging crews, who were practically leaping with excitement and diagramming the shot with their hands. "It was a good hit. They are certainly going down. It is a pity the Texican scum did not venture a little farther, where we could have captured them and taught them a lesson for their insolence."

Joe translated like an automaton, without inflection.

Evan judged it best if he showed no more emotion than anyone might at a hitch in their usual relentless routine. But it was difficult, and he was not sure of his success, particularly when Joe bumped his shoulder as they were marching across the parade ground to their cell at sunset.

"Whatever you're thinking about that ship they shot down, keep it to yourself," he murmured. "Are you crazed, to let them know you're on the side of the Texicans?"

"But I'm—"

"Silencio!" That needed no translation, so Joe didn't bother. But it was a sign that Evan's status had changed slightly since the night he had interpreted the commander's dream. Instead of a rifle butt between the shoulder blades, he merely got a shove.

It was not until they were locked up again and their paltry dinner distributed that Joe told the others about the ship, and Evan was forced to wait until he was able to speak without falling to pieces before he could join in the speculation. "It was not a Texican ship," he said, his voice hoarse with suppressed emotion.

Instead of mocking him—for what knowledge of aeronautics had he ever shown before?—his companions simply waited.

"What makes you so sure?" Barnaby asked at last. "I saw it, too, as did every man with eyes in the camp. It is a Zeppelin B2 long-distance vessel. An older model, to be sure, but one the Texicans have been known to fly."

"But that particular ship has been modified—its fuselage is silver and blue, not blue alone. It is captained by Alice Chalmers, and is the ship in which I came to this godforsaken country." He leaned forward, putting his tin plate on the stone floor. "They have come back for me. I must get out of here. If she has gone down, they will be needing help. We must all escape without delay and go to their aid."

"If it were possible to do that, I'd have gone to my own aid long before this," Joe pointed out in a tone that indicated it was accompanied by a rolling of the eyes.

"What do you propose?" Dutch asked. "For we have already concluded that as the situation remains, it is impossible."

"I must confess something to you," Evan said. Shame rose to engulf him, and it was difficult to meet their eyes.

"You?" Barnaby shook his head. "The most you would have to confess, my friend, is taking a mouthful of another man's water. And that's nothing the rest of us haven't done."

"No." He dragged in a breath. "I confess I had ... given up hope. I have been working and eating and sleeping like a dead man, just waiting for that eventuality. Not like you. You three have never given up—I've seen you watching the sky, watching for your chance. I haven't bothered. Because I, too, believed it to be impossible."

"And watching a ship shot down has changed your mind?" Joe said. He could never be guilty of excessive sympathy ... or words, for that matter.

"It is one thing to give up on oneself," Dutch mused. "It is quite another to give up on one's friends ... if what you say is true, and this ship is known to you."

Exactly. He had expressed precisely Evan's thoughts, and he gave the other man a grateful look at having saved him from speaking them aloud.

"It is true." He took in their faces, though it was dark and all he could see was the plane of a masculine cheek here, the glitter of an eye there, illuminated by the lamp outside. "We all agree that escape using normal means is impossible. So now we must employ abnormal means. We must use the tools available to us—and that means the behemoth."

"It is under guard at night, as are we," Barney reminded him. "And only a madman would attempt to escape during the day, with the guard they have on you—and especially now that they have that cannon. It is no old model, that I will tell you."

"I know," Evan acknowledged with a sigh. "I have intimate knowledge of the wretched thing, having been employed by the only other person on the planet to have owned one."

Dutch stirred, as though someone had prodded him. Perhaps a rat had run over his leg.

"You talk as if the cannon is our only difficulty," Joe said impatiently. "The cannon, the guards and their rifles, the sheer numbers of men they will force to bring us down, the landscape, the face of the dam ... if we're talking abnormal means, just get the behemoth to fire the cannon. That would eliminate two things on your list, at least." The sarcasm in Joe's tone only served to remind Evan again why no one seemed to attempt escape very often anymore since he'd been here.

It was ridiculous for a sane man even to think of it.

But there was always insanity.

He laughed without humor. "Yes, that's it. I shall fire the cannon into the dam, toss it down from the turret, and while the water is carrying everyone away, skip over the mountains and go rescue my friends." It was only by the narrowest margin that he kept the helpless, enraged tears from welling into his eyes.

"Are you telling me that you were employed by Charles de Maupassant?" came Dutch's voice out of the dark, hollow with horror.

"De Maupassant, the traitor who attempted to kill the Prince of Wales?" Barney's voice sounded like that of a stranger—or a judge facing a prisoner in the dock.

"Yes," Evan said a little blankly. How strange to hear that once familiar name in this remote corner of the world. "Last year. I told you—my cousins—one of them is his daughter. Or was. He is dead now, of course. That is why I came aboard *Swan*. Because I could not bear what my life had become in his service. I needed to do something ... something positive to rebalance my accounts. To put good entries in the ledger instead of what I knew was there."

"And you know that cannon?" Barney said. "Can you fire it?"

"Of course. But since I will be in the behemoth, the point is moot."

"But you could tell me, and I could fire it."

"Certainly."

FIELDS OF IRON

Barney let out a sigh and the tension left his body. "Well, of all things, to be locked in a gaol halfway across the world with the one person who has ever got their hands on a pressure cannon..." He glanced up. "It was destroyed, you know. Somehow in that lightning storm that killed de Maupassant. Melted past all recognition—and past all scientific ability to reverse engineer it."

Now it was Evan's turn to straighten and feel his muscles pulling tight with tension. "How do you know that?" he whispered. "There are not six people in the world who know that."

"He is dead?" Dutch demanded. "De Maupassant? Are you sure?"

"Of course I am sure. I saw the body ... afterward. Between the lightning bolt and the fall from the castle roof ... most definitely dead."

"We are talking about the same Charles de Maupassant—business leader, investor?" Dutch said.

"Also known as Seacombe. The very one," Barney told him. "Were you acquainted with him, too?"

Dutch passed a shaking hand over his forehead. "Why cannot I remember? Only a flash of recognition of his name—and revulsion—and elation at the news that he is dead. I knew him, but I cannot tell you where we met, or even what he looked like. It is like knowing someone about whom you've read in a novel. Oh, it is maddening." Now he pressed both hands to his face.

"If you're finished catching up on old friends," Joe put in harshly, "can we get back to *el Gigante?*"

"I would rather get back to Barney, here, and what he said about de Maupassant's cannon," Evan said. "Tell me how you knew it was destroyed."

Barney sighed. "It was my business to know." He paused, and seemed to make up his mind to something. "The business of espionage. Gentlemen, we have become friends, and since we are all in the same boat, with greater things ahead, I find that now more than ever we must trust one another. My name is not Barney."

"I bet you're glad about that," Joe said to no one in particular.

"I am an agent in the service of Her Majesty, attached to the Walsingham Office in London."

Evan eyed him. "That is a grand title for a man locked in a Californio gaol."

"You know what they say ... the best laid plans and all that. I was foolish for less than a minute—and that was all it took to be captured. But if we manage to escape, what I have learned here will be invaluable. Priceless."

"That is a big *if*," Dutch pointed out.

"What is your name, then?" Joe wanted to know.

Seated on his noisome pallet, Barney gave a little bow from the waist. "Captain Barnaby Hayes, of Her Majesty's Secret Service Bureau. Gentlemen, I am a spy, and I am very tired of being locked up."

"Aren't we all." Evan had had just about enough surprises for today. "And what is the Walsingham Office going to do for us now, pray?"

"It is what we are going to do for it." He gave Joe a nudge. "We are going to carry out Joe's plan to the letter—though if we can find a way to get the workmen and prisoners out from under the dam before we blow it up, that would be my preference."

"My plan?" Joe squeaked. "That wasn't a plan. That was a joke."

Barney—Barnaby—whatever his name was—grinned in a way that Evan was very glad was not directed at him. "When we are finished, my clever friends, the joke will definitely be on them."

8

Alice had gone down with white knuckles on the helm a number of times in her life, but never like this. Bullet holes in the gondola, yes. A dead or dying engine (especially in the case of the *Stalwart Lass*, poor cobbled-together old girl), certainly. But not like this. Not a bloody great billowing hole in her fuselage and no idea if the remaining gas would get them to the ground or simply spindle up and let them plummet out of the sky.

"Vanes full horizontal, propellers heading due north," she ordered tersely.

"Aye," Jake said, white to the lips, already hauling on the wheels. "Captain Hollys, don't shut down the engines until the last moment. We need every ounce of propulsion we can coax out of her."

FIELDS OF IRON

"She won't fail us," came Ian's beloved voice through the speaking horn, sounding every bit as confident as though he were simply on review. As he'd been trained to be in a crisis. "Not *Swan*."

"If I have to fall out of the sky, I'm glad it's with you," Alice said recklessly into the horn.

"Likewise," came the cheerful reply, while Jake rolled his eyes and blushed at his captain's flagrant lack of decorum in the last ten minutes she had in this life.

If it came to that, she'd abandon the helm to spend her final minute in Ian's arms, and die happy. But she still had nine minutes in which to try to get them all out of this, for Benny's and Jake's life stories should not have a period put to them on her watch if she could possibly help it.

If they could stay out of the canyon, they had a chance to survive. But once they came within the grip of those sheer cliffs, the downdraft from the cooling air would push them into a free fall, and without the loft from the gasbags, there was no hope.

Swan floated to earth rather faster than Alice was used to. Far faster. The enormous half-mile-wide gash carved in the sere landscape by the river far below appeared to widen like a mouth getting ready to ingest them, and she flung her body on the helm hard alee. Jake leaped from one propeller wheel to the other, spinning them in the same direction as the helm, his skinny arms working like a pump gone mad.

"Alice?" came her husband's voice, still cheerful, but filled with an underlying tension that told her the enormity of the gift she was receiving at his hands—

hands that were not at this moment tearing the helm from her. This was her command, and he had not forgotten it even in this moment of extremity.

"Six degrees," she gasped, hugging the wheel, its spokes digging into her stomach and prodding her ribs. "Five. We must have three to make it. Four. Shut down engines."

A moment of breathless silence as Ian cut the engines and they heard nothing but the whistle of wind in the ropes … and the yawning, bottomless drop below was replaced with a grand sweep of mesa top, not twenty feet beneath the keel.

"We made it!" she screeched, releasing the helm and leaping clear as it spun with killing force and the ship wobbled back into a semblance of level flight. "Prepare to run aground!"

There was no need to steer now—nor any ability to do so. She and Jake tightened up their safety lines and her feet left the deck. "Benny!" she screamed.

"I've got him," Ian called. "Secure for landing."

With a scrape like a giant's moan of pain, the keel of the gondola grounded, leaving a long gouge in the earth but also putting such a drag on the ship that it bounced once, twice, and then settled with a jerk, nose down in a shallow arroyo.

The fuselage, which she expected to blow overhead and spread across the mesa top for a thousand feet, settled ungracefully across the stern. Alice felt as though she had been punched, though to her knowledge the lines had kept her from hitting anything. She loosened the clips on the lines in the rings on her corselet and settled slowly to the deck.

Where her knees failed to hold her up.

She sat there, breathing hard, as Jake lowered himself beside her. His knees were clearly made of sterner stuff, but his face was as pale as milk, and his staring eyes looked as though panic were only seconds away. He gave her a hand up. "Are we alive, Captain?" he croaked.

"We are, thank God, and what's more, the forward gas bags are, too. That missile, whatever it was, must have gone straight through the stern as we heeled over, and out the other side."

"I'm glad their aim wasn't any better."

"So am I. Come on." She jogged along the corridor to the engine room, where Ian met her at the door, stained with steam, his perfectly cut uniform jacket torn at the shoulder, and his eyes—

Alice flung herself into his arms and burst into tears.

When, minutes later, she finally regained control of herself, it was to look up and see a telltale track through the dust and sweat on Ian's face. He smoothed the curls back from her forehead. "Well done, darling," he said softly. "I could not have done better myself— nor could any man flying in the Royal Aeronautic Corps today."

"I had very good help from my brave crew." She laid her cheek on his chest and could not prevent a glimmer of satisfaction. It was one thing to know she had brought the people she cared about to earth safely, but another thing entirely to know that one of the finest captains in the skies had acknowledged it, too.

"Pity Her Majesty wasn't here to see it," Jake said. "She might have another think about women captaining their own ships in the Corps."

"If I have anything to say about it, she certainly will know," Ian said stoutly. "I shall wax rather fulsome in my report—if we ever see England again."

"We will." Alice straightened and set her shirt and pants to rights, twisting her corselet so that the rings for the lines lay once again over each hip. "And the first step in that direction is to see how badly we're damaged and how soon we can be skyworthy again."

"I'll check the gangway." Benny Stringfellow scampered down the corridor, but not before Alice had a chance to tousle his hair with affection. Nothing seemed to faze her young Gunner Second Class—not even crashing in the middle of a desert that she knew better than anyone was as remote and inhospitable as the moon.

Though not quite as remote and inhospitable as some places she'd been—the northern reaches of the Canadas, for one, where her real father had been a spy. Or in that foreign world behind the black iron railings of Belgravia. She supposed she ought to be grateful that, in spite of her own colossal foolishness in poking her nose into the Royal Kingdom's air space, the land upon which her ship now lay was at least familiar.

Dangerous and unforgiving, yes, but familiar.

Her gunner was back in a moment with a report. "The hull is dug in and we can't use the gangway, Captain."

Her body had already told her so, the cant of the deck reporting the angle at which the hull had plowed into the earth. At least it was earth, and not the red sandstone that might well have torn it out altogether. "Very well. We shall do as the Mopsies do, and go out the stern through the communications cage."

"And send a pigeon while we're at it," Jake muttered. "Can't see us getting ourselves out of this without a hand from someone."

"Jake is right." Ian followed Alice and Benny down the corridor. "We should send for the Rangers and request their assistance."

Alice had never in her life asked the Texican Rangers for anything—mostly because the stepdaughter of Ned Mose was not so stupid as to bring herself to their attention, and Lady Hollys was not convinced she wouldn't be arrested on sight, title or no. "Ian, you know we can't do that. I'd be recognized."

"You were not recognized in the hospital in Santa Fe."

"That was because none of the Rangers but one set foot in there, and you didn't let him see me." And before his frown became too pronounced, she held open the wire door of the communications cage and motioned him ahead of her. "Let's take a look at the damage first. We can't make plans until we do."

Stooping, he slipped through the opening in the back where the pigeons came in. A second later they heard a grunt as he landed. "Be careful, especially Mr. Stringfellow. It's a good eight-foot drop, with the deck at this angle."

Benny went out next, then Alice, then Jake. When she landed once again in her husband's arms, she smiled up at him. "We forgot one thing."

"And what is that?" he asked tenderly. "I have all I need right here."

She grinned. "We don't have a way to get back in."

"If the two of you would stop spooning for one minute, you'd see that I'm the only one with the sense to hook up one of the rope ladders before I dropped." Jake's tone held more humor than disgust.

"I knew I hired you for a good reason," she told him cheerfully. "Come on, let's see how my girl survived her landing."

Even at her most optimistic, Alice could not say that in a contest between *Swan* and the mesa, her ship had come out the winner. The gondola had sustained most of its damage to the bow, which was not surprising. But their greatest loss was the propellers at the stern, particularly to port. The blades were now a flattened, useless mess under the tilted hull.

While Ian climbed back into the engine compartment to check that the boilers were cooling despite the odd angle at which they sat in their cowlings, Alice walked forward with Jake to have a look at the fuselage.

The gasbag pierced by the missile lay forlornly in a thick, rubbery heap across the ventral vane, while the remaining three hung aloft, dragged earthward a few degrees by the unsupported weight of the fuselage.

"At least they're aloft," Jake said, his sharp eyes scanning for obvious tears outside of the great rent in the stern quarter. "What are the chances she'll fly with three?"

Alice had been asking herself that very question from the moment she'd realized they'd been hit. "I've been doing the arithmetic, as I'm sure you have, too."

Jake nodded, walking slowly along the port side, furthest from the cliff and the river canyon. The sun had sunk enough to hang on the mountains to the west, burning like an accusing eye even as the remaining upright gasbags threw Alice and Jake into shadow.

"Three might get us into Santa Fe and landbound for repairs," he said, considering. "But never back to Philadelphia, and certainly not to England."

"Without a port propeller, we might not even make it to Santa Fe," Alice said. "We have a spare, but it looks as though the housing itself might have got crushed in the landing. And I'll tell you now, I'm not going back to Resolution to dig around in my old stash of parts to build one."

"That's a relief," was all Jake said. He pointed to the bow. "Even without a fourth gas bag, we still have to find something resembling a mooring mast. One big gust southerly and there's a good chance she'll wind up in the river."

"Don't even say that." Alice was too old to make the sign to ward off evil, as children might, but still, her hand twitched a little. That was the stuff nightmares were made of. "But you're right. Let's see if we can make do with something."

"Captain!" Benny's voice came from far astern, on the starboard side.

"Over here, Benny," Alice called. "We're going to try to moor her."

"Captain, don't—they've got us—"

"What's got up his britches?" Jake wondered. "There's nothing out here but burrowing creatures and vultures."

Alice walked around the bow, gazing upward to check for damage, and caught the dangling mooring line in one hand. "Not even a dead tree up here, or a pinnacle like the Navapai use in Alaia's village. There's only—"

She stopped dead and stared.

Ranged along the cliff edge were dozens of dead people.

Skulls, skeletons, bony hands holding rifles, wearing thrown-together bits of castoff clothing. And embroidered blouses. And roses woven into crowns on their heads. Benny struggled in the grip of a particularly large skeleton who seemed to be quite deep in the keel for a cadaver.

"Captain!" he shouted. "The lightning pistols!"

"Now, now, no need for violence," *la bruja* said, shaking him as though he'd been a carpet and she a housewife. "Not unless it's us dishing it out."

Alice drew in a long breath to try to settle her heartbeat—and the plunging alarm in her stomach. Witches. She'd heard the legends and the stories, but had never actually seen one. Never really believed they were true. And now, here they were, trapping herself and her crew as surely as though they'd been run into a box canyon.

"Release my gunner, if you please," she said. "He's only doing his duty."

"His duty, my foot," said a skeleton next to the large one. "He's a little wolverine, he is."

Benny stomped on the witch's foot, and when she loosened her grip with a cry, he shot across the twenty feet between them and straight into Alice's arms.

"They're dead!" he gasped. "They're dead and they almost killed me!"

"I haven't changed my mind about that yet, you little monster." The witch surged forward, limping. "No one may cross our borders and live. Come, sisters. The river welcomes the Texican as well as the Californio."

"Stand back!"

The surge of witches halted at the command in Ian's voice, and skulls tilted skyward toward the viewing ports of the gondola.

"One move out of any of you and I'll fire," he warned.

Thank heavens for Ian. Alice couldn't see him above her head, because the deck was tilted away, but she had an imagination. He had his lightning pistol trained on the large witch, she'd bet her life on it.

In fact, she *was* betting her life on it.

"We've been shot down by the Californios," she said. "We mean no one any harm. All we need is to make some repairs, and we'll be out of your territory as fast as we can pull up ropes."

"No one leaves our borders alive," the second witch repeated flatly.

"Dadburn it, we haven't done anything wrong!" Alice exclaimed. "In fact, if you'd let us, we want to help you. Do you know what my hold is full of?"

"Alice, no!" came from above.

Why on earth shouldn't she tell them? They'd set a course for the Navapai villages, hadn't they, with the goal of getting these horses and rifles to the people living along the river. Well, here they were, and darned if they weren't going to kill her and her friends for their courtesy.

"Alice?" said someone in the very rear of the crowd. "Did you say *Alice?* Here, let me through. Dadgummit, sister, out of the way!"

The crowd moved and shifted and the hands of the witch that Benny had kicked stiffened into claws of rage. "Blast it, Betsy, what are you playing at? This is serious business!"

A slender, less colorful edition of the leader pushed between two others and halted, breathing heavily, a few paces away. "Alice. By all that's great and good, it is you! Alice Chalmers!"

Alice stared. Her mouth fell open. "Great Caesar's ghost. Betsy Trelawney, is that you?"

The girl darted forward. "It's me!" And before Alice could even move, she'd grabbed her in a bony hug. One arm was held stiffly from when that rat Bert Blake had broke it one night when she wouldn't do what he wanted down at the Desert Rose. Alice had splinted that arm herself.

"Well dang, Betsy, this is a fine fix. Would you please explain to the lady here that we mean no harm to any of you?"

The girl turned to her leader. "Mother Mary, it's true. This is Alice Chalmers, Ned Mose's girl. But she ain't like him. She's a friend to us—a friend to all witches, ain't you?" She appealed to Alice over her shoulder.

"I certainly am." The large personage that Betsy had called Mother Mary didn't seem convinced, so Alice threw all her cards on the table. "In fact, I've been trying to find you. My hold is stuffed full of the Californios' mechanicals and weapons that we stole from them. We know there's going to be a war, and we want you to arm yourselves so you're ready for it."

Mother Mary stood stock still. "A war."

"Also true," said Ian from above. "The Texicans do not believe it, but we came all the way here to stop it."

"You ain't the only one. Dang." Mother Mary shook her head, and in the dying light, the silk roses twined in her graying black hair looked as though they were glowing. "And here I thought that girl was as crazy as a jackrabbit, but maybe she ain't."

Jake clutched Alice's arm hard enough to make her wince. "What girl?" he said harshly. "Who are you talking about?"

"That Meriwether-Astor girl, who gave her name as Meredith Aster. But whatever handle she goes by, she says exactly the same as you. And I expect them mechanicals you say you have in there—" She jerked her chin at *Swan.* "—are the ones she was trying to keep out of the Viceroy's hands. So you've done her a good turn, if you're telling true."

"Gloria Meriwether-Astor," Jake repeated. "You've seen her. Where is she? We thought she was dead."

"Oh, she ain't dead," Betsy said helpfully. "In fact, she was married yesterday morning. We were all there. Our very first wedding."

"Married?" Jake's voice cracked.

Under this second shock, Alice's voice came back. "Married? Who to? Not Evan Douglas—is he alive, too?"

"Don't know any Evan Douglas. But Meredith—Gloria, I should say—married our Captain Stan in Santa Croce church yesterday. They'll be almost to Nuestra Señora la Reyna de los Ángeles by now."

This was making no sense. "Why would she go to Reyna de los Ángeles—deeper into the Royal Kingdom? She could be killed."

"Well, now, that's why she married Captain Stan. So she wouldn't be."

"But why? What is she doing?" Between the twin forces of incredulity and fear, Alice could hardly breathe.

"She's going to San Francisco de Asis, the capital, to talk the Viceroy out of his war." Betsy took her arm, as friends did. "Why, Alice, what is wrong? You've gone white as paint."

FIELDS OF IRON

9

Gloria had been to the Moorish coast of the Royal Kingdom of Spain and seen the white plastered houses with their curvy tiled roofs, draped in bougainvillea. It was a distinctly odd sensation to see that same architecture replicated here on another continent with such loving exactitude that it had to have been the result either of law or a kind of civic homesickness. The mission at Nuestra Señora la Reyna de los Ángeles was a massive example of the same, with the addition of a huge stained-glass window at the end of the nave that recalled the rose windows of Chartres or Notre Dame.

By the end of the second day of her married life, they had registered the certificate Padre Emilio had given them, and were as officially bound together as it was possible for a couple to be.

Except for one detail that Gloria was determined not to think about.

"There is a caravan leaving for San Gregorio in the morning," her husband said, coming along the lavender walk in the shady cloister of the mission. "We can be among its number—I have already sent Riley to make the arrangements." He sat beside her on the bench under a myrtle dripping purple flowers all over the walk. "Does that meet with your approval?"

"Of course." She moved to make room for him. "Isn't this a lovely spot?"

He glanced about him, taking in the unglazed windows in the colonnade, and the two gates leading in and out of the garden. "If you say so. Please don't wander off alone like this, Gloria. Even in the mission, it isn't safe."

"Is there any safe place for a woman in this country, if the mission is not?" She wasn't being ironic or sarcastic. She really wanted to know.

"On the ranchos, if one is the owner's wife or daughter, I imagine there is."

"So only a handful of women may truly feel secure—as long as they are in their own houses?" She sighed and drew in a breath of lavender. "How terribly sad and ... dreadful. These caravans, then, are groups of people who must band together to travel?"

"Yes. Between thirty and forty, usually. They travel up the King's Road by horse and wagon from mission to mission if they are on pilgrimage, or by train from rancho to rancho if they have more secular errands, as we do."

"That seems awkward for the people on the ranchos, doesn't it? To always be playing host to bands of strangers?"

"It's part of the culture. Travelers, I am told, don't stay with the family, but at inns. One of the monks here told me the ranchos are like small towns, with hostelries, stables, markets, and each with its own train station. Travelers can be invited to socialize, too, if it is appropriate. That is the point of it all. Hospitality, the exchange of news, that kind of thing. The rancho families make a life of it, you know, traveling from one hacienda to another to celebrate fiestas ... and, I suppose, to get their children acquainted with one another so that they may marry when they are old enough."

She could not imagine a life constrained to the properties along a single road or railway line. How could their women not die of suffocation? "How very strange."

"Speaking of news, I picked up a tidbit that might affect us at some point or another. Apparently the Viceroy is not well."

Gloria shifted on the bench to look at him more directly. "Is it serious?"

"Difficult to say. Who knows how long the rumor has taken to reach them here in the south. The priest said he was 'beset by visions,' whatever that means."

"Dear me." That didn't sound very serious. She had been beset by quite a number of visions herself during the night before she made up her mind to accept the captain's proposal. "But as you say, if they do not have pigeons or mail tubes, then news might take quite a while to travel. He could be recovered by now."

A silence fell. Then, "Since we do not leave until dawn, I took rooms at an inn close to the station. I hope that is satisfactory?"

"Of course. I'm sure Ella and I will be quite comfortable."

"Ella ... and you?"

"Yes." She turned a limpid gaze upon him. "She and I can share a bed, if there is only one."

His lashes flickered, as if he had been quite taken aback. "Once one has registered one's marriage, it is customary for husband and wife to share a bed, you know, dear."

She settled her skirts about her, and smoothed the ruffle on the front of her secondhand dress. "But we are not husband and wife in the conventional sense. We are more like ... companions in arms. Of course, when we are in public I will behave as wifely as you like. But I see no need to take the ruse in which we are engaged to ... such an extreme."

He exhaled. "I do not agree. We are married, Gloria."

Her cheeks burned with the impropriety of conversing about such a subject, but she straightened her spine. "I made it clear from the beginning that this is a marriage of convenience. A—a battle strategy. We have only known each other less than a week, Captain. It is simply not possible to manufacture the feelings that lead to—to the intimacy of marriage in so short a time."

"Then you concede it might be possible, given more time and better acquaintance?"

She slanted a glance at him. "I cannot see that happening, can you?"

It took him a moment to reply, so rapt was he in contemplation of ... something. Perhaps she had smuts on her cheek from that wretched train. It would not be surprising. She had splashed her face in the fountain, but there were probably still quite a number in her hair, and burning tiny holes in her hat.

"I am not in the habit of predicting the future," he said at last, "but yes, I could see the degree of liking between us progressing to something more, given time."

"I am glad you think so. But it won't do, you know. Once our task is concluded and I go back to Philadelphia, you may divorce me as quickly as you like."

"Oh, I may?" he said in quite a changed tone.

"Yes, certainly. Unless—that is—you would prefer that I do so?" She hadn't actually thought this through, and yet words were pouring out of her mouth that she wasn't convinced she meant. "Perhaps on grounds of— of adultery, or some such?"

Now his mouth fell open and it was a moment before he could speak. *"Adultery!"*

Her own mouth primmed up in spite of herself. Really, this was the most distasteful conversation she had ever had. It was almost as though some other woman were saying these things, using words that had never crossed her lips before.

But ... she *was* some other woman now. She was Mrs. Stanford Fremont, and there were subjects which that lady must discuss without delay.

"I am sorry to be indelicate. I might have had a sheltered upbringing, but I am not unaware of the ways of the world. Mother Mary was quick to tell me that you'd had plenty of practice ... er, between the sheets. I should not blame you if you looked elsewhere." She swallowed. "I do hope, however, that you would be discreet, and not shame me in front of our companions."

He had been leaning away from her by degrees, and at this he leaped up and took a few short, jerky steps across the gravel path. "Do I understand you correctly? You are denying me a husband's prerogative and giving me permission to *break my marriage vows instead?*"

"Well ... I would not put it quite so bluntly, but yes. I suppose I am."

"Good God!" He spun away, and his bowler hat fell into the box hedge. He didn't seem to notice, clutching his hair as though in a paroxysm of distress.

"Captain, I ... have I upset you?" Goodness, his eyes seemed almost wild.

But in a moment, his back turned to her and his hands on his hips, he seemed to regain control of himself. After a few deep, cleansing breaths of the lavender-scented air, he was able to face her again.

"I have never in all my life heard such a proposal—and that is saying something, let me tell you."

She did not know whether or not she ought to apologize, so she merely folded her hands in silence. She had heard that men placed a much greater importance on the marriage bed than did women, but she had been nothing but honest with him about her reasons for accepting him. If one were getting down to brass tacks, she had much more to find objectionable in this conversation than he did.

"Do you—" He clenched his jaw and then forcibly relaxed it. "Do you honestly believe me capable of breaking my vows so quickly and so—so cavalierly as that?"

"I do not know you well enough to entertain beliefs about anything."

"Except for what Mother Mary says, evidently."

"She has known you for much longer than I. And while I understand that she was passing on hearsay—" And suddenly she saw where her error lay. On an indrawn breath, she touched her fingers to her lips. "Oh, dear."

"Now what? More gossip to judge me by?"

"No, only your own words. Captain, I am so dreadfully sorry. Your father … he is the one who broke his vows 'so quickly and cavalierly,' isn't he?"

He glared at her as though she had betrayed him by bringing it up.

"You have disavowed your father and his behavior just as I have disavowed mine. Of course you would never behave as he did." She felt ill at how badly she had misjudged him, and how foolish had been those thoughtless words. "Please forgive me for suggesting that you would." He did not look very forgiving. She tried once more. "I shall never say or even think such a thing again."

"You can hardly control your thoughts."

"No, but I shall not let them run away with me on no evidence."

His shoulders relaxed a fraction, and he shook back his hair. She got up and reached into the hedge for his hat, dusting it off and handing it to him. "Am I forgiven?"

"Does it matter to you?"

"Of course. I want the air to be completely clear between us. Particularly if it is scented with lavender. Though in this case it may not apply, since the language of flowers would have us believe it stands for serenity ... and enchantment." Goodness, now she was babbling. She really ought to find Ella and then the room at the inn he had reserved for them.

"The language of flowers, eh? That's one I don't speak."

"Never mind, then. Will you show me the inn?" He offered her his arm, and she took it. "We have not yet resolved the question of the sleeping arrangements."

They strolled up the walk. "All moral considerations aside," he said, "I believe it best that we begin as we mean to go on. The first time someone sees us go into separate rooms, the questions will begin, and that is the last thing we want. We must be so circumspect as to be nearly invisible, particularly on the ranchos. The farther north we go and the closer to the capital, the more we are likely to encounter those who wish to prevent you from succeeding in your mission."

There was certainly no arguing with his logic.

"I must confess that I have never shared a bed with anyone save a governess or maid," she said, a little shyly.

"I am quite capable of assisting you in a maid's capacity, if that would help."

Her eyes widened in shock and chagrin. "That is hardly proper!"

When he laughed, she felt almost as shocked, but for a different reason. Real, unaffected laughter transformed that sardonic face, lightening its planes and showing her that the crow's feet at the corners of his eyes might have come from humor as well as squinting into the sun on the river.

"And besides, I am quite capable of dressing and undressing myself. My corset is a front-fastener, and I possess no waists of the kind that button down the back."

"An opportunity lost," he said with mock regret. "Perhaps you will be called upon to valet me, for I am not in the habit of wearing these confounded string ties that it appears one must put on in public to seem respectable in these parts."

"I think that tie looks nice on you. As does the waistcoat."

"One more compliment and I shall be quite overcome, Mrs. Fremont. I may not be responsible for my actions."

"Oh, I think that of all the men I have met in the past week, you are the most responsible for your actions of any. I value that in a man."

But they had reached the arched door into the mission proper, and there was no more opportunity for conversation of the conjugal kind. Nor was there later, over dinner in the inn's public room with Ella and Riley and the two crewmen who had joined their party to make it look more impressive—and who consequently carried an astonishing number of concealed weapons. Gloria wondered that they did not clank when they sat down.

Ella had found a room upstairs with one of the barmaids, and the men were to sleep in the bunkhouse behind the inn, with their ears open for any gossip that might further their purposes. Ella paused on the stairs when Gloria turned off at the corridor to the room she was to share with her husband.

"You'll be all right, won't you, Mer—I mean, Gloria?" She lifted her chin in the direction of the room. "With Captain Stan? For if you're not, you could always come bunk with me. I won't mind."

Gloria smiled and gave her a one-armed hug, then rested her head against that of her friend. "You are a dear to be concerned, but the captain and I have come to an understanding."

"You have?" Ella did not pull away. Which was just as well, since this was the kind of conversation best held in whispers anyway.

"He understands the purpose of our marriage. That it ... you know ... is not like other marriages formed under more ... conventional circumstances."

"What does that mean?" Ella whispered back, looking puzzled. "He doesn't have the clap, does he?"

FIELDS OF IRON

Gloria gaped at her. "What on earth is that?"

In a few brief words, Ella enlightened her. "Dear me. I do not know. I certainly hope not. The point is—that is not the point. There will be no ... er, activity of that kind."

"There won't?" Ella looked as though Gloria had just delivered the happiest of news, and it suddenly struck her like two notes on a gong—that one should not discuss such matters with a girl who was in love with one's husband, and that the fewer people who knew about this, the better.

"But you must not tell anyone," she said urgently. "Not a soul, Ella. We must appear to be exactly who we are—even in the dark."

"Oh, to be sure," Ella said eagerly. "Not a word."

"Not even to Riley and the others."

"I promise."

"Good night, my dear friend." Gloria gave her a squeeze. "We shall see each other at breakfast in the morning."

Ella squeezed back. "Good luck."

Which was not exactly the sentiment one wanted to hear as one approached the doorway for one's delayed wedding night.

10

If *Swan* had gone down on the eastern side of the mountains, which Evan knew for a fact were inhospitable and did not even provide shelter from the sun, much less food or water, then they had no time to lose.

They must destroy the dam and escape in the behemoth today.

Between their hasty plans of last night and the complete lack of sleep as a result, Evan felt a little light-headed. A little reckless. Who would ever have thought that it would be up to him to mount a rescue of Alice, who embodied capability and command? What had she been thinking of to attempt to cross the border? But it didn't matter. She had been shot down, and the only person within hundreds of miles who could help was himself.

How close he and the others had come to simply giving up—how blind to their own resources hopelessness had made them! Their situation had not changed, but their attitude toward it certainly had—if wild foolhardiness could be called an attitude.

He and Joe climbed up into the behemoth, guarded fore and aft by the usual soldiers. Had it been Evan in command, he would have changed the troops daily. But no, it was always the same pair, and up until now Evan and Joe had given them no trouble at all. They were hanging their hopes on a slight sense of complacency in their captors—a confidence in their power. A disbelief that model prisoners could be anything else but.

Evan and Joe exchanged a glance of anticipation as Joe passed behind him to man the engine. Evan settled into the pilot's harness with his usual nod and raised eyebrow, and when the larger of the guards nodded his permission, he began the ignition sequence. Both of them knew perfectly well they could not overpower the soldiers by sheer brute force. At least, not the kind they personally possessed, since Joe was a slight, underfed-looking individual, and Evan, while more robust than he had been when he'd left England, did not have much confidence in his ability to wrestle a rifle from a trained military man. No, they would use the brute force of the behemoth, and Evan had a difficult time keeping the glee out of his expression. But he must school his face to its usual expressionless misery, lest the guards detect that today, something was different.

In the distance, he saw the work crews boarding the steam drays that carted them across the few miles of water meadow and desert to the dam site. Barnaby would be among them, and Dutch, too. Their task, in his mind, was the more difficult. Frankly, one would think a man from the Walsingham Office would have escaped long ago, but since he had not, Evan hoped he would be up to it now. Dutch, on the other hand, was flying blind. He had no memory of what he had been capable of, and his frustration was palpable as he had committed to doing what came to hand, hoping that the mists in his mind would clear enough to make him useful.

"Pressure has equalized," came Joe's voice from the engine compartment. "You may proceed. All is secure."

The same words he used every morning. Except for the last three, delivered just as tonelessly as the others. But what it meant was that Joe had located the unused security line and clipped it to his pants.

Evan swung into motion, lifting his arms and legs and turning the behemoth about. They proceeded out of the stockade and stumped down the road as they did every morning. But today, Evan increased his speed just enough to overtake the drays and their clouds of dust and pass them. Once he was in the clear, he threw up the two levers that allowed air into the cabin, and raised the protective isinglass shield about a foot.

"What are you doing?" the tall guard snapped. "Close that at once."

"I am to place the topmost beams on the structure today," Evan explained. "The shield distorts my vision, and the job requires delicate precision."

When Joe translated, the guard frowned. "Close it, and open it up later."

"No, don't," said the other guard. "Breathe fresh air while you can. Once we get to that hell-hole it will be nothing but sweat and dust. Be grateful for your blessings while you have them."

Frowning, the taller guard subsided, but not before backhanding Joe for having had the temerity to translate private remarks. Evan bit back a smile, and a twinge of regret that no more blessings would be forthcoming for those two today.

But before they could reach the pile of girders where he had been working for the last several days, and put the first stage of their impossible plan into motion, an entire troop of men strung themselves across the road, rifles on their shoulders, blocking the way.

"Stop, in the Viceroy's name!"

The shorter of the two guards leaned into the speaking horn. "What is it, countrymen? We are bound for the dam, as usual."

Cursing internally, Evan had no choice but to bring the behemoth to a halt, steaming, its joints hissing as he released the pressure in their pistons. Blast and be-bother it! Barnaby and Dutch could not know that his side of their two-pronged plan was being delayed. Unless somehow they could see the road, and see him stalled here in a cloud of dust and steam.

"What is it?" he asked the tall one. "Why are they stopping us?"

"Proceed back to the barracks," came the command from the man on horseback in the middle of the roadblock. "The foreigner is wanted on His Highness's business."

"Foreigner?" Evan said aloud. "Does he mean me?"

This question had clearly occurred to the short one, too, for he called down for confirmation. The leader's horse backed and sidestepped as the man stood in the stirrups. "Obey me at once! Do you want to keep the commander waiting? He wants the operator of *el Gigante*, and he wants him now, you fools!"

Evan bit back a groan of frustration. On this morning of all mornings—when Alice and what was left of her crew could be bleeding in the desert just beyond those peaks, when he and his three companions had screwed their courage to the sticking point—*now* he was summoned into the commander's presence? He could not have done this last night? What did he want—for Evan to interpret another of his nightmares?

He exchanged an agonized glance with Joe, who gripped a pressure lever so tightly his fingers were white as bone. Joe's eyes were wide with apprehension as he mouthed, *Go! Go!*

But he could not. If he did, the element of surprise would be utterly lost, to say nothing of the necessary proximity to the dam. If they broke through the line here, it would be a premature act of war, and all they would get for their pains would be a missile from the cannon on the platform above the road.

"Tell them we shall return immediately, and to clear the road," Evan said at last. "Joe, apply some pressure to our legs, if you please."

"But—"

"If you please."

His mouth locked in a grim line, Joe did as he was told, and Evan moved the behemoth in a slow circle. His blood ran cold through his veins with disappointment and the poisonous dregs of a battle lust that had nowhere now to go. Then they stumped back down the road in the direction of the barracks, passing the steam drays with their loads of men—Barnaby and Dutch gaping up at them in dismay. By the time they came to a halt once more inside the stockade, Evan's limbs were shaking and it was all he could do to keep the tears of frustration from leaking down his cheeks.

He had no desire to explain *that* to anyone.

To his surprise, when he and Joe were escorted into the commander's quarters, it was not to the man's sleeping chamber, but to the audience hall, whose support beams had been made from the slender trunks of trees, adzed and carved with festive garlands and the suns that were the Viceroy's symbol. At the far end was a throne covered in gold leaf, presumably for those rare occasions when the Viceroy visited, and below that, a long, heavily carved table at which the commander presided.

He was not sitting now. Instead, he paced back and forth in front of it, his hands clasped behind his back, clearly waiting for them and not happy about it.

"Ah. At last," he said when they approached, their shirts dusty and stained with sweat, though the sun was barely above the mountains. "Please, be seated. Coffee?"

Evan couldn't stand the bitter beverage, but Joe was happy to allow a steward to pour him some in a delicate porcelain cup.

"I regret the necessity for interrupting your work on the dam, but word has come of a most extraordinary nature, and I fear that you, Senor Douglas, are the man to answer it."

"In what way, sir?" Evan's mouth was so dry that his tongue clicked on the consonants. The steward handed him a thick, greenish glass full of water, and he drank it gratefully.

"You recall the service that you rendered me a few nights ago."

"Of course, sir. I trust your slumbers have been more peaceful since?"

"Oddly, they have. But even were they not, they are the cause of a chain of events that has resulted in a letter on this morning's train. A letter from the Viceroy himself."

The commander picked up a creamy piece of stationery, its paper thick enough to accommodate the heavy engraving of the royal crest. It was covered in small, spiky handwriting that looked as though an irritated bird had run back and forth across the page.

The commander's resolute eye now fell on Joe, whose own eye was assessing whether there was enough coffee in the elegant pot to ask for a second cup. "I understand that you, sir, have some ability with the language of God?"

It took Joe a moment to understand first, that he was being directly addressed, and second, what this question meant. And a good thing he did, for Evan hadn't the least idea. In the Californio tongue, Joe answered smoothly and with what Evan felt was rather an elegance of pronunciation, compared to the way he usually spoke it.

The commander held out the letter. "Translate this for Senor Douglas, then, if you would."

Joe took the paper as though it were Holy Writ and cleared his throat with a squeak.

> *Senor de Sola, Commander of the fort at Las Vegas de la Colorado, greetings.*
>
> *It is no doubt common knowledge in the Royal Kingdom that I have not slept in many nights, and in fact, have been disturbed by dreams and phantasms of an alarming nature even during my waking hours. I am at my wits' end, sir, and my patience came to a similar end some days ago.*
>
> *I understand that in the gaol under your supervision is a man who, like Joseph of old, is an interpreter of dreams. Bring him to me at once. I shall leave San Francisco de Asis on Silver Wind—*

At Evan's gasp, Joe looked up. "Nothing," Evan said hastily. "Go on."

—on Silver Wind, and receive this man at Rancho San Luis Obispo de Tolosa, where he will interpret my dreams. I must have peace. I demand peace, and at once. If I do not receive satisfaction, he will pay with his life for deceiving us both.

Evan fumbled for a chair and fell into it as his knees gave out.

Go with God, and may His angels rally to our cause.

Carlos Filipe

Viceroy of the Royal Kingdom of Spain and the Californias, Defender of the True Faith, and General of the Armies of Heaven

Carefully, holding it by its edges in his filthy fingers, Joe replaced the royal command on the glossy surface of the table.

"Well done," the commander said. "Your accent is almost perfect."

"Thank you, sir."

"Where did you learn to speak our language so very well?"

"Excuse me, but did anyone just hear that I am to be executed if I cannot interpret the boy's damned dreams?" Evan hardly recognized his own voice, so harsh and commanding was it. "May we dispense with the pleasantries and come to an agreement? I am a citizen of Her Majesty Queen Victoria, and neither she nor

I will take kindly to the threat of execution under such trivial circumstances!"

"Would you prefer it be under more serious circumstances?" the commander inquired.

Evan lost his tenuous hold on his temper. "Do not patronize me, sir! I have lived under threat of execution since I was tricked by your ambassador into crossing your borders. Believe me, I should never have come of my own volition. What I want to know is, how am I to refuse this ridiculous command, and when may I return to my duty? The behemoth's abilities are being wasted while you sport with us, sir!"

Commander de Sola gazed at him, his dark eyes assessing, until at last he picked up the sweating pitcher of water and poured Evan another glass. "I regret to say that a royal command may not be refused. I realize you are ignorant of our customs—and ignorant of how close you came just now to execution with your intemperate words. Even to refuse the Viceroy in principle is treason."

"Must make it difficult when he passes people things at dinner," Joe muttered.

"Do not make light of it, young man," the commander said quietly. "Consider this a lesson and guard your tongues better in future. No, there is no refusing it. I must deliver you to him in San Luis Obispo de Tolosa, and there is an end to it. I am afraid *el Gigante* must remain idle for as long as the journey takes— unless you have managed to train someone in your place?"

Evan snorted, his temper still at a rolling boil. "Your guards have been so assiduous in their duties that they have not allowed the man Barney—the only person I would trust in the behemoth's harness, since he is not a complete idiot—to be in the pilot's chamber with me. They fear we will cause mischief. Stage a coup in the stockade or some nonsense. So no, there is no one trained in its operation who can keep the work going on the dam." He glared at his guards, who stood at attention on either side of the audience chamber's door. "And you have no one to blame but yourselves!"

The commander allowed Evan's angry tones to die away into the rafters. "Very well. There are no doubt other areas of the dam that can be constructed in your absence. Come. We must get you both ready and on the northbound train. I have enough influence to make it wait a short time, but not for longer."

"Wait. Us both?" Joe squeaked.

"Do you know of someone else proficient enough with our language who can be spared in order to translate?" the commander inquired.

"Well ... you, sir."

The smallest smile curved the commander's lips below his moustache. "I will not be on my knees in the Viceroy's private chambers, translating the interpretation of his dreams. That will be your task. I am required to deliver you into his presence, no more."

"I cannot go." Evan couldn't quite believe they were having this conversation. He couldn't go meet the Viceroy hundreds of miles north. He had to save Alice!

"You must."

"I must stay here. I have my duty—I have—"

"You will be executed at sunset if you do not leave with me on that train."

All the air rushed out of Evan's lungs, and his spine wilted against the carved chair back. "What?"

"I am quite serious. The Viceroy requires you. I must deliver you. If you do not come willingly, I am still required to do so, even if it is in chains ... or a coffin." He regarded Evan with some sympathy. "It is not forever, sir. We will have you back in the prison cell you seem to value so highly within a few days."

A few days would be too late. Evan dared not look at Joe, but he heard his breathing change as the same realization dawned on him.

A few days in the desert was all it would take to put paid to his friends. If dehydration did not kill them, the witches would, and the destruction of all the dams in the world would not bring back the closest thing to family he had ever known.

Alice had heard of *las brujas*, of course—everyone in Resolution had, since the river and the lands the witches controlled were only an hour's flight away. But she had never seen them. Had half believed them a myth conjured up to scare disobedient children into behaving, much as the legend of their gold kept prospectors exploring the river canyons though the legend had never been proven true.

"How did you ever find them?" she asked Betsy Trelawney as the former desert flower showed her and her crew into rounded rooms chipped out of the soft rock. These were well behind the towers and homes made of mud brick that housed witches and equipment and food, while below, terraces and laddered ledges tumbled to the river.

"They say that a woman truly in need will find them, and it turned out to be true," Betsy said simply. "After you fixed up my arm, I made my way to the river overland. When I got there, I found a group of them fishing. They fed and clothed me, since I'd left with next to nothing, and so I stayed."

"It seems almost miraculous, that a group of women could accomplish all this." Ian's gesture took in the room, the village, and by extension, the vast canyons of the territory the witches controlled.

"I don't know about miraculous," Betsy said with a laugh. "If a group of men had done the same, would you call it so?"

With a smile, he had to admit the flaw in his logic. "But I must say, you have some engineering here that I have not seen even in London. The—the conveyance in which we came down the cliff face! What a marvel!"

"I must have a closer look at it," Alice agreed. "Half ascender, half spider ... I wanted to close my eyes in fright, but its operation was too fascinating for me to lose a moment watching it work."

"That was invented years ago by a woman who has since climbed the starlight stair," Betsy said. "Her daughter runs it now. I'll warn you now before you sit next to them at the evening meal, May Lin and Stella will go on for hours about mechanics."

"I can't think of anything I'd like better. Maybe she can give us some help getting *Swan* back in the air."

"And maybe you can give us some help in return."

Alice turned at Mother Mary's voice to see her leaning on the door jamb. "Of course. You've given us hospitality freely. The least we can do is share what we know, if it will help."

Mother Mary nodded, and Alice wondered how she had crept up on them with no one hearing.

"I've sent for Stella and Gretchen upriver—the two girls who left with Captain Stan's party to spy out the dam. I'll want a report from them before we put our heads together."

Alice wasn't sure what she had in mind, but she nodded anyway.

"You may join us in church if you want," Mother Mary said, "and the evening meal is at sunset. The others should be here by then. We don't have much time. I don't mean to hold an axe over your heads, your being allies and friends of Betsy's and all, but we won't be able to put our minds to your ship until we come up with a plan to set the Californios dead to rights."

"Now, see here—" Ian began, but she cut him off with an upraised hand.

"There are four of you, and hundreds of us," she said simply. "If you help us, then you have my word we will help you. Until the river is out of danger from that dam, I must think of *las brujas* first."

Of course there was nothing to do but be gracious and assure the woman who commanded these lands that they would do everything they could to help.

When she and Betsy were gone, Ian folded himself onto the hammock bed and drew Alice down beside him. In the safety of his arm about her, Alice could almost be positive about what waited for them outside.

"I wish I knew what they needed our help with," she murmured, her head resting on Ian's shoulder. "If they plan to declare war on the Royal Kingdom, I'd rather not be mixed up in that. I'd rather go after Gloria."

"Married to a stranger," Ian marveled. "I cannot believe it. I knew she was a woman with a strong will and iron principles, but I would not have expected they would carry her to such an extreme."

"I hope he's an honorable man," Alice mused. "I wouldn't like to think of her tied to a scoundrel, or someone who would hurt her."

"A woman who can escape a party of mercenaries and form an alliance with a nation of witches is not likely to allow a man to hurt her, dearest."

"But still. She's only as big as a minute, though I have to say she's the best dressed and the finest shot of all of us. What she doesn't know about her father's guns would probably fit in a teaspoon."

"The guns will stand her in better stead than the clothes, I must say. Let us hope her new husband is a poor shot."

Alice bumped his shoulder with a fist. "You are not helping. You know it wasn't so very long ago I thought Gloria would be a better match for you than I."

He tucked her more securely against his side and gazed deeply into her eyes in that way that always made her shiver inside. "I am very glad you no longer think so. If I am to be stranded in the desert with only my wits to save me, all the wealth and fine clothes in the world are worth nothing. But with a woman like you at my side—a woman who can outfly, outshoot, and out-invent me—a woman I can depend on when the chips are down? My dear girl, I would rather be with no one else." He punctuated these happy facts with a kiss that emptied her mind of what could have been and filled her with delight at what was.

"You forgot one thing," she said, snuggling into him in a glow of complete satisfaction.

"And what is that, my darling outlaw?"

"I know how to make two people comfortable in one of these hammock beds. Want me to show you?"

They were almost late for dinner.

Alice saw by the expressions on Jake's and Benny's faces that the evening meal had far exceeded their expectations. After his third helping of pork and chile stew rolled up in a corn pancake, Benny's eyes rolled back in his head in an expression of complete satisfaction. Clara, who seemed to be second in command in the village and in charge of foodstuffs in general, beamed at him.

"I like a youngster who appreciates good cooking."

"I ent had food like this since I left Carrick House," he assured her, wiping his mouth on his sleeve. "I never would've suspected this landscape could produce such a meal, ma'am."

"And polite, too," Mother Mary murmured.

"The land does part of it—the chile, the hogs, the corn. But we enjoy trade with parts up and downriver to round things out. In the winter sometimes, pickings can be slim, but we've never starved yet."

"But this is the winter," Benny objected. "It's March, though you'd never know it. I've never been in a place so warm in March. Beats London and the Canadas both."

"It can be plenty cold, with snow to boot. But the village is warm and with the hydraulic heating system, we don't need to burn valuable wood to enjoy it." Mother Mary looked down the table toward the two young women who had been eating with great concentration, as though they'd been rationed for the past while. "Stella and Gretchen, we'll have your report on the dam now, if you please."

With a gulp, a girl with long, dark hair twined up with silk roses swallowed the last of her corn pancake and swigged from her clay mug some kind of clear spirits diluted with what Alice had been told was cactus nectar.

"We spent two days spying out the dam, Mother," she began. "On both the north and south sides, though the access is better from the south."

"Which we know because two soldiers shot at us, and when we returned fire, we had to go dispose of the bodies before the birds gave us away." Gretchen tossed a long blond braid over one shoulder. "Salvaged two rifles, four pocket pressure bombs, and two nice uniforms, in case we ever need the disguise."

Alice saw with a tingle of realization that the girl was wearing a clean white shirt with gold suns on the collar points. She had only a nodding acquaintance with

Californio insignia, from having done some trading and deliveries in Reno, but if memory served, that meant the previous owner of that shirt had been a new recruit. Inexperience had likely led to overconfidence, and then death.

Mother Mary nodded. "Good. Go on."

"They are putting every man they can conscript, impress, or shanghai into the work." Stella took up the report. "The dam is now forty or fifty feet high, and they've built a release valve in the base of it to allow the river to flow freely while it's under construction. Even with the valve only a quarter closed, the river is rising ... as we see here." She looked over her shoulder a moment, where on the opposite bank the water was lapping against a sheer face.

Alice saw that the stone had been marked at regular intervals. So they were recording the speed of the waters' rise, then.

"How many days before the village is flooded?" she asked. When Stella looked surprised at the interruption, Alice said, "I'm sorry. But I see that you have marked the water's rise, and I imagine each interval means something."

"Yes," Stella inclined her head. "I did that this afternoon. Each mark is one day, with smaller markings for each quarter that the valve is closed. At one quarter closed, the river will flood the village in thirty days. Fully closed, about seven, I think."

"You mean if someone takes it into his head to close that valve all the way, we could be flooded out of here in a week?" Clara exclaimed.

FIELDS OF IRON

Stella nodded slowly. "That is exactly what I mean. While it is under construction, we are fairly safe, because the dam is low. But there is a new problem—*el Gigante*."

"The what?" Mother Mary said sharply.

"A mechanical giant has been put to work. Before he died, the soldier told me," Gretchen said. "He thought he would frighten me, poor boy. The work is proceeding at three times its previous pace, because they use this thing as a crane, placing girders higher and higher, and moving gigantic boulders to backfill and strengthen the dam."

"You mean they've replaced the Gatling gun and the cannon with—with hands?" Alice exclaimed. "But it was made for war!"

"How do you know what its arms were?" Gretchen's stare was the kind that Alice would not want to face at the business end of a rifle—even across a wide river.

"There are two of them, aren't there?" Alice didn't answer her. Instead, her mind was already leaping ahead. "Or did Gloria say they'd ordered only one of those monsters?"

"We saw only the one, and it was being used for construction, not war." Gretchen's tone was stiff, as though she appreciated neither the interruption nor the implication that her information was faulty.

"Only one." Alice turned to Ian. "Do you see what this means? We found no trace of Evan or the behemoth in Resolution, yet we know for a fact they were both there, shooting at us."

"Do you think—surely not, Alice."

"Evan is alive?" Jake finished his sentence. "Alive, and operating that monster for the Californios?"

"He can barely shoot a gun, never mind walk about the country in a battle machine," Benny said. "It can't be him."

"It fits the facts," Alice insisted. "I don't know how or when, but we know that someone is operating that thing—and it's not the original operator. They would never put a Californio officer to manual labor."

"I think that hope is making you jump to conclusions," Mother Mary said. "Gloria knew nothing of this Evan. She thought he was dead."

"So did we," Ian told her. "But enough of that. We know where the behemoth is now, and what it is doing. Who is inside it is not really pertinent."

"Quite so," Gretchen said frostily. "But we need more information, and we need it quickly."

"Ella will see to that," Mother Mary said. Then, at Alice's questioning look, added, "She is my daughter. She went with Gloria to act as her maid, but she will be sending us information as she can."

"Not fast enough," said one of the crew of the *Colorado Queen*, seated at the far end of the table. "And too easily pinched. We need feet on the ground. I'll go."

"You'll be captured and pressed into the building work, and of no use to us," Stella said. "We know what we know, and we'll have to make do with it. We are going to have to destroy the dam from this side. There is no time for anything else."

"From this side!" Mother Mary sat back in her carved chair—the only one besides Clara's that pos-

FIELDS OF IRON

sessed a back. "How are we going to do that? The water is rising every moment."

A picture unfolded itself in Alice's mind. "How deep is the water behind the dam?" she asked. "Right there, I mean, not upstream."

"The dam is fifty feet high, so there is perhaps the height of a person between the top and the water's surface. It is backing up quickly—much more quickly than here."

"Forty feet of water will hide quite a bit," Alice said. "What we need is one of Gloria's undersea dirigibles. Swim right up to it and toss a bomb into the release valve, and it'll bring the whole thing down."

"Along with all the men working on the other side," Gretchen pointed out. "Innocent men who have been captured, including men we know."

"Do you have another solution?"

"I do not think *you* have one." Gretchen glared at her, and Alice felt her hackles rise. "It is all very well to talk of undersea dirigibles when we have neither sea nor dirigible to hand."

Alice gazed thoughtfully at the *Colorado Queen*, tugging at her mooring ropes several hundred yards away.

"No," she said slowly. "But we might have the next best thing."

12

There was no better way for a nation to isolate itself than to make travel so dangerous that no one would come to visit.

Gloria gripped the wooden bench in a first-class compartment that made train travel not only beastly uncomfortable but downright painful, and watched in suspense as the soldiers that traveled with every train dealt with a band of mounted brigands. The latter had dragged a wagon across the track, forcing the train to stop, but clearly had not counted on the passengers being at least as well armed as the soldiers. Two or three of the desperadoes lay abandoned where they had fallen off their horses, while their companions pounded across the desert and up into the barren hills, followed by parting shots. Her husband and some of the other men dragged the wagon aside so that the train might get back underway with no further loss of time.

They were scheduled to arrive in San Luis Obispo de Tolosa tomorrow before sunset. Though the captain had assured her there would be accommodation in the town, Gloria fully expected that they would be locked out of the mission's gates and left to fend for themselves if they arrived after dark. For all the monks knew, they could be brigands themselves.

How did any civilized person live in such an archaic society? How was it possible it had survived for two hundred years without falling apart from the sheer weight of inconvenience? Perhaps she would ask the Viceroy when she was finally able to speak with him.

Captain Stan fell into the seat beside her, wiping the sweat from his face. "Are you all right, Gloria?"

"Of course," she said. "I was not the one running off bandits and dragging wagons from railroad tracks. Are you hurt?" His shirtsleeve had been torn partly out of the arm's eye, and his waistcoat was soaked with what she devoutly hoped was sweat.

"Not at all. I tore my sleeve trying to make my tussle with José look convincing." His eyes crinkled at the corners. "From your tone of wifely concern, I gather I succeeded."

"My concern is very real. What on earth do you mean? Who is José?"

He leaned against her and whispered in her ear, "The attack was very real, too, except for José's and my little tussle. He had news for me and that was the only way he could convey it—while I had him in a head lock."

Gloria got her mouth closed with difficulty. "You mean—you mean those poor men died for nothing?"

"Oh, no. They were dead set on robbing the train. Their families are starving while the men are forced to join the rancho musters of soldiers and dam builders. The caravans, at least, provide a temporary means of getting food and coin."

"Barbaric," Gloria whispered. "But what news could possibly come at so high a cost?"

"The Viceroy is on his way south," he breathed, his lips practically touching her ear.

She shivered and moved away just enough to let him know she would not permit such a liberty. Though it felt wicked. Delightfully wicked. She crushed her wayward thoughts with the certainty that it was a trick he likely used on desert flowers and cancan girls alike, and no respectable woman would allow it.

"Why?" she whispered back.

"José didn't know. But think how this changes our plans. What are the odds that we might meet in the middle, at one of the ranchos?"

"I am sure you know better than I."

"Approximately one in fourteen."

"Good heavens, captain. Your mathematics instructor would be proud," she said in a normal tone.

"It isn't mathematics at all. There are fourteen missions with ranchos associated with them between here and San Francisco de Asis, the capital. The question is, what can we do to increase those odds enough to put us in the right place at the right time?"

"Hope that there are no more bandit attacks?"

"That will certainly help to keep this train on schedule. He left the capital yesterday on a private train—quite a marvel of engineering, I understand."

"For this country that is astonishing. Though the train on which I was conveyed here—*Silver Wind*—was certainly a marvel. It could travel overland without tracks. It possesses two sets of wheels, you see, and..."

She forgot the rest of what she'd been going to say. He had frozen, his relaxed posture tensing as though he was about to leap to his feet. He bent his intent, green-eyed stare upon her and she felt rather like a rabbit under a raptor's eye.

"What was the name of the train?"

"*S*—*Silver Wind.* Captain, what have I said?"

"You came out here on *Silver Wind?*"

"I was kidnapped here on *Silver Wind*," she corrected him with some asperity. "It was the train from which I escaped into the witches' church. Do you not remember? The Ambassador to the Fifteen Colonies, His Excellency Augusto de Aragon y Villarreal, was transporting the mechanical horses and the behemoth to the Royal Kingdom when we tried to stop him. In the resulting battle, I was knocked unconscious and brought aboard. Instead of the locomotive being trapped on a spur line, it simply let down a second set of wheels and the Ambassador and all the soldiers and mercenaries left alive departed the battlefield in perfect comfort."

He stared at her in astonishment. "I can see that my musings as to your past have been wildly off the mark."

He had mused about her?

Never mind. "The point is, I spent two days aboard that train before I was able to escape. If only I knew how to operate the wretched thing, I would steal it myself and go home."

His astonishment melted into a smile. "I would not put it past you."

"But how did you know of it?" she asked. "As soon as I mentioned its name, your face changed and you looked rather dreadful."

"I only know what anyone knows of trains," he said with irritating vagueness. "I expect it wasn't built here, though."

"It was not. It is a Fremont train—my father commissioned a number of them from Stanf—"

Oh, dear Lord in heaven. How could she have been so stupid? No wonder his name had sounded so familiar!

"Stanford—" She tried again, but her mind was going at such a pace her mouth could not keep up. "A Stanford Fremont train," she finally said. "Your father is Stanford Fremont."

"I thought we had already established that."

Ooh, she could just whack him with her pocketbook! If she possessed a pocketbook.

"Now I remember."

"I would prefer you did not."

"But—but—"

"Gloria. I mean it. I neither use that name nor wish to be reminded of it."

She could barely breathe, and it was not because of her very comfortable corset, either. *"But you are the missing heir!"* she finally hissed. "They have been searching the entire country for you for years!"

"The mysterious 'they' must not be very good at it," was all he said.

"But Stanford—"

"Gloria. Please. I beg of you. *Captain* will do nicely while we are out in public."

"But—"

But he had finally had enough. He leaped to his feet and slid open the door of their compartment, and before she could complete one sensible sentence, he had vanished down the corridor.

Ella ducked inside and closed the door behind her. "He didn't look very happy. Have you had a quarrel?"

Gloria had gone so deeply into memory, ferreting out bits of information, that it took her a moment to journey back and realize she was no longer alone. "I beg your pardon?"

"Captain Stan. Have you had a quarrel? He left just now looking like a thundercloud."

"A quarrel? No indeed." What had they been talking about? Trains. *Silver Wind.* The Viceroy. Ah, politics was a much safer subject. She dropped her voice. "One of the bandits gave him a message. The Viceroy is on his way south."

Ella nodded. "Riley told me. That's good news for us. Riley thinks he'll break his journey at San Luis Obispo de Tolosa, too. It is a pleasant place, from all accounts ... and with the Viceroy's retinue the size of a town, it's one of the few ranchos that can handle a royal progress."

Gloria touched her forehead and dabbed at her upper lip with the ruffle on her sleeve. "Ella, I'm feeling a little faint. I think it was the shock of the bandits, and the motion of the train. Would you be so kind as to find me some water?"

"Of course." Ella sprang up, as if happy to have something useful to do. "There is a barrel and tin cup a few cars back. I'll get you some."

She vanished in the direction opposite of the one the captain had taken, and Gloria sagged against the horrid slat back of the bench.

It had been all over the papers ten years ago, when she had been a schoolgirl still in London. When her most pressing concern had been convincing Lady Julia Wellesley that her wealth made her a friend worth having, and that her wit and elegance would prove Julia's excellent taste in including her in her circle.

The lurid headline in the *Evening Standard* had shouted, RAILROAD BARON'S SON KIDNAPPED! For of course the boy, fresh out of school and on the first leg of the obligatory European tour, must have been kidnapped. A young man simply didn't walk away from a fortune that vast, disavow his father's name, and disappear. However, unless he *had* been kidnapped and had managed to escape his captors, that appeared to be exactly what he'd done.

She had followed the newspaper reports for some time, with a schoolgirl's crush on a daguerreotype of a young man only a few years older than she. But as time went on and no ransom demands were made, and save for the first and only withdrawal of funds from his bank, no money was ever requested, the reports became less frequent. Finally, in the absence of any clues, they faded away altogether, to be revived five years ago when Stanford Fremont II had been killed in a locomotive explosion that had also taken the lives of Garrison Polk and Lord James Selwyn, Lady Claire Trevelyan's then fiancé.

How strange life was. Claire had met the father. Then she and Gloria had become fast friends. And now Gloria had met the son, out here in a vast desert that people called the Wild West for good reason.

She was married to the missing heir of the Fremont fortune.

With a laugh that sounded more like a disbelieving exhalation of breath, she gazed out of the isinglass at the rolling green hills through which they passed. Say rather that *he* had married the missing heiress to the Meriwether-Astor fortune. After all her slippery maneuvering to scotch her father's plans and avoid the stuffy, stiff-collared scions of politics and industry in Philadelphia, here she'd gone and married the most sought-after scion of all!

It would be funny if it hadn't been so ironic, and so dreadfully, maddeningly real.

When Ella came in with the tin cup full of cold water, Gloria had recovered sufficiently to smile at her in thanks, and drink it with gratitude. "I hope you had some for yourself?"

"Oh, yes. We should be stopping soon, to visit the next rancho and buy food. We've eaten everything that Mother Mary sent with us. And they say we shall be able to see the sea! I have never seen it. I wonder what it is like."

"It is vast, and cold, and full of creatures," Gloria said absently. "I must say, I take food much more seriously now than I once did."

"Food is serious," Ella agreed. "Would you like me to keep you company?"

"Certainly." Gloria shook herself and made room for her friend on the bench. "I trust the seating is equally as comfortable in your compartment with the men?"

"It's awful, isn't it?" Ella wriggled a little. "I'll never complain about the stone benches at home again."

Home. Gloria stifled a sigh.

"Tell me, what do you know of Captain Stan? How many years has he been on the river?"

Ella shrugged and clasped one knee, her serviceable cotton skirts riding up a little. "A couple, I guess. The *Queen* used to be captained by a terrible old goat with a beard as long and white as snow. He was so proud of that beard—I heard he washed it more frequently than he bathed the rest of him. I believe Stan was among his crew then, but I don't know what he did. All I know is that one night the captain fell overboard—or was pushed—and the next thing you know, Stan was at the tiller."

"Goodness. He didn't do the pushing, did he?" A scion of industry was one thing. But Gloria was quite sure she did not want to be married to a murderer.

FIELDS OF IRON

"Oh, no, that was Riley."

"Riley. The very Riley who is in our party?"

"The very one." Ella glanced at her. "Don't be afraid, Mere—er, Gloria. Nobody knows for sure that he was pushed. And he was awful—a cruel master. No one regrets his passing, including Mother. Goodness, the fights they used to have! He never bothered her after she shot him, though."

"Good for her," Gloria said faintly.

"Anyhow, that was quite a while back. Everyone likes Captain Stan—or if they don't, they're smart enough not to show it."

"And you?" Gloria hardly dared ask, fearing to tread on sensitive ground. "Do you like him, too?"

"Sure, as well as I like any man. But then, we don't see many outside his riverboat crews. There are three other boats besides the *Queen*, you know. The captain owns them all."

"Does he?" Any fears she might have had about having to fish one of her gold guineas out of her corset to buy food faded away. "He has done well for himself."

"He's educated," Ella said simply. "Not too many folks out here can say that. And he's the kind of man the rivermen are willing to crew for." She glanced at Gloria sidelong. "You could've done worse."

"I still feel badly, though."

"About what?"

"About—" Dear me, this was very awkward. "Well, about any hopes you might have cherished in that direction."

"Hopes?" The color drained from Ella's face.

Her foot was in it now. There was nothing for it but to wade on through the morass she had embarked upon, as treacherous as the muskeg up at the Firstwater Mine. "Yes. For Captain Stan. Believe me, if there had been any other way, I would not have—"

"Hopes for Captain Stan?" The color flooded back into Ella's tanned cheeks. "Is that what you think? That I—that we—"

The door slid open and the object of their discussion stepped into the compartment. He looked from Ella's scarlet face and wide eyes to Gloria's distress and the trembling of her lips. "Seems we've gone from bad to worse. Shall I go away?"

Ella jumped up and was out into the corridor before he even finished the question. He gazed after her, then shook his head and slid the door shut. "I must remember to knock next time."

"It is not that." Gloria tucked in her skirts so that he could take his seat beside her. "I do not know what I said to distress her so. Well, yes, I do. I pried where I had no business doing so, and I upset her." With a sigh, she added, "That makes two in a row. Please forgive me for prying into your life, too. It was clearly a subject that pains you. I will not do it again."

But he shook his head, and to her surprise, took her hand, folding it between both of his, which were warm, but not sweaty. She resisted the instinctive urge to snatch it back, and did her best to relax.

He is your husband. He has every right to take your hand, and more besides. It is to his credit that he is willing to give you time.

FIELDS OF IRON

"No, I am the one who overreacted. You of all people have the right to know my story."

"Not if you do not wish to tell me."

"But I do." Again that green glance, alive now with the first hint of humor. "I may not meet with honesty very often, but I have observed that in my own household I may count upon it."

In spite of herself, she smiled. "If you mean that I am blunt and need to think more often before I speak, then you had better say so straight out."

"I wouldn't dream of it. So, you know who I am. May I ask how?"

"The newspapers in London had a field day, believing that you had been kidnapped by the Famiglia Rosa or a band of slavers or the royal family of some impoverished nation. I was young, but I still followed the story. There was a very flattering daguerreotype of you in the *Evening Standard*, you know. I was not the only one of my set who sighed over it before she blew out her candle."

"Heavens." He made a rueful mouth, as though this idea were distasteful to him. "The truth is not nearly so romantic or exciting. I simply took the opportunity that presented itself in Paris, and boarded *Persephone* for New York instead of *Hera* for St. Petersburg. Once I reached this side of the pond, it was simple enough to disappear. Went to the Louisiana Territory first, where I worked on the riverboats on the mighty Mississip. I was good at cards—not as good as you, mind, but good enough to make a living once the money ran out."

"But the trust—you could have drawn upon it at any time."

"Not my father's money." His tone was flat, and Gloria took the message as it was intended. "I knew where he got it. Running track through non-treaty Navapai lands, opening up the West to every cheat and well-dressed criminal who cared to come. He even had his fingers in the Klondike, making a fortune off the dreams of miners. I couldn't bear it, Gloria, and knowing that he wanted me in the business with him, learning how to steal and trick with all the skill he had … well, I simply walked away."

"Cheer up," she said with a half-smile. "At least he wasn't an arms dealer, starting wars all over the world simply to create markets for his weapons."

After a moment, he tilted his head toward her in acknowledgment. "There is that."

"After my father died saving my life—one of the few times he actually paid attention to me, I might add—I took over the business. I was voted president by the board of directors just before I came out west."

"I think you will make an admirable president. What are you going to do once you talk the Viceroy out of this war?"

"Well, I must go back. I have undersea dirigibles to manage, and factories to instruct to make ploughshares instead of swords. But after that, I do not know." She cocked an eyebrow at him. "What about you? Are the trains still running despite your absence?"

"They seem to be, if *Silver Wind* is out here. She was my father's flagship—his dream. It is quite astonishing to know she was actually built. I remember seeing the drawings for her on his desk, years ago."

"Apparently the late Viceroy had a hand in her design. I was told the double wheels were his idea."

"Do not think I have not noticed your use of singular pronouns, Mrs. Fremont. Nor have I forgotten your use of the word *divorce* in earlier conversations. But at some time or another, may we not consider whether our futures might be brought into parallel, like a railroad track? Or if they might meet and become one track altogether?"

She did not know how to answer. How could she, when any given day might see her—and him—dead or imprisoned or who knew what? What was the point of building castles in the air when one did not know if one were ever going to live there? And she had merely brought up the subject of divorce in the mission garden because it had never occurred to her he would want anything else.

But in her efforts to put such thoughts into words, she hesitated too long.

"Never mind." He rose and took her empty tin cup. "How foolish. We must concentrate on saving the world, mustn't we? Excuse me."

And for the second time in an hour, he left her alone.

She liked it even less than the first.

13

Next to being the Viceroy, or a commander in the militia, Evan thought, the way to make a living in this strange and backward country was to own a railroad. The lines ran down the eastern and western borders, roughly north to south, with a station at each mission and its attached rancho. Since there were well over twenty missions along the rocky length of the coastline, the ranchos extending for miles into the fertile lands to the east, many of them were less than an hour apart. Lines ran from east to west, as well, but only three of them crossed the mountain range, one running through the water meadows known as Las Vegas, one through a mountain pass to Reno, and one farther north where, the post commander said with some regret, "I have never been."

They occupied a private car—Commander Joaquin de Sola, Evan, Joe, and four soldiers whose sole duty it was to make sure the two of them didn't try to escape. Evan thought that was rather overdoing it—he and Joe, fit though they might have become from their labors at the dam, were unlikely to succeed in overpowering three men, let alone five.

Commander de Sola was a pleasant fellow, however, especially given the secret that lay between them. Since the night Evan had interpreted the man's dream and subsequently discovered that he was not quite as supportive of the Ambassador's ambition as might be supposed of a good servant of the Crown, the commander had not treated Evan as a prisoner. And now, his conversation was not only civil, but downright informative.

"Rancho San Luis Obispo de Tolosa is the largest between Nuestra Señora la Reyna de los Ángeles and the capital, San Francisco de Asis," he explained as the train chuffed through one of the smaller stations without stopping, people's faces turning to gape at the ornate private car that brought up the rear. They were flying the Viceroy's own flag of the crowned sun, its benevolent rays extending over stripes meant to represent the green of earth and the blue of sea. On the occasions when they had stopped, the soldiers had disembarked to stand on the platform, one at each door, warding off the unwary who might try to board. And, of course, making it impossible for anyone to leave the car.

"I have had a message by express that we are to stop there and await His Serene Highness."

"How long will it take him and his party to reach it?" Evan asked, his gut rolling uneasily at the thought of Alice and *Swan*, crippled under some red cliff, possibly injured, and the great black desert birds slowly circling.

"One does not ask such questions of royalty," the commander told him with a smile. "One simply puts oneself at the prince's disposal."

Evan gritted his teeth and tried not to show his unease.

"However, the correspondence seems to indicate a degree of urgency, so I do not think we will be waiting long. The earliest he could arrive is tomorrow night, so our task now is to anticipate him by the widest margin possible."

"I did not thank you for the suit of clothes in which to attend him," Evan said. "I appreciate your forethought."

"One does not appear before a prince in rags, smelling of urine and sweat, Senor Douglas."

"Certainly not. But one is no less a prisoner, despite a bath, fine wool, and a clean shirt." He plucked at the sleeve of the short black jacket he had been given, and the chains between the buttons at his wrists jingled. Chains of a decorative sort ran down the outside of the pant legs, and the belt buckle was silver, embossed with the insignia of the commander's company. His boots, however, were his own and told the tale of his hard journey. He had attempted to clean them, but some of

FIELDS OF IRON

the gouges from the battle of Resolution and the many scratches from his labors on the dam could not be eradicated.

At least they were comfortable. Should he find an opportunity to run, he would not be crippled by blisters, at any rate.

"And what of you?" he asked Evan's translator. "Does your suit fit?"

Actually, it suited him much better than Evan imagined his own borrowed feathers did. His tanned skin and fine bones lent it an elegance that Evan had not seen in his own reflection when he had been permitted to use the water closet and the mirror over the sink.

"It does," Joe said with his usual brevity. "Sleeves are a bit long."

"Alas, we had no tailor to hand," the commander said. "But you both look presentable. Perhaps, Senor José, you have a little Californio blood?"

"I might." Joe sat stiffly on a settee bolted to the floor, his hands on his knees. "My father, best I can tell, was a San Gregorio man."

"Is that so?" The commander leaned forward, and replaced his dram of port on the table by his elbow. "That makes you a citizen, then."

"I don't see how. I was born on the river, and my mother is from back East somewhere. Or the Canadas. Can't rightly say."

"Do you know your father's name?"

"It was the same as the rancho."

"Ah." The commander looked thoughtful. "Then he was likely illegitimate. It is the custom for baseborn boys to take the name of the rancho on which they were born rather than of a father who may not wish to acknowledge them. Still, that does not have any bearing on your citizenship. Though you are a half-breed, you are entitled to some rights, at any event."

"Don't see 'em doing much good now," Joe said, though it was clear from his face that this was all news to him.

"What was your crime, senor?" the commander asked. He offered Joe and Evan tiny glasses of port, which he had not done before. Clearly this was one of the rights to which young Joe was now entitled—as well as the address of *senor* rather than nothing in particular.

"Don't know." Joe shrugged. "Being in the wrong place at the wrong time, I guess. Came in to Santa Croce to trade for supplies, and was impressed into the work gang. Never even had a chance to see my friends, or tell them what happened. My mother probably thinks I'm dead."

The commander frowned, and the soldiers shifted from foot to foot. What did that mean?

"A citizen, baseborn or not, may not be impressed. Why did you not tell them? You would have been returned to San Gregorio and received training in the militia, or some other employment, not condemned to brute labor in the camp."

Joe gazed at him in the manner of one listening to the ramblings of an old man who is not quite all there. "You've never been impressed, senor."

"Of course not. What a thing to say!"

"Then perhaps you do not realize that there is no asking of questions or giving of information. There is simply a cudgel, and a whip, and a cell." His tone was flat, and the commander's gaze settled on his face a moment, where the scar of an old knife wound formed a pale comma shape in front of his right ear.

The commander gave a single nod. "Then allow me to correct this error with what powers I possess. When we reach San Luis Obispo de Tolosa, I will have citizenship papers drawn up and filed with the monks at the mission. Once you are in possession of papers, you cannot be sent back to the work gang. Instead, you will have the choice of performing your current service for His Serene Highness, or going on to San Gregorio, which lies north, between there and the capital."

Joe glanced at Evan. "I will do what I have said I will do." A ghost of a smile curved his finely drawn mouth. "Can't leave Evan on his own—he's likely to get himself hurt."

"I think you underestimate the man who controls *el Gigante*, senor."

Perhaps—when Evan was actually controlling the mechanical behemoth. Outside of it, Evan was just as vulnerable as anyone else to sword or propelled bullet. Perhaps more so, for he was a doctor, a scientist, not a trained military man who, presumably, knew how to avoid being run through or shot.

Who was learning to operate the behemoth now? If the commander was correct, no one would be assigned to replace him, but then again, no one would have deemed it important enough to tell him if they had. Ah well, if some fool climbed into the harness and tipped the behemoth over, or sent it walking into the nearest barracks, it would serve them right. And, if the truth were told, he rather missed the beast. Missed the safety inside the pilot's cabin, the view of the surrounding countryside, the knowledge that as a giant, he could travel great distances and no one could tell him not to.

As opposed to this present moment, when he was traveling great distances and feeling as insignificant and trapped as ever he had as a child in the small but drafty house belonging to his grandmother.

They broke their journey that night at a rancho set in the middle of acres of orange trees that stretched as far as the eye could see. What a strange time of year for trees to fruit. But there they were in March, branches heavy with orange and yellow, bristling with ladders as men harvested, the air sweet with the scent of citrus. Perhaps this was the source of the oranges each man received in the prison camp.

He and Joe were assigned a room in the mission dormitory with two comfortable cots, no window, and the obligatory soldier posted at the door. After a more substantial dinner than Evan had enjoyed in weeks, he and Joe retired.

"If a man were inclined to escape," Evan said in a low tone once the door had been bolted behind them, "this would be the place to do it. One could make one's way halfway back to the mountains concealed by fruit trees."

"At harvest?" Joe cocked an eyebrow at him. "Place is crawling with workers, and the reward would likely feed a man's family for six months."

"They wouldn't be picking at night."

"You did see the lock and the guard on our door, didn't you? I'm getting papers, remember? He ain't there for me."

Evan sighed. "Just thinking aloud."

"Keep it to yourself, then, until you come up with something practical." Joe paused. "Besides, I promised to translate for you, and it means I get a look at the Viceroy. He's said to be the same age as me."

"Nineteen? Twenty?"

"Thereabouts."

"I wish I knew more about his dreams," Evan said rather fretfully. "From what de Sola says, they are not pleasant. More like hallucinations, really, since they can occur at any time of day or night."

"Guess we'll find out." And Joe rolled himself up in a blanket that smelled of clean wool and nothing else, leaving Evan alone in the dark with his thoughts.

In the morning, the train waited for them, steaming, at the village platform, and their journey continued. Evan, who had not slept well, nodded off, lulled to sleep by the endless rolling vista that parted only occasionally to show a glimpse of the sea. Thus it seemed to him that they arrived at their destination quickly, in mid-afternoon.

He climbed down to the platform, gawking from the sea on one side to the mission of San Luis Obispo de Tolosa above, commanding a majestic view from a long hill above the fishing village and train station. Its towers thrust up into the sky with authority, and even the tenants, fishermen, and visiting citizens in the square seemed to have an idea of their own importance simply from being there.

Evan and Joe were loaded into a steam conveyance of about a decade's vintage, and carried up the hill to make their obeisances in the church, be registered, and taken to the rancho.

The rancho itself lay a quarter mile away down a broad gravel avenue that practically blinded one in the sunlight. Cypress and orange trees, fields of lavender, and knot gardens filled with roses even at this time of year lay on either side as they crunched briskly down the avenue.

"It's like bloody Versailles in miniature," he murmured. Perhaps the grandee was an educated man, and had made his own tour of Europe.

Joe was silent, his gaze moving from trees to buildings to beds of flowers as though cataloguing everything for future escape plans. If Evan had any sense, he would be doing the same, but he could not. It was all too much to take in—the leap from stinking prisoner to this spreading, sunlit luxury and the prospect of the inevitable fall back again.

He was still a prisoner. Still had no control over his own life. Only his surroundings had changed, and he must not forget it. Even the civility of Commander de Sola was no more than expediency, a means to getting a job done about which he too had no choice.

FIELDS OF IRON

The conveyance puffed around a circular drive and under a graceful portico draped in a vine with such brilliant fuchsia flowers that it hurt to look at them. Double doors swung wide to admit them into a courtyard nearly as big as the parade ground back at the barracks. Fountains played at either end, flinging up cool water with a sound like music. On the far side, a doorway draped in roses opened and a family trooped down the steps.

"Welcome to the servants of His Serene Highness," boomed the man at the head of the procession.

"Long may he reign," responded the commander, saluting smartly while the soldiers followed his lead in perfect unison.

"Welcome to Rancho San Luis Obispo de Tolosa." The man's teeth flashed white under a luxurious moustache. The silver on his suit winked enough to blind a man, and his hair was pomaded and brushed back from a noble forehead above a hawklike nose. "I am Ignatio de la Carrera y Borreaga. This is my wife, Liliana, and our daughters Beatriz, Esperanza, and Isabel. Our son is away at university in the mother country."

While Joe translated rapidly, the women sank into graceful curtsies, their black, beribboned silk gowns spreading around them like blooming roses. The commander bowed low and expressed his gratitude for their hospitality, then introduced Evan "and his manservant, José, who acts as translator."

The fierce gaze passed over Joe and stooped upon Evan. "So this is the interpreter of dreams. Far be it from me to deny the wishes of our prince, but I find it strange that a godless foreigner should be given this honor."

Joe's murmured translation hitched in the middle, and Evan realized that if he did not call upon the spirit of *el Gigante* at this moment, he and Joe would be relegated to the likes of the poor sods who cleaned water closets for the duration of their stay here.

He took in the grandee's person down the length of his nose. "I am far from godless, sir, and you may address me as *el Doctor* or Senor Douglas. I possess a medical degree from the University of Edinburgh, which boasts the most impeccable reputation in Europe, surpassing even that of the Universidad de Sevilla."

When Joe finished translating, the three girls gasped and watched their father, clearly expecting him to order Evan into prison, or at the very least, back into the conveyance for a fast trip down to the train station.

The grandee took a long breath that to Evan seemed to increase his size. The red sash wrapped about his waist positively creaked. Then his clean-shaven chin dipped sharply in a nod of acknowledgment. "You are welcome here, Doctor Douglas," he said in accented English.

Joe opened his mouth to translate, and closed it again.

"Forgive me. I was not informed of your credentials in the manner that I should have been, and misspoke."

"Of course, sir." Evan tried to look as calm as though this was not the first time an impossibly wealthy man had apologized to him. "You speak my language very well. Were you educated abroad?"

The grandee smiled. "All the sons of our noble houses are educated in Spain, sir. But I was fortunate enough to spend some months at the very university of which you speak. I was never so cold in all my life, and hope never to enjoy such good fortune again."

Evan could not help a smile. "There we are in perfect agreement, sir. Though I will say that the whiskey cannot be improved upon, and went some way toward mitigating the situation."

De la Carrera laughed and clapped him on the back. "That it did, sir. Please, allow me to offer you the small comforts of my home with the assurance that, while we do not stock Scots whiskey, at least it is not cold."

Evan could not tell who was more astonished—Joe or Commander de Sola. But he was not so foolish as to believe he had just made an ally in this peculiar country. If anything, he had just made it exponentially more difficult for he and Joe to escape.

Taking their cue from the grandee, the ladies clustered around the two of them, giggling and chattering to the point that Joe could only translate in snatches.

"Delighted and honored—so handsome—that must be you, amigo, it can't be me—dinner at eight—oh, there's a fiesta tomorrow night in the plaza here when the Viceroy comes—the whole countryside is invited."

Carried away by the feminine tide, he and Joe were deposited in an airy ground-floor room overlooking the sea that boasted velvet curtains and carved black furniture that had to be two hundred years old. Then, with flirtatious glances from long-lashed dark eyes, the one called Isabel pulled the door closed and he and Joe were alone.

Joe walked over to the basin and ewer and splashed cool water on his face and the back of his neck. "Nicely done," he said, pulling a towel from the rack and patting himself dry. "You'll notice they haven't posted a guard."

"There must be one outside."

Joe pulled open the heavy, ornately carved door and looked both ways down the colonnade. "Nope. I wouldn't have believed it if I hadn't seen it myself."

"It means nothing," Evan said. "There are thousands of men on this land and every man Jack of them loyal to de la Carrera. They need no guards, for everyone is a guard."

"Maybe not."

"I grant you, perhaps there are a few who do not support this way of life, but finding one placed where he or she might assist us will be more than both of us can manage."

"They might find us."

"They have no motivation to do so. What are we to them?"

Joe's gaze was half quizzical, half impatient. "Look at yourself. You took on a grandee and got us put in this room instead of the barn—or gaol. You're about to have the ear of the monarch. I would say that if we haven't been approached by midnight, they'll have lost a bloody good chance."

"And how do we know who to trust?"

"We don't trust anyone," Joe said flatly. "You have a job to do, and I—"

He turned away to hang up the towel and Evan felt a moment of surprise at such a tidy habit. "And you? You're about to have your citizenship restored and be sent off to join the militia."

With a snort, Joe shrugged out of the short black jacket and hung it on a peg, then walked to the window to gaze at the ocean lying at their feet in all its vast, unknowable beauty. *"Si,* that's what I want. To fight against my own people, in a prison just as real as the one we left."

"But you would be a free man. And aren't these your people?"

Joe's jaw flexed. "My mother became *una bruja* because they were the only ones who would take her in after he beat her and left her for dead, pregnant with me."

"Who? Your father?"

"I don't know who my father is."

"But you told de Sola—"

"I did. But San Gregorio wasn't my father. He just happened to be single and of an age to marry a woman who was already pregnant by someone else. A little gold for a wedding gift and it was done."

"Oh." Evan sat on the bed. "And he treated her … badly. I'm sorry."

A quick shake of the head. "Not your fault. He was a blacksmith, so he traveled around to the ranchos. Near Las Vegas he got tired of being tied down, and in these parts, there's only one way a woman leaves her marriage."

Evan felt sick. "Then *las brujas* are not entirely evil."

"They're not evil at all." His movements jerky, Joe spun to face him, and Evan realized too late he ought to have chosen his words better. "They're clever, and generous, and there is more love in one of their stone villages than there probably is on this whole rancho." A sweep of his skinny arm took it all in. "The moment I can, I'm going back. There's someone—" Again, he cut himself off.

Wisely, Evan managed not to ask the obvious question. Instead, he said, "So we are still in this together, then."

"Don't know how we're going to get out of it, but it'll be together. And then we do our best to take care of business in Las Vegas." Which was as close as one could get to the river canyons and the place—or person—Joe called home.

Joe offered his hand and Evan shook it, feeling every bit as though he were making an unbreakable vow.

FIELDS OF IRON

14

It could be said of Captain Stan that once he gave his word, he was good for it, which was more than Gloria could say of his men. They were good for giving the appearance of a party of gentlemen and none of the substance, which meant that the only place she could allow herself to be alone in their company was at the card table, and sometimes not even then. They could not be trusted not to hold an ace up their sleeves, protesting ever so sincerely to their captain's wife that they were as clean as the proverbial whistle.

Fortunately, she was as good at spotting a cheat as each of the four was at being one, so on the whole she came out even. By the third evening, she was able to trounce them so soundly at Cowboy Poker that it was difficult to believe any of them would have the nerve to try cheating her again.

At first her husband had allowed her to play simply to see if the luck she'd had back at Mother Mary's village was real or accidental. It didn't take long before he realized that luck was only part of it, and powers of observation combined with an excellent memory had far more to do with the pile of chips in front of her than anything else. The simple fact was that they needed money, and in the absence of a trust fund and dividends, gambling would have to do. Carefully, she secreted the gold and silver coins about her person, with only a few of lesser value in the shabby reticule Ella had managed to find for her in the market.

The captain escorted her from the hotel with its cheerfully raucous gambling parlors to the much more modest inn at the far end of the waterfront below the enormous and imposing mission. "I dare not let you out of my sight, with all the money you carry," he said as she strolled along beside him, her hands clasped on his arm.

"I am happy to have your company." She swerved a little to allow three drunken seamen to pass. The ships they had presumably come from were moored along a wooden pier farther down. "I have not forgotten what can happen to a woman alone here."

"Never forget it for a moment. While you were making your fortune, I was gathering information. I would rather not tell you indoors—may we walk a little farther along the shore?"

"Certainly. The climate here is almost as warm as Italy, is it not?"

"I never got as far as Italy, so I will have to take your word for it."

The moon had risen over the hills to their left, turning the heaving waves to silver. The lights of the town were reflected in the harbor, tossed in hectic motion as jolly boats came and went out to the frigates, and the air smelled of seaweed and oranges and a medicinal scent that she remembered from Italy as well. Eucalyptus, it was called.

"This should be far enough," she prompted the captain. "Not even the starfish can hear us." The tide was low, and creatures of that kind adhered to the rocks below them.

"I'm quite sure they're being paid by the monks to listen," he said solemnly, "but I will take the risk. The Viceroy is to arrive tomorrow, and there will be a fiesta."

Something prickled through her stomach—unease mixed with anticipation. "It is certain he will come here, then, and not to one of the other ranchos?"

"Quite certain. The whole town is in an uproar. You cannot imagine it is like this under normal circumstances."

"You forget I grew up in Philadelphia and London, which are in an uproar all the time," she said. "I'll wager there will be a frenzy of cleaning in the morning to wash away the debauchery of tonight."

"He will be staying with the grandee and his family, of course, so our task will be to get you in to speak with him before the entire country descends to have their cases and grievances heard."

"Is that what usually happens?"

"So I am informed. The trouble is that the young man is unwell."

"Which may make it difficult for us or anyone else to see him."

"Exactly. However, he must appear at the fiesta, to which all the surrounding noble families have been invited. If he does not, the rumors will become twice as thick, and may even go so far as to say he is on his deathbed. Which would not do the government any favors. The country is in enough unrest as it is."

"The poor boy," Gloria said with some sympathy. "Is there no doctor to treat him?"

"I'm sure there must be an army of them. But whatever his condition, it does not seem to be improving. Quite the opposite. Of course, this is all hearsay. But I suppose it is best to plan for the worst and be pleasantly surprised when it doesn't happen."

"So what you are saying is that we cannot simply make an appointment with his secretary and take our place in line."

"No. But here is another little piece of news. I have been asking myself why he is here at all, if he is so unwell, and in the jakes behind the hotel I had my answer."

"Spare me the details, if you would."

He leaned in a little and lowered his voice. "He is apparently here to meet an interpreter of dreams. Like Joseph in the Bible, I was told. I was also told to expect to see signs and miracles, so I am not sanguine as to the reliability of my informant. He was in the righteous stage of drunk."

"Good heavens." Gloria shook her head. "Is there no end to the foolishness and superstition of these folk? First airships fly in the face of God, and now dreams may be interpreted by prophets. Next they will be killing poor chickens to examine their entrails and predict whether or not he will live."

"Don't say that—you will start a rumor."

"If I see any chickens about to be used for that purpose, you can be certain I will do more than that. I have a very good friend who makes a habit of rescuing the birds when it is necessary. I am quite prepared to follow her excellent example."

"If one rescues a chicken, it is merely so that one may have it for one's own dinner, I am sure."

Gloria lifted her chin. "Not among my acquaintance, I assure you. Claire's hens fly as members of the crew in her ship, and have their own domicile in the garden when she is ashore. Her ward Maggie is studying the field of genetics, and the hens she and her grandfather breed in Cornwall are renowned throughout the country for their beauty and productivity."

After a moment in which she peered at him to be sure he was not trying to stifle a laugh, he said, "I shall be sure not to order chicken for dinner in future, given your feelings on the matter."

"Thank you. That is very thoughtful of you." She paused, then said, "So if the rumors prove to be true, and the Viceroy will be receiving no one, how are we to approach him?"

"And now I note your use of plural pronouns, my dear."

"You have just reminded me that I must not go about alone," she said with some asperity. "I merely assumed this meant bearding monarchs in their dens as well."

"You are quite right. It is clear that we must join the fiesta, and attempt to close the deal in a social setting, not an official one."

Gloria allowed that this was likely their best plan.

"I hope you will be succinct. A waltz is not much time in which to put the case for peace to a man who has had many months to plan for war."

Now, wait just a moment!

It was dark, but the moon illuminated enough of his face that she could examine it to see whether he was serious. "A waltz? You cannot be suggesting that I dance with the Viceroy. With a house full of noble families? If it is anything like London, the mamas will be pushing their daughters in his path like ninepins, hoping he will choose one of them to be Vicereine. We shall be lucky to be allowed on the property, much less be in the same room, or the same set of dancers."

"You underestimate yourself, Mrs. Fremont."

"This is not Philadelphia, where I had my fortune to recommend me," she said tartly. She had become a realist long ago.

"You still do. You are a wealthy woman, and in fact are his partner, if one may be so bold as to bring it up.

FIELDS OF IRON

You have as much right to waltz with him and discuss business as anyone in the room."

Gloria stopped her slow stroll and released his arm abruptly. "I am not his partner. I am the farthest thing from that you can imagine."

"I know that, and you know that, but he does not know that."

"And the moment I step into the room, the Ambassador to the Fifteen Colonies, Augusto de Aragon y Villarreal—" The syllables rolled grandly off her tongue. "—will spot me and clap me in irons. That is how I was to have come here, you know. As a penitent, to apologize to the Viceroy for losing his shipment of mechanicals."

"And what was to have happened to you afterward?"

"The clapping in irons, I imagine. One doesn't simply admit to losing hundreds of thousands of pounds in arms and then walk away to spend the afternoon in the shops."

"I don't see why not. My father did, on one memorable occasion."

"I am not your father. Or mine, for that matter. No, we must approach him in a different way. If I cannot use business, I must use—" What? What on earth did she possess that would entice a prince to spend a single moment in her company?

"Guile?" her husband suggested. "Blandishments? Beauty?"

"You are not helping."

"I thought I was. You may walk into that fiesta like a queen, expecting to be paid homage, and you will get it. I've seen you do it myself."

"Nonsense." Her cheeks burned at the very thought. "Even in my salad days I could not do so."

"I beg your pardon, but those days are not over. Come. Ella should be back by now."

"Ella?" What had she to do with it? And where had she gone without telling Gloria? It wasn't safe for a young woman to be out in the streets of the port with all these sailors reeling about.

"Yes. I sent her on a mission for which she is uniquely equipped."

"Alone?"

"Of course not. She is a lady's maid, and Riley accompanied her."

"To do what?"

"Come and see." And, maddening man, he would not say another word all the way back to the inn—though their pace was satisfyingly fast.

Ella met her at the door of their room with dancing eyes. "Come see, Gloria, how lucky we are."

Considering she'd won quite a sum earlier that evening, Gloria assumed the surprise had something to do with Cowboy Poker. But with a flourish, Ella shook out a beribboned black skirt and a silk bodice that was clearly meant to go with it.

"A new dress for fiesta!"

Or nearly new, anyway, for of course there had been no time to have anything made up. Gloria had assumed she would have her audience with the Viceroy in one of the shabby, out-of-fashion dresses the witches had lent her. This was indeed a surprise.

"Where did you get it? Oh Ella, such fabric. I haven't seen silk like this since Italy."

"We're so lucky it's fiesta." Ella was delighted at Gloria's pleasure. "It's the custom for the noble ladies to get new dresses for each holiday, you know, and they give away their old ones. I just happened to hear of it, and sure enough, the ladies of Rancho San Luis Obispo de Tolosa had given several at the mission. I do hope this will fit you. The one I got is tight, but manageable if I don't overeat."

Gloria was sick to death of the blue dress in which she'd been married and been traveling all this time, but her only other options were the white ruffled petticoat and embroidered blouse she'd worn with her leather corselet, or the yellow day dress, neither of which were exactly suitable for meeting royalty.

"Goodness, I hope it does, after all the trouble you took. Can you unhook me?"

Captain Stan, looking on from the doorway, suddenly seemed to realize that he was *de trop*. "I trust you are in good hands, my dear. Join us downstairs once you are decent, so that I may see the final result."

"Of course." She could barely wait for the door to close behind him. "Ella, you are the best and cleverest friend a girl could have. I had no idea of this customs of the ladies in these parts."

Ella's skillful fingers made quick work of the blue bodice and skirt, and then Gloria stepped into the black silk skirt. "Goodness, how full it is!" She spun, and the layers and flounces with their colorful ribbon trim spun in a full circle with her. How lovely it would look during the waltz!

"It is a little large in the waist," Ella eyed the skirt critically. "We will have to pin it."

"I do not mind that at all. I would not mind if it were as big as a tent, as long as I do not have to wear that blue dress again for a day or two. Now the bodice." She slipped her arms into the bodice and settled it on her shoulders. "Sensible ladies, these. It hooks up the front."

"We are lucky its previous owner was not as heavy on the top as on the bottom. I am not much of a seamstress, but we would have had to take it in somehow."

"I can sew enough for that, thanks to having embroidered enough samplers in my girlhood to paper a room." She hooked up the front and turned this way and that in front of the little mirror over the sink. "What do you think?"

The neckline was much lower than Gloria was used to—clearly the Californio ladies had no compunction about displaying skin and curves in the evening. Covering the hooks was a series of pink and blue ribbons crisscrossing down the front, matching those on the skirt, and the neckline was edged in a deep flounce of lace as fine as a spider's web.

"I think you look lovely." Ella smiled with satisfaction. "Mine is silk, too, though not quite so fine, but that is appropriate. I didn't think it would do to have a lady's dress when I am not."

FIELDS OF IRON

Gloria touched her cheek. "If a lady is measured by her loyalty, her ingenuity, and her kindness, then you are a lady as fine as any I have ever met."

For a moment, tears filled Ella's soft brown eyes, and she blinked them back. "That is the nicest thing anyone has ever said to me. Oh Gloria, if only—"

"Dear heart, do not say it. No one ever made herself happier by a sentence that began with those two words. Come. Let us get you dressed, and we will go down and show the gentlemen what they must live up to."

Ella bit her lip, and her gaze fell as she nodded. Then she brightened a little. "Wait—there were silk roses, too. We won't tell anyone what the roses mean, will we?"

Gloria's breath caught with mischief that matched Ella's own. "We certainly will not. But I do believe there will not be two ladies more proud of their roses—"

"—*for in death will bloom life, and none will take it from her,*" Ella recited simultaneously with her, smiling a wicked smile. The words were straight out of the morning service in the witches' church, so many miles away.

She and Ella pinned the roses in their hair in such a way that they looked almost like crowns, yet not enough to arouse suspicion or questions. Gloria felt quite sure that, with her blond chignon and blue eyes, she would be the last one in the room one might suspect of being a witch. Ella simply fit in with the dark-haired, dark-eyed ladies they had already seen going about their business in the town, though in Gloria's admittedly biased opinion, her sweet temper made her prettier than most.

Hand in hand, chins tilted proudly, they went down to present themselves for inspection.

For the first time since they had met, Gloria witnessed Captain Stan Fremont struck dumb. She tried not to show it, for that would be dreadfully vain, but there was no denying that a little stunned silence from a man usually so sure of himself was just the thing to give a woman confidence in her secondhand clothes and not-quite-seditious hair ornaments.

"Ella, you look a right lady in that rig," Riley said with undisguised admiration.

Ella primmed up her mouth, but at a smiling glance from Gloria, unbent enough to thank him rather solemnly.

"And what of you, Captain?" Gloria said half playfully, half seriously. "Will I pass for a lady?"

Wordlessly, he shook his head, taking her in from head to foot.

Gloria was suddenly acutely aware of the two pins in her waistband, the arrangement of her silk roses, and the fact that the bodice had been designed for a woman slightly shallower in the draft than she. The tilt of her chin became more pronounced.

At which he seemed to come back to himself. "No," he said, "not a lady."

"Well, I am afraid this will have to do, unless you have a way to raid the closets of the ladies up on the hill."

FIELDS OF IRON

What was the matter with her? She had no doubt he had the skills to inveigle himself into any woman's private chamber, but it was badly bred of her to bring it up right here in front of everyone.

His eyes met hers. "Not a lady. You look like a queen."

With difficulty, she broke the intensity of his gaze, her own dropping in shame at her thoughts, which might have been true at one time, but which were certainly unworthy of him now.

"Every man in the room will wish himself your partner, and the Viceroy is a fool if he doesn't lead off the second set with you."

"Only the second?" she said a little breathlessly, striving for a playfulness she no longer felt.

"He will have to dance the first with the ladies of the house."

Of course. She knew that. It seemed that some customs were the same no matter what the culture.

Again her gaze met his. Again she was unable to look away.

"It is I who will dance the first with you," he said, "if you will permit me?"

Gloria hardly knew whether she was standing on her head or on her heels. All she could do was nod, and wonder what else she might agree to if only he would look at her like that once more.

15

Ian Hollys lay behind a rocky outcrop overlooking the east side of the Californios' dam, and with one finger, turned the brass gear that adjusted the focus on the dualocular. The twin lenses moved slightly farther apart. "Well," he said, squinting, "We have one thing acting in our favor."

"And what is that—besides our new friends' skill with mechanics, their bravery, and their complete loyalty to one another?" Alice bumped his shoulder, propping herself up on her elbows to peer over a rock.

"That is three advantages, and you are quite right. No, I meant you and I and the crew of *Swan*. We may be thankful that the Royal Kingdom does not possess airships, for if we have one weakness at the moment, it is our own ship."

In the four days since they had crashed on the mesa, the bulk of their efforts had been focused out of necessity on the dam and the rising water, and not on repairing poor *Swan*, which still lay exactly as they had left her. Besides caring daily for the three chickens in the communications cage, Jake and Benny between them had finished scoping out the task that lay ahead of them. This involved getting *Swan* aloft enough to allow them to replace the crushed propeller on the port side, and to hammer her stove-in hull back into shape enough that they might get a temporary plate bolted to it so that nothing would fall out. But scoping out a job and getting it done were two different things, and meanwhile they had no means of escape if everything went sideways.

"I don't know how to get it all done," Alice admitted. "It seems we must commit ourselves either to helping the witches destroy the dam, or abandoning them to their fate and taking our chances with wind and sky."

"It seems we have already made that choice, or I for one would not be making a target of myself this close to enemy territory." Ian handed her the dualocular. "Tell me what you think."

"I think that's another reason we have to be thankful for the rules against flying in the face of God." She took the instrument and panned slowly across the chasm below. "No one can shoot at us from above."

They had chosen their location carefully, a party of witches that included Gretchen coming with them in the darkness of the small hours. They had steered the least of the riverboats downriver as far as they dared, and then taken to the hills to walk the final mile in the cool dawn. Now their party of engineers was hidden behind rocks and on the sharp edges of cliff faces, broiling in the sun.

Since the original reconnoitering party had returned, it looked like the dam had not gone up very much more. Try as she might, Alice could not see the behemoth, which might account for the slowdown in the work. Still, the dam's scaffolding teemed with men stripped to the waist, working with barrow and mallet and bucket. Men who were thin and starving, and who occasionally collapsed, to be dragged away by their companions and replaced by someone just as hungry and ragged.

"I'll have no regrets about blowing it up," she said at last, handing the viewing instrument back to Ian. "Those poor men."

"You still agree that our best chance of success is the water flow regulation port in the bottom?"

She nodded. "I can see it in my mind—a steerable vessel wedged into that port as far as it will go, detonating right in the center of the dam. The whole thing will collapse."

"We might consider a night attack," Ian said thoughtfully. "I should not like to be responsible for the deaths of those poor devils—both from the collapse and from the subsequent flood."

"How would you pull that off?" Alice rolled over in the dust to stare at the sky, empty except for the massive carrion birds that always seemed to be circling lazily, waiting with infinite patience for some earthbound creature to make a mistake.

"I leave that to my brilliant wife and her friend Gretchen." Ian leaned over to kiss her, dust and all.

"None of that, sir," she said with mock sternness. "We are reconnoitering."

"I do not know how many chances I may have left to kiss you," he said mildly. "I must take them when I can."

There was a degree of truth in that, though Alice didn't like to think in such terms. But she had learned long ago that every day was a gift, and a day spent with Ian and the people she loved was twice as valuable to her as any day she had passed in old times, flying alone.

Gravel pattered down upon them and Alice searched the rocks for the source of the disturbance. A small blue and gray bird scratched briefly among the roots of a pine growing out of a cleft, then flew away in a flurry of startled wings.

"Something's coming," she breathed to Ian, pulling the lightning pistol from her leather jacket.

"Impossible," he whispered. "We are at the highest point above the dam, and the cliff above us is impassable."

A shadow floated along the walls of the canyon below them—too large for a bird, too small for a cloud. With a gasp, Alice scrambled to her knees and craned to look upward, past the rocks, past the sheer cliff that loomed at their backs.

An airship bearing the star and swords of the Texican Rangers banked over the mesa and prepared to make another pass. "It's the Rangers!" Alice fell flat to the ground, though heaven only knew if she'd been spotted already. "What are they doing here, so close to the border?"

"The same thing we are?" Ian suggested, his voice low.

They could hear the drone of the ship's engines now—old ones, with the peculiar clank on the upstroke of the piston that every aeronaut could recognize.

"Crocketts," Ian said contemptuously. "*Swan* could outfly her even disabled. My touring balloon could outfly her."

"I'd give a lot for your touring balloon and Claire's Helios Membrane right now," Alice said, shading her eyes. But it had been rescued from the field in which it had gone down, and was in Andrew Malvern's laboratory in London, the repairs no doubt long finished.

The ship cruised down the vast canyon that had been carved into the earth by the river. They had to have spotted *Swan*. The only question was what they would do about it.

"You don't suppose they'll come back and offer a rescue, do you?" Ian suggested as the gleaming blue fuselage faded into the distant haze. "I would much rather drop a pressure bomb on that dam from a safe vertical distance than to spend days building a submersible."

"Ian, you know the facts as well as I do. Not only would I be instantly recognized, but if you tried to drop a bomb, you would be just as instantly accused of committing an act of war on Her Majesty's behalf," Alice reminded him.

"Yes, I know," Ian admitted. He got up, dusted himself off, and held out a hand to her. "Come. Let us find Gretchen and her team at the meeting point, and compare notes. I know you have that missile built in your mind, but her expertise seems to be explosive loads and displacement. In this business the two go hand in hand."

"What business? Clandestine acts of sabotage?"

"If you must be so distressingly blunt." Ian scrambled down a chute of rock and waited for her to land beside him. "I am of two minds whether or not to include our submersible in my report to Her Majesty."

"You are such a Corps man," she chided him, taking the lead along a shelf of rock that they had negotiated earlier and trying to ignore the fact that a hundred feet of empty air lay between her and the deep arroyo with its feathery ironwood trees that provided shade for the meeting place. "Always thinking about the paperwork."

"It is a failing in my character," he admitted, sliding along beside her, his back to the rock and both hands pressed to it. "I can think of nothing I would like better at this moment than to be in my office at Hollys Park, filling out the forms from the seed catalogues, a cup of tea at my elbow and my wife puttering among her plans and drawings across the corridor."

It did sound heavenly. So heavenly that she lost her concentration in the contemplation of it, and a stone turned under her boot.

Alice shrieked in sudden terror, her arms windmilling as she fought to keep her balance on the narrow ledge.

"Alice!" Ian shouted. He grabbed for her hand and caught the back of her shirt instead. Inside a single second, he had rammed the other hand inside her leather corselet and hauled her in. Her head smacked smartly on the rock as he pinned her against it, breathing in gasps that sounded almost like sobs.

"Darling, are you all right? Did I hurt you?"

Alice's head spun and she blinked away the stars that crowded the edges of her vision. "The alternative ... was worse. Thank heavens ... you have quick reflexes. You saved my life."

Still breathing hard, he pressed her against the sheer sandstone, his boots planted between hers as though he thought she might pitch forward again. "Then we are even, my dearest, for you saved mine weeks ago."

Trembling, the sore spot on her skull making itself felt with a vengeance, Alice held him tightly and wondered, not for the first time, how out of all the skies she had flown in the world, she had managed to be so lucky as to cross flight paths with this man.

When they reached the meeting point a half hour of heavy scrambling later, Gretchen had already completed her calculations of how much explosive they would need in order to decimate the dam.

She lifted an imperious eyebrow in Alice's direction. "I do not think that your plan for a submersible will work. We can never pack that much in one of the kettle buoys from the riverboat. We would need three at least, and there are only two."

Alice was reminded a little too forcibly of the man at the Admiralty in London, explaining to her why she could not captain her own ship in the Royal Aeronautic Corps when it was perfectly clear she was more capable than he.

Perhaps this was why she was a little testier than was wise. Perhaps it was the result of her brush with death on the cliff. In any case, she found Gretchen's tone insupportable. "I have no intention of using the kettle buoys. I intend to use the ship's boiler, of course. Anyone could see it's the only iron receptacle large enough to be turned into a missile without too much trouble."

"The boiler?"

Alice amused herself by imagining Gretchen in a monocle, and it falling out of her protuberant blue eye in her slack astonishment.

"You must be mad. That will cripple the riverboat, and Captain Stan's fleet will be down to two. How will we get supplies up and down the river?"

"If we don't act quickly," Ian put in, "the question will be moot. You will have to be displaced for miles upriver, every man and woman in your villages moved halfway to Denver."

"If you can only repeat what we already know, be silent," she spat. *"Las brujas* do not need the obvious pointed out to them by men." Clearly she resented Ian's tone, which Alice found to be merely businesslike, as much as Alice herself resented Gretchen's.

They were in a difficult spot all around, and snapping at each other was not going to help. Alice tried to catch Ian's eye, but he was looking toward the cliffs, affronted and trying not to show it.

Stella stepped up and laid a hand on Gretchen's arm. "Peace," she said. "We all know the danger, and we are running out of time."

"Then we will take the boiler out of their airship." Gretchen tossed a tight smile of triumph in Alice's direction. "They are not using it at the moment."

"I'd buy a ticket to see you get it down the side of the mesa," Alice said with her best attempt at cheer. If anyone laid a hand on *Swan*, it would be the last thing they did. "The steamboat's boiler is right there to hand, and with a few adjustments to your cliff-crawling engine, we can have it out and on the dock inside of a day."

"What are you doing to my ascending spider?" A woman with glossy blue-black hair pushed to the front of the little group standing in the shade. "No one touches it without my say-so."

"It would make an excellent crane," Alice suggested, "unless you can think of another way to get the boiler out of the hull? You are May Lin, aren't you? The daughter of the woman who developed the ascender, and the underwater weir-and-chain system?"

The woman looked at her in some surprise. "How do you know my name?"

Alice grinned, her tension easing. "Betsy told me. When Mother Mary asked me who I needed for this reconnoiter, she recommended you. She said yours,

Stella's, and Gretchen's are the best engineering minds she has."

May Lin's face softened into a grin, too, though Gretchen merely crossed her arms and looked impatient, as though all this chitchat were holding her back from doing something more important.

"Mother Mary never lies, unless it's to a man. So yes, I suppose I might make a few adjustments to my spider and turn her into a crane, just this once."

Alice dusted off her hands on her pants. "Excellent. Let's get moving, then. If we're lucky, we'll make it back to the village by dark."

"Not so fast," Gretchen said, and all the witches came to a halt, telling Alice a little more than she wanted to know about the esteem in which the other woman was held. "Perhaps Mother Mary forgot to remind you who was in charge here."

Ian's hand jerked, as though he had barely stopped himself from reaching for the lightning pistol at his hip, and now it was Alice's turn to put a hand on his arm. "I never said it was. But we should hurry—the sun will be down behind the mesa soon."

Oops. Telling her what she already knew again. What was it about this woman that rubbed Alice's fur the wrong way?

"Mother Mary assigned this reconnoiter to me. We go when I say so and not before."

"Nonsense." Alice's temper, not in the best of shape since her own foolishness had brought them to this pretty pass, finally slipped its reins. "You're not my captain." She stomped off down the trail, pushing the branches of the tree out of her face with such force that she snapped one.

"Hold it right there!"

"Oh, for the love of—" Alice whirled to see the dad-burned fool woman sighting down a rifle barrel like she meant business. "Is this your idea of a joke?"

"Put that down at once!" Ian commanded, drawing his pistol, only to have the rifle slowly swing and sight in on him.

"What did I just say about who's in command here?"

"I'll give you that command when you show me some evidence you are a competent commander," Ian said in the tone he used when instructing the middies.

Alice just had time to raise a placating hand when three things happened simultaneously.

The rifle went off.

Ian shouted, spun around, and was flung to the ground, bright blood blossoming on his shirt.

And the Ranger ship floated back over the mesa and settled into a hovering pattern directly overhead.

16

The royal train puffed into the station at San Luis Obispo de Tolosa at noon, belching so much steam into the clear sky that it obscured its sleek blue body. It was a moment before Evan recognized the great locomotive pulling the ornate red-and-gold carriages.

"Well, knock me down and call me a bollard—Joe, that's *Silver Wind!*"

"That magical train you were chasing?"

"The very one. What is it doing here?"

"Seems obvious." Joe joined him at the window, where both of them had a center-balcony view of the station below. A band struck up a tune that was so ponderously earnest it could only be the Royal Kingdom's version of "God Save the King," and the enormous crowd that had gathered burst into song.

"I wish we could see him." Crane as he might, Evan could not tell which of the several hundred tiny figures might be the royal personage. "But there's no mistaking that train—there can't be another like it in all the world. It must have taken the Ambassador on to the capital when I was clapped in gaol with you."

"To tattle to the Viceroy about what you and this Gloria girl had done with his mechanicals?"

"Presumably. Which doesn't bode well for me if he returned with His Serene Highness … or if the latter dislikes my interpretation of his dreams."

"Nothing about this bodes well for either of us, *amigo.*" Joe gripped his shoulder briefly.

Evan accepted the moment of wry comfort for what it was, and pointed to the crowd below. "Poor people, looks as though they have to listen to a royal address."

"I didn't think he was well enough for that."

"I don't think he is the speaker."

Sure enough, a large, enclosed horse-drawn carriage shouldered its way through the crowd while most of the welcoming citizens listened to the address from the station platform. It looked as though the young prince was being escorted up the hill, if the mounted troops surrounding his carriage with the flashing metal epaulets and waving plumes upon bucket-shaped helmets were any indication.

"Come," he said to Joe. "Let's watch from the colonnade."

"What's the matter, never seen a prince before?" Joe complained, but he came along anyway.

No one stopped them as they left their room and made their way along the cool, shady colonnade. No guard stood at the door, and it was soon clear why, for every member of the household was ranged in order of rank—from the majordomo to the lowliest kitchen maid—out in the courtyard where tonight's fiesta was even now being prepared.

Evan and Joe took up a good position behind a spiral-turned post covered in the violently pink plant that seemed to be native to the area, and watched as the vehicle came to a halt before Ignatio de la Carrera y Borreaga and his family. The grandee held the carriage door himself as the young prince stepped down.

Evan examined him curiously. He was tallish, though probably shorter than Evan himself, and weedy-looking, as though he needed to put on a little muscle to match his height. He wore a short jacket and silver-adorned pants similar to those most of the men wore, with the addition of a scarlet ribbon running diagonally across his white shirt front and a large medal in the shape of the royal sun at his throat, between the points of his collar. His hat was round and flat, like the one the grandee had swept from his own head. His hair was black and curly, his face thin, his nose aquiline.

Evan had seen that nose before. In fact, the Viceroy's entire person looked deuced familiar.

But he couldn't be. Evan had never laid eyes on the fellow in his life—even at university or during his travels, he would have remembered meeting a future king.

Nor had he seen an illustration of him in a newspaper account, for until recently he had been at school. It must be a trick of the light, or the way the shade fell under the brim of his hat.

The girls were sinking into curtseys now, all flirting and batting of eyelashes forgotten in the solemnity of the moment. The Viceroy lifted their mother to her feet with awkward gallantry, and then the girls rose to cluster together, eyes cast down and hands clasped nervously before them.

"I don't suppose we'll get an introduction," Joe whispered, trying not to look interested and failing utterly.

"I don't suppose so. What are we but prisoners, after all? We don't even rank as high as the kitchen maids. What are they saying?"

"Welcomes, the house is his, anything they can do for his comfort, that kind of thing. About what you'd expect."

And then the Viceroy lifted his head to look beyond his host and hostess. He asked a question and Joe drew a sharp breath.

"What?"

"He just asked where you were," Joe breathed. "And here comes the majordomo. Lucky job we put on jackets."

Evan tugged on his, and Joe ran a hand jerkily through his poorly cropped hair. They stepped out of the deep shade of the colonnade into the sunlight, and the majordomo caught sight of them.

"His Serene Highness wishes to see you," he said rapidly. "Address him as such, do not speak unless spoken to, and bow from the waist."

Evan had met the Prince Consort of England once, shortly after he'd graduated and the prince was attending the graduation of one of his nephews from the engineering department. And then at Lady Claire's wedding celebration a few months ago, he'd been presented to the Queen. He supposed he could be grateful he'd had a little practice. Poor Joe had had none.

"Your Serene Highness, may I present Senor Evan Douglas and his translator, José San Gregorio," de la Carrera said with ceremony. "Gentlemen, make your bows before our beloved prince, Carlos Filipe, Viceroy of the Royal Kingdom of Spain and the Californias, Defender of the True Faith, and General of the Armies of Heaven."

Evan bent gracefully at the waist and even remembered to extend both toe and hand. From the corner of his eye, he saw Joe copy him exactly, and they straightened at the same moment. "Your Serene Highness," he murmured. "It is an honor."

The majordomo shifted, and Evan remembered too late he was only to speak when spoken to.

"You have pretty manners," the Viceroy said.

While Joe translated, Evan dared to look up as far as the young man's chin, and then met his eyes. Eyes that were wretched—hollow from lack of sleep, haunted from nightmares, and most of all, desperately unhappy and awkward. Evan had seen street children in London who looked worse, but not very. His heart went out to the boy—for boy he was, hardly a year or two older than his cousins Maggie and Lizzie.

"It is lucky I met the Prince Consort in London," he said with a smile. "Otherwise I would not have known what to do."

When Joe began to translate, the Viceroy held up his hand and looked at him as though he were a person, not an automaton or even a prisoner. "Thank you," he said in slightly accented English, "but I speak Senor Douglas's tongue. We shall carry on all our conversations in English, then, while we are together."

"Then ... you won't be needing me, Your Serene Highness?" Joe ventured.

Behind him, the majordomo went into a coughing fit.

"I always need good, loyal men," the Viceroy said, though it sounded a little as though he said it because he was expected to, not because it was what he really thought. His face turned a little pale. "We will go in, out of the sun."

Hastily, the grandee escorted his prince across the courtyard, apologizing all the while, and the latter nodded to the ranks of servants and workmen who stood as straight as posts in the warmth of the day, sweat beading on a brow here and soaking through a shirt there. "You may return to your tasks," he said with what Evan thought was great kindness. "Thank you for your attention."

"Are we to go in, too?" Evan whispered to Joe. "We are not guests."

But the youngest daughter must have had sharp ears, for she turned and took Evan's arm. Isabela, that was her name.

"Senorita," he addressed her awkwardly, "is this quite proper?"

"You are a guest in my father's home." Her eyes were long-lashed, dark, and sparkling with mischief. "Why should you not come in and take some refreshment?"

"Because I am a prisoner?" he suggested.

Her pretty, heart-shaped face clouded. "Do not dwell on such unpleasant things. It is fiesta, and we all have the honor of serving His Serene Highness!"

"Well, yes, and I am very sensible of that honor, but—" How did one explain one's circumstances to a pretty, sheltered, unimaginably rich young lady? Perhaps it would be more polite to pretend he was merely here as a tenant or a man of business.

"Do not imagine me ignorant of your situation," she said, lowering her voice. "I read Papa's correspondence. I know all about you."

"A girl after my own heart," Joe said to no one in particular, his hand brushing the petals of the vine as they passed through the front doors. "What is this plant called?"

"That is bougainvillea," she said, "and do not change the subject."

But now her mother's sharp eye had counted heads, and dropped to her daughter's hand nestled so confidingly in the crook of Evan's elbow. She said something tersely to Isabela, who looked suitably chastened and released him.

"I must go with my sisters," she said, and then added rapidly, "but you must promise me a dance each tonight."

"Certainly," Evan replied, but Joe only looked amazed.

"That one is a trial to her parents, I'll wager," he said as they followed the party in to the long dining room, where the carved, heavy tables were spread with every manner of meat and vegetable and fruit and drink.

Evan's mouth began to water, and though he could see Isabela chattering with her sisters, he could not focus on her. It was everything he could do to control himself and not dive straight into the middle of a platter of pork slices and figs gleaming with oil and smelling like a gift from heaven.

Servants attended each guest, helping them to plates of food and delicate glasses of liquor. The grandee served the Viceroy himself, choosing the best and first from each platter, and plying him with drink. But the young man seemed to have an abstemious appetite, eating only a very little roast beef, figs, and an odd vegetable that looked like a massive thistle, whose leaves were dipped in oil and eaten one by one. Evan passed over a pyramid of the strange things—it seemed like far too much work for too little nourishment.

He and Joe were permitted to serve themselves just ahead of people who must be tenants, dressed in their best and too overcome with the honor of being in the same room as the Viceroy to do much more than stare and murmur among themselves.

The sun had barely traveled the width of one window, and Evan had only just cleaned his first plate, when the Viceroy stood. Every person in the room leaped to his or her feet in a great scraping of chairs and rustling of silk.

"Thank you for your hospitality," he said with a nod to the grandee, "but I will rest now, in preparation for the festivities this evening. No, do not trouble yourselves. Finish your meals."

"I would hope so," Joe murmured as he concluded the translation, starting in on his second plate with gusto.

"Perhaps one must be given permission," Evan replied, filling his own with everything within reach. "Though I should hate to think we had to stop when he did. No wonder the poor lad is so thin."

"I'd refrain from referring to the absolute monarch as *the poor lad*," Joe said. "Might be dangerous, him being General of the Armies of Heaven and all."

"Quite right. I shall watch my tongue. When it is not occupied with this excellent wine." He knocked back the tiny glass of golden liquid with satisfaction.

"Watch that stuff," Joe warned him. "It's got more of a kick than you'd think, and the last thing we need is to draw attention to ourselves."

Evan was not the kind of man to disdain good advice, but he did suffer a pang of regret as he set the little glass down and refused another.

The grandee returned from escorting his royal guest to the wing of the house that was to be for his exclusive use, and with the royal staff gone to attend their master, the room seemed somewhat emptier. Isabela made her way over to them, her skirts frothing in an appealing way about her ankles.

"Did you enjoy your lunch?" she asked with a smile at their empty plates.

"That was a lunch?" Evan said. "It seemed like a feast fit for a king."

"I hope it was, or Papa will never bear up under the shame," she said merrily. "Come. If you want nothing more, perhaps we might walk in the gardens. Dessert will be served later, with tea."

Joe gazed at her with one brow raised. "Does your mother know you are making shocking advances to the political prisoners?"

"Pish." The girl waved a hand as though this hardly bore thinking of. "I am simply playing the role of hostess, and you two are much more interesting than the mayor or the daughters of lesser grandees. But if it will make you feel more comfortable, I will call my duenna to attend us at a suitable distance."

"Soldiers would be more appropriate, don't you think?" Evan couldn't help but smile. Really, she and Lizzie would get along famously. "We might be tempted to capture you in exchange for our freedom."

"If you did, I shouldn't complain." She tossed her head. "I can help you steal some horses, if you like."

Evan laughed, which netted him a glance from her watchful mama like a spear thrown the length of the

FIELDS OF IRON

room. "I am afraid we are not nearly so dashing as you think. But after long weeks in the gaol at Las Vegas, I should be glad of a walk in the garden, if only to settle what could be my last meal."

"I hope it will not be." Imperiously, she signaled, and a lady of uncertain age rose to join them, her lunch left unfinished. "Come, this way."

Evan had a moment to feel sorry for the woman, who was thin enough to indicate that this might happen fairly often, before Isabela took his arm once more and their little party sallied forth into the gardens on the opposite side of the house, now pleasantly shady and cool.

"Are the gardens your mother's work?" Evan asked as they paced the gravel walks between knot gardens and arbors covered in climbing roses on the point of blooming.

"Oh no. Our family has lived here for two hundred years. They are pleasant, but terribly old-fashioned. My great-grandmother was interested in botany, as you see there." She indicated a long garden full of what Evan instantly recognized as medicinal herbs—lady's mantle, echinacea, lemon balm—and growing above them, elder trees in early flower like a drift of snow, their sweetness hanging in the air.

"I should have liked to talk with her," Evan said. "I am a doctor, you know, and we are sometimes obliged to take our medicines where we can get them. In one of my examinations, we were given a case and instructed to take a day in the countryside, collect the herbs needed for a cure, and compile them."

"That seems a waste, if there was only a teacher to give them to," Joe remarked.

"Oh, no, the cases were real. We administered our cures to patients at the hospital. It was one of my more anxious moments—for if she did not recover, you see, I would have failed the examination."

"And did she?" Isabela asked.

"Fortunately, yes." And Evan had gained a healthy respect for even the most humble plants that grew in kail yard and field as well as formal garden. "Do you have any ability along that line? Perhaps you might have inherited it from your great-grandmother."

"Heavens, no," Isabela said, skipping ahead to crush a leaf of lemon balm in her fingers and inhale the scent. "Mama says I have no talents save dancing and gossip."

"I do not believe that, for you have just chosen lemon balm, one of the most useful herbs in this garden."

"It smells nice." She shrugged and dropped the remains of the leaf in the path. "Shall you and Senor San Gregorio dance with me this evening? You promised, and I shall hold you to it."

"I would not dream of disappointing a lady so kind," Evan said, "though I am afraid it will be far past your bedtime."

The look she cast over her shoulder told him his error at once. "I am eighteen, and old enough to be courted," she informed him with a tilt of her chin. "But do not get your hopes up—Papa is quite determined that I shall marry the heir to … San Gregorio."

FIELDS OF IRON

Joe stopped fingering the lemon balm, and gave her his full attention. "Why that one, in particular?"

She moved away to follow an orange butterfly whose wings were rimmed in black. "Beatriz is determined to be a nun, and Esperanza is already being courted by the heir to San Carlos Borromeo de Carmelo, so it is up to me to capture the heart of the Ambassador's son."

"He has a son?" Joe turned away to gaze at what appeared to be a pasture in the distance. Horses grazed and leaned against the fence, black and glossy and as beautiful as any Evan had ever seen.

"He has three, but only the eldest matters. He is fourteen and said to be only moderately attractive. He was certainly a homely child when I saw him last. I'll wager he has pimples." She made a face but only succeeded in looking utterly charming.

"And what does he think of you?" Evan asked with some amusement.

But she only shrugged. "It does not matter. I shall be mistress of the second largest rancho in the kingdom, with a father-in-law who is the Viceroy's closest councilor. There will be visits to the capital, and balls, and there I will be, second lady in the land after the Vicereine." She dimpled, the mischief back. "And both my sisters will have to curtsey to me."

"Why not aim for the top?" Joe asked with an edge that put his tone just on the near side of polite. "Why not be the first lady if you can—and to a man who is not a pimply wretch of fourteen?"

"Because I have the sense God gave a goose," she replied tartly. "Did you not observe our glorious Viceroy? He is said to be chosen of God—a prophet—a mystic whose visions are divine. Set apart from other men not only by blood and birthright, but by the hand of God. One cannot see such a man taking a girl to the marriage bed and dandling children on his knee, can one? One can barely imagine him surviving his dreadful burden for much longer."

Evan blinked, a little taken aback by a girl who could dance along the edge of treason with two strangers for partner. "Keep your voice down, senorita, if you please," he managed.

"Oh, no one here would betray me, and you two are already prisoners. What difference does it make? In truth, I find honesty quite refreshing. I am able to indulge in it so seldom."

In Evan's mind, it made quite a lot of difference, but he did not say so. Clearly she believed them both so far out of her world that they made safe receptacles for shocking confidences—like whispering into the ear of a horse or a dog.

"But how will marrying the Ambassador's boy be any better? Are you content to settle for being only the second lady in the land?"

The sparkle was back, and she wagged a finger at him. "How little you know of women—or of politics, sir. Clearly my father wants the best for me. It does not take a gazing ball to see that if the Viceroy is consumed by the fires of holiness, as some say, there will be a Regent appointed. And who better but the man who practically rules the kingdom now?"

"But surely the people will not accept a ruler—be he Viceroy or Regent—who is not of the blood royal?" Joe objected.

Evan had slept and eaten and labored next to him for weeks, but he had never heard this new note in his voice. A note borne of the same dawning realization that Evan himself was feeling, prickling in his fingertips and along the back of his neck.

"Oh, there is blood royal," she assured him. "In the mother country. I'm sure they will flush an heir out of the thicket of cousins and nephews of *el Rey*, but settling on one could take years. Do you not read your history books? The same thing happened in 1869 and 1802, and before that in 1751."

"So years pass, and then a new Viceroy arrives, and in the meanwhile, a Regent rules?"

She smiled happily at Evan, a student who has given the right answer without prompting. "*Si*. Just so."

And what would Ambassador de Aragon y Villarreal make of that individual's arrival? Evan could not see a man who would force his prince to declare war for the sake of imaginary gold as likely to accept a new ruler without a fight. "But what if—"

"Isabela!" Fifty feet away, the duenna turned in fright at the sound of Senora de la Carrera y Borreaga's voice, floating down from a casement window above them. "Return to the house at once. I need you here in my solar."

With a sigh and a roll of the eyes, Isabela called up, "*Yo voy, Mama.*" To Evan and Joe, she said, "I knew our walk would not last long. Mama is convinced that I shall be taken up by brigands—it is only a matter of time."

Joe touched his brow with two fingers. "Let us know when we can oblige. Thank you for showing us around."

With a giggle, she flitted down the gravel walk, collecting her unhappy duenna as she went.

"I expect they will meet our soldiers on the path," Evan predicted with some regret.

"I expect so," Joe agreed. "This family would do well to teach its daughters discretion, along with dancing and music, wouldn't you say?"

"I would indeed. Is she really that innocent, or has she been coached in order to lead us astray?"

"From what?"

"I have no idea. Why bother to lead us anywhere but back to a prison cell?"

"Unless the family feels that in your efforts to interpret the Viceroy's dreams, you will slant your words in one direction or another, and better to their advantage than not."

"That seems a bit convoluted," Evan objected. "Why risk my telling their prince that the Ambassador plans to wrest the kingdom from him?"

"Perhaps they secretly want him to know. Perhaps they are royalists to the core," Joe said. "Though leaving such an important task to one so young and foolish seems risky."

"That is the understatement of the year." Evan tucked a stem of the lemon balm through the buttonhole of his short jacket, where its refreshing scent would travel with him. "One would think, no matter the visions God is giving him, that the Viceroy and his councilors would have made contingency plans."

"He is young."

"He can't be any older than you, and you are far from young—at heart, anyway."

"I haven't lived as sheltered a life, nor had a book education. It is one thing to read about 1769 and 1802, and quite another to imagine it happening to oneself, I suppose. Ah, here they are."

The soldiers marched smartly around the corner of the house, shouting as though Evan and Joe were at this moment pelting toward the horses to make a break for it. "We should have escaped while we had the chance," Joe said as they were surrounded.

But Evan realized he would not have gone even if the paddock had been wide open and the horses saddled and ready. He wanted to hear the Viceroy's dreams. He wanted to listen to that boy's voice, to discern whether he was intelligent enough to realize what his most trusted councilor was up to.

And most of all, he wanted to exercise his skills as a doctor. For it was clear to him, if not anyone else on all these hundreds of thousands of acres, that the Viceroy was not merely a prophet of God, worn thin with reflecting the light of Heaven.

He was very, very ill, and his time was running out.

17

Gloria took a deep, fortifying breath as her husband gave their names to the majordomo, and that gentleman turned to announce them to the room.

"*El Capitan* and Senora Stanford Fremont, of New York, London, and Philadelphia!"

Dear me. That is laying it on a bit thick, isn't it?

They proceeded forward in the receiving line, Gloria's hand in the crook of her husband's elbow, her chin held high, her hair piled up in the latest fashion (or what had been the latest when she'd left Philadelphia in January, at any rate).

"Senorita Ella Balboa and Senor James Kilpatrick of Denver, Colorado!"

FIELDS OF IRON

Gloria did her best to ignore the admiring glances—she appeared to be the only blonde in the great quadrangle of the grand house, and therefore looked quite exotic. Instead, she focused on the receiving line, and the young man whose uniform was so covered in ribbons and medals that he must be the Viceroy, sinking under the weight of them.

Her only goal. The culmination of days of travel, of significant personal danger ... and the sole reason, blast and bebother it, that there was a gold ring on her finger.

She reached him, and sank into the deepest curtsey of which she was capable. "Your Serene Highness." Beside her, Captain Stan bowed with the flourish of toe and hand due to persons of high standing, but the Viceroy did not seem to see him.

"Rise, Senora Fremont." A cold hand took hers and raised her, and she looked up into his eyes. "We are honored by guests who have come so far."

A shiver of shock ran through her. Goodness gracious, he was only a boy! But the eyes—dark, hollow, miserable—these were the eyes of someone who had been in a prison cell for years, or been afflicted with pain for so long he had forgotten what it meant to be free of it.

He had not released her hand.

Some compulsion, some flood of sympathy, overwhelmed her and she clasped his cold fingers in her warm ones. "Oh, sir," she murmured, "what can we do to help you?"

He blinked in shock, and removed his hand from hers abruptly. "I am in no need of help," he said. "You forget yourself, Senora."

And she had. She had probably just thrown away her one chance to be asked to dance, too. "I am so sorry, I—"

The majordomo announced the family of a neighboring rancho amid much fanfare, and Gloria and the captain were forced to move along the line to the grandee and his wife, their three daughters surrounding them like a flock of pretty birds. She had the presence of mind to curtsey and keep her mouth shut, and to allow her husband to murmur thanks and pleasantries.

She did not, however, miss the sharp look that the eldest daughter gave her gown, and when they rose out of their mutual curtsey, Gloria realized she must be looking at its former owner, who did not seem to know whether to be amused or affronted.

Perhaps she had better leave now, before the evening became any worse.

"What was that about?" the captain whispered to her as they moved off toward the loaded tables, where there actually appeared to be a fountain dispensing wine. "What possessed you to be so familiar with the Viceroy?"

"I—I don't know," she moaned. "I don't know what came over me. He looks dreadful. I couldn't help myself."

"Word has it that he is possessed of the Holy Spirit," Ella said as she and Riley joined them at a table spread with more food than Gloria had seen in months. "They say he is like a lamp worn thin with the effort to contain the power of God."

"He's worn thin with something, that's certain." Captain Stan loaded a plate for her and one for himself, and after a moment, Riley attempted to do the same for Ella.

"I can feed myself, thank you," she said rather crisply, and took the plate away from him. "The poor man. His hands are very cold. The power of God must not be the sort that keeps you warm."

"Looks like poison to me." Riley didn't talk very much when he was sober, but when he did, Gloria had noticed her husband listened.

"Keep your voice down," the captain told him tersely, "or you may find yourself in gaol facing charges of treason."

"Just saying."

Gloria opened her mouth to protest—for surely there was a much less sinister explanation—when a voice spoke behind her.

"Gloria? Heavens above, can it be you?"

She turned. Her mouth fell open. And if it hadn't been for Ella's quick hand, her plate of food would have crashed to the floor.

"Evan? *Evan!*" She leaped across the flagstones and threw herself into his arms. "I thought you were dead!" And with that, she forgot dignity altogether and burst into tears. Oh, he was so blessedly, impossibly solid and alive and ... thin. So dreadfully thin! What was wrong with the men in this country?

But it was Evan! He was *alive!*

She could not let him go, the wool of his black jacket scratchy under her wet cheek, and when she felt a weight upon her shoulder, she realized that his head was bowed and he was sobbing in joy, too, his arms locked about her as though she were a treasure he thought he had lost forever.

And then she heard a sound like a cry, like an animal that has been suddenly wounded—or had a thorn removed that has been a source of torture for a long time. It had not been she. It had not been Evan.

Gasping, she looked up. What...?

Ella, her face so white it looked almost green in the flickering light of the torches and festive lamps set all around the huge courtyard, staggered. Riley managed to remove the plates in both her hands, and set them on the table behind him. A strange man who had been standing beside Evan darted in to hold her up, both hands spanning her waist, as she stared into his eyes.

"Dios mio." Ella's voice trembled. "It cannot be. Is this a dream? Have we all died, and are reunited in heaven?"

"Perhaps we might find somewhere a little more private in which to express our joy," Captain Stan suggested. "This seems to be a most welcome reunion, but I'm afraid it is attracting attention."

Gloria clung to Evan, feeling quite certain that he would disappear from the fiesta as suddenly as he had disappeared from the Battle of Resolution, if she did not keep a hand upon him. Captain Stan shepherded them over to the colonnade, where tables and chairs had been arranged in groups so that people who had not seen one another since the last fiesta could converse in relative privacy.

She sank into a chair, her skirts poufing around her, as she clung to Evan's hand. "Captain," she said breathlessly, "it is a miracle! I cannot believe it, even with the proof in my own hands."

"Evidently," her husband said.

"This is Evan Douglas, who traveled from England with us aboard *Swan*. He disappeared during the Battle of Resolution, and I thought he was dead!" She shook Evan's hand between her own as though he had been naughty not to tell her the opposite was true. "You must tell us what happened. What in heaven's name are you doing here?"

"I might ask you the same." His gaze devoured her, his hand gripping her own tightly. "You are the one who disappeared. It was only by the process of elimination that I concluded you had gone on *Silver Wind*—so I followed you in the behemoth."

"The behemoth!" The captain and Riley exchanged a glance, but Gloria was too intent on Evan's story to heed it.

"Yes, I taught myself how to operate it, and followed the railroad for days until I saw *Silver Wind* sitting at a siding, at which point I learned that the crew were out in the rocks, looking for you."

She could hardly believe it. "You were so close—but the flash flood—it swept me into the Sangre Colorado de Christo. It killed so many men—but how—"

"That is how the Ambassador tricked me into walking the behemoth right over the border into the Royal

Kingdom of Spain, and delivering it handily to His Highness." Evan's mouth trembled with disgust—at himself? At the Ambassador? Gloria could not tell. "At every crossing, it seemed, you had been seen just a little further downstream. I searched the banks for days, and when I met the Ambassador and his men again, they said you were in a hospital in Las Vegas—the water meadows where the river comes into the valley."

"But I wasn't. I've never been there in my life."

"So I was told when they arrested me and tossed me into gaol with Joe, here." He indicated the tall, slender man whose appearance had nearly made Ella faint.

"Joe?" Ella croaked. Her gaze searched that of the man, as though she had been expecting ... something else.

"The same," Joe said, and then added something rapidly in the Californio tongue that Gloria could not understand.

Ella flushed scarlet and pressed her hands to her cheeks. When she caught Gloria's eyebrows raised in question, she said, "Hon—Joe—is Clara's, um, son. He was shanghaied a year ago and we all thought he was dead also." Her gaze returned to him, and she shook her head slowly, as though acknowledging a miracle. "But he is not. Oh, thank the holy angels, he is not. Clara will be transported with joy."

"I'm quite resurrected, in fact," Joe said with a grin.

"This is wonderful." Gloria felt as though she had downed a glass of champagne, so fizzy inside did she feel, so dizzy with happiness. "I do believe I have never been so happy in my life as I am at this moment ...

other than the night Claire rescued me from Hay House, that is."

"Oh!" Evan caught her hand again as if he could not bear its absence. "That's something else. You'll never guess who our fellow cellmate was."

"I could not. What other unfortunates among our acquaintance have found his way to this godforsaken place?"

He grinned. "None other than Captain Barnaby Hayes."

"No!" Gloria felt quite breathless at this fresh revelation. The scoundrel who had kidnapped her from Venice in an undersea dirigible in order to bait a trap for her father's capture? The wretch who had practically proposed marriage and who had imposed on her affections most abominably? She released Evan's hand. "Impossible."

"Quite possible—if you are a spy with the Walsingham Office."

"If he's in gaol with you, he must not be a very good one," the captain observed.

Really, he might be a little more pleasant on such a joyful night. Could her husband not share a little of her happiness at being reunited with one of her friends? Frankly, it was a miracle and they all ought to be thanking God for it!

"Bad luck happens to everyone," Joe observed. "He was shanghaied, same as me."

Gloria observed that Joe's gaze had not left Ella's face—nor had hers left his. They sat across the white damask tablecloth from one another, their food cooling on their plates, in another world altogether.

Deep inside, under the happiness of seeing her friend safe and mostly unharmed, ran a tiny trickle of relief. It was clear now that she would no longer have to feel guilt at having stolen Captain Stan away from the woman who loved him. Clearly, Ella's feelings for Clara's son were of the deeper, more reliable kind, and of a longstanding nature. What must she be feeling, seeing him in this crowd and being unable to give voice to her emotions?

"Yes, he was captured," Evan said, returning to his dinner with a vengeance. "But he is very much the spy—we came literally within inches of carrying out a plan—" He lowered his voice to a whisper. "—to destroy the dam."

Only this would have brought Ella back to the corporeal plane. "What stopped you?" she breathed after a glance at the chattering family at the next table. "The entire nation of witches—to say nothing of the Navapai—both are in mortal danger with every inch the river rises."

Evan gestured with his fork toward the Viceroy at the high table, flanked on either side by the grandee and his family, then the royal equerries and councilors. "I was summoned."

"By whom? For what?" Gloria could not imagine what connection Evan Douglas might have with a prince.

"By the Viceroy. To interpret his dreams."

Captain Stan put down his knife, with which he had been spearing olives. "I beg your pardon? *You* are the one we heard of?"

Evan finally stopped shoveling in his food. Now he too laid down fork and knife neatly in the middle of a clean plate. "I do not know what you have heard, but in England, I have something of a reputation for inventing the mnemosomniograph—a device for recording and understanding dreams. The garrison commander discovered my experience with dreams, and one night when he had a nightmare, he sent for me to interpret one of his. I did so—whether rightly or wrongly, I cannot say. But the word must have traveled, for the next thing we knew, I was on a train heading north under full escort, with Joe here to act as my translator. I am apparently to perform the same service for His Highness."

"When?" Gloria asked him, her brevity the result of surprise at this turn of events.

"I do not know. We only just arrived. I expect I will receive a summons soon, probably in the middle of the night."

"But why?" Captain Stan asked. "The people say that these dreams are sent by God, and that His Serene Highness is a prophet."

"His Serene Highness is ill." Evan leaned in toward them. "I say this as a medical doctor."

"Told you," Riley said. "Poison."

"Anything is possible, but whatever it is, I doubt that God is behind it," Evan said. "I am anxious to examine him, and if interpreting dreams is to be the pretext, then I will oblige to the best of my ability."

Gloria put her left hand on his. "You must be careful. This country is a powder keg, and one spark could set it off. That is why I am here—my goal has not changed one whit. I must see the Viceroy in private and convince him not to pursue this war."

If she had expected a declaration of support, or even reassurance, she did not get it. For Evan was staring at her hand as though a scorpion decorated it rather than a gold ring.

"Gloria, what is this?" He lifted her hand, then met her gaze.

Oh, dear. Oh, dear. If she had thought Ella's heart had been broken, this was much worse. Evan's eyes—

She had not realized—

Oh, dear.

"That is my wife's wedding ring," the captain said evenly when Gloria did not reply.

"Wife?"

She must say something. She must do something. Under no circumstances must he be made to feel small, or rejected, or any of the other unpleasant things ascribed to unhappy suitors. He deserved better, after pursuing her halfway across the territory and getting himself captured and imprisoned for her sake.

"It was the only way for me to accomplish my mission," she explained awkwardly. "A woman cannot travel in this country alone, so the captain made the only offer possible under the circumstances. It was most generous and courageous of him."

She did not dare meet her husband's eyes at this speech, though it was the literal truth.

"You mean—it is a union of necessity? You are married to a man you do not love?" Evan's gaze searched hers, looking for ... looking for ... the impossible.

"That, sir, is taking the privilege of friendship too far." Captain Stan pushed his plate away. "The orchestra has just indicated that sets may form. Gloria, will you do me the honor?"

"But—" Evan began.

The captain's arm was as hard as iron under her hand, and she had no choice but to accompany him out into the center of the plaza, and to take her place opposite him in the lines of dancers.

Only I could manage to break two men's hearts in the space of three minutes, she thought in despair.

And then, as the music began, she realized that Stanford had put them at the very bottom of the Viceroy's set, where, when the pattern of the dance brought her to him, the prince could not avoid speaking to her.

"Are you in love with him?" Captain Stan asked as they swung in a circle between the lines of dancers in a waltz hold, then separated.

Her thoughts scattered like birds. "This is hardly the time or place."

"You are the one who suggested divorce on the very day we were married, my dear."

She fumed as they separated, each circling the person next to them in the line, then coming together again, one place down.

"You cannot ask me that, when your ring and a very elaborate wedding certificate make the question irrelevant."

She circled a grandee, smiled prettily, and was handed back down the line to the captain, who turned her in an inescapably polite hold between the two lines once more.

"The legalities do not preclude an emotional tie," he pointed out. "Answer me."

She had eight beats of music to smile and wrestle with her temper. Honestly, did he think she was going to break her marriage vows with poor Evan? And he had become so angry when she had suggested he might do the same, at the very beginning of their journey!

"No, I am not in love with him, though several weeks ago I thought I might be." There. Let him find a way to apologize for casting such aspersions on her character.

It took two patterns danced in silence, and two places moved up the line, before he finally said, "I suspect the same may not be true on his side."

"I cannot help that, though I am sorry."

"For me, or for him?"

"For him, you goose. I have no reason to be sorry for you."

"Yes, I am quite sure you will wear black for precisely the required number of months if I should be killed in the course of this adventure."

The pattern of the dance separated them as her mouth fell open in dismay. How could he say such a dreadful, heartless thing! Did their growing friendship, the strengthening of her regard for him—blast it, the effect he had on her heartbeat—did that all mean nothing? Why, she had a mind to—

She looked up into her new partner's face and closed her mouth with a gulp. "Your Serene Highness."

"Senora Fremont. Are you quite well? You look flushed."

"I shall not take offense at the inquiry," she said, summoning the smile she gave her closest friends, "when I know it springs from honest concern. I am quite well, thank you. My husband was teasing me."

He bit his lip. "I will apologize for my earlier conduct at greater length when you accept me as a partner for the waltz. If your husband does not object."

"He will be as honored as I, Your Serene Highness."

"Until the waltz, then."

He moved down the line and Gloria found herself once more in the captain's arms. "Well?"

"I am not speaking to you, sir."

"That is immaterial. Are you speaking to the Viceroy, is the question."

"Yes. He has requested the waltz."

"Then your mission could be accomplished by the end of the evening. This could be the shortest union of necessity in the history of such things."

The dance parted them, and when next she could speak, she said, "I hardly think so. The most I could accomplish is to request an audience."

"I have much greater faith in your abilities than that, Mrs. Fremont."

"What a pity you do not have as great a faith in other things," she retorted.

He would have replied, but the orchestra leader, observing that the Viceroy had reached the end of the set, brought the music to a close. Gloria took the opportunity to turn and cross the room without waiting for her escort, but he anticipated her. When she found her way to the punch bowl, he had already ladled a cup for her, a decorative orange slice as thin as paper floating on top.

"Gloria—"

She had gulped down most of the punch before she realized that it contained a generous helping of that fiery gold wine. "I cannot speak of this now," she told him. "The waltz will begin at any moment, and besides—no, I must think quickly of what I shall say."

"But it seems we must speak together."

"I thought we had," she choked out, and then with a start, noticed the slender gentleman next to her.

He bowed and said something in the Californio tongue.

"This gentleman will conduct you to the Viceroy," the captain said with a bow of his own. "Good luck."

Luck! If Gloria had possessed a fan, she might have smacked him with it. Now that he had reduced her nearly to tears, he could launch her off on her mission, could he? Evan would not have done so. Evan would have been supportive, and encouraging, and made her feel as though her task were actually possible.

Well, she would have to do the best she could on her own. Her entire life had been leading up to this. One waltz—one chance—one moment in which she might be like dear Claire, and change history.

Gloria took a deep breath and gave a smile of thanks to her escort as he delivered her to the Viceroy, then sank into a curtsey. The prince raised her, and the orchestra conductor, ever vigilant, struck up the first notes of a Strauss waltz.

The Viceroy whirled her out onto the floor and to her horror, the other dancers stepped back along the fringes, as though it would be a social faux pas to crowd them.

"Dear me," she said a little shakily. "I did not expect to monopolize you to quite this extent, Your Serene Highness."

"Oh, do please dispense with that long title," he murmured, sounding so young that it took her a moment to adjust. "Call me *sir* if you must."

"Sir," she said obligingly. "Please ask the other dancers to join us. What if I should stumble? The entire kingdom would see it."

"Then I should take the blame," he said gallantly, and with a lift of his chin, indicated to Senor de la Carrera y Borreaga that he and his wife, and the other dancers might join them.

How did one introduce the subject of war into such an elegant, festive scene, while one whirled in a man's arms? Gloria's mind raced through one line of conversation after another, discarding them as quickly as a housewife examining apples at the market. Too bruised. Too soft. The wrong color.

"How long have you been married?" the Viceroy asked. "Your husband seems a handsome gentleman."

"He is that, thank you, sir. Not more than a week."

"You are newlyweds, then." He smiled in delight. "Is it too soon to ask after the prospect of children?"

"Goodness me, yes," she blurted. "Does one discuss such a subject in public in the Royal Kingdom?"

"Children are a topic of discussion anywhere and at any time during fiesta," he told her. "Think of this plaza on which we dance as one great map of bloodlines, ebbing and flowing this way and that."

"And you the prize at the center, I should imagine," she said pertly. "I must take advantage of my chance, must I not, for there are at least forty young ladies of marriageable age watching for theirs."

"Ah, but I alone may choose," he said, his cheeks reddening. "I chose not for expediency, but for pleasure. I chose the most beautiful woman in the room."

"You are very kind, sir, though since I am at least five years older, I will say nothing of your taste—or the strength of your eyesight."

He laughed, and around them, the dancers obligingly smiled.

Gloria took a breath and plunged. "But I confess I am glad to be your choice, for I have a question of some urgency, and we are already halfway through this waltz."

"And what is that? If it is in my power, I will grant your request."

"Oh, it is," she assured him. "I have come all the way from Philadelphia to ask you to meet with me, and discuss ending the war that is brewing before it begins in earnest."

A hitch in the smoothness of his turn was the only indication of the depth of his surprise—and of his training as a gentleman. "And what reason would a respectable woman have for a request so far outside her sphere?"

The waltz would end in one minute—Gloria knew it well. She must be frank without being rude, or politically foolish.

"My maiden name is Meriwether-Astor, sir. I believe you knew my father, Gerald."

His long-lashed brown eyes widened as they met hers, and she took advantage of his momentary speechlessness.

"I believe that your nature and mine might share a similar desire for peace, not the machinations of our fathers to bring war upon a country and a people as beautiful as this. All I ask is half an hour of your time—tomorrow, perhaps, or when it is convenient—in order to put my case before you."

His arms had slackened about her. Now they tightened again. "I have heard about you."

"From my father? He has visited San Francisco de Asis on a number of occasions, I believe."

"No. From my Ambassador to your Fifteen Colonies. He tells me that not only did you lose my mechanical horses, you escaped while he was bringing you to me to apologize for your carelessness."

She must not faint.

She could not flee.

She must take one step after another, and spin, and smile, while she waited for him to call the armed guards that stood at attention at every column surrounding the plaza.

18

Evan's grandmother had used a word now and again in connection with both cooking and life. When he'd asked her the meaning of it, she'd laughed. "Bittersweet? Why, silly boy, it means the combination of those two things, nothing more."

"But that is impossible," he had objected, his orderly mind offended by paradox even at nine years of age. "They cannot exist simultaneously in nature."

She had gazed at him. "Not in the nature you are thinking of, boy. But in human nature—oh, yes. You will learn that soon enough."

He hadn't. Not until now, as he sat, stunned silent, at the table under the colonnade, watching the dancers spin and twirl in and out of the pools of light cast by cheerful hanging lamps.

Gloria, alive. Oh, sweet, sweet joy, enough to render a man overcome with tears!

And married. Bitterest gall, sickening disappointment like a fatal wave poised to crash and carry him away into darkness.

He watched her in the lines of the *contredanse*, her hair gleaming gold, her lithe figure bending and twirling with a grace that seemed to etch itself in the light. When she stepped into the Viceroy's arms and smiled up at him, Evan realized as he had never before the depth of his own failure.

He had crossed an ocean and then a desert to help her in her mission. But he had not.

He had learned to operate the greatest weapon devised by humankind so that he could rescue her. But he had not.

All he had managed to accomplish was to get himself captured, while a pirate in a bowler hat had swept in somehow, married her, and delivered her like a package tied up in pink and lavender ribbons, right into the arms of the Viceroy.

Evan's dinner threatened to come up, and he stood uncertainly. He must escape. He could not face this crowd and allow them to bear witness to his shame. He had failed at Collingford Castle. He had failed at the Battle of Resolution. Three times was the charm ... and of what use was a life charmed in such a way?

Even Joe had deserted him, dancing in a lower set with the young woman who had come with Gloria.

Well, why should he not dance with a pretty girl? He had not failed *her* in every way it was possible to do so.

"Are you ill, Senor Douglas?"

For a moment, he could not find the source of the voice, and then he realized she was standing right in front of him, so small and fragile that her head came only a little higher than his heart.

"Senorita Isabela," he managed to say with a good impression of civility. "I confess I feel rather ill."

"A feast after a famine will often cause an upset stomach," she said as sympathetically as though she had actually experienced the latter. "I came to claim the dance you promised me, but I do not wish your dinner to make a reappearance out on the floor."

Now he really did feel ill. "Nor do I."

"Come. Let us walk, then. Mama has had lights put up in the gardens for those who do not dance. Let me show them to you, and perhaps the air will do you good."

He might remind her they were already outside, where there was no shortage of fresh air.

He might protest the impropriety of a young lady of good family walking in the dark with a prisoner.

He might decline and make his way up to his room, where he could gaze out at the sea and imagine how it would feel to sink under the waves and hope that people would forget that a person called Evan Douglas had ever existed.

Or he could simply do as she asked, since he did not have the energy for any of the other options.

FIELDS OF IRON

She led him down the nearest walk, which was lit by cheerful orange, red, and yellow paper lanterns every three feet or so, and in the lavender-scented darkness, he did begin to feel a little better. Or maybe it was the effect of his companion, clinging to his arm and quite content to remain silent until he felt well enough to speak.

He finally cleared his throat. "Are you always this concerned with the welfare of your guests?"

"Not usually," she said. "Beatriz and Esperanza tend to monopolize the young men at fiesta, but now that Bea has declared for the missions, I fully intend to take her place."

"Until the heir of San Gregorio comes up to scratch," he suggested.

"What odd expressions you English use! But *si,* until then, I shall be the most popular girl at fiesta, and all the heirs will jostle for a space on my dance card."

It took so little to make some people happy.

"Do you know her, that blond girl?" she asked. "I saw you greet her and her party, and caught you looking at her like a man in love."

Was he that transparent? Had Gloria seen him staring at her like a lovesick puppy? Scalding shame flooded his face. "You think everyone must be in love."

"I think everyone should be. I cannot wait until I am. But that girl—she is very beautiful. Look." She stopped him, and pointed through one of the arches of the colonnade behind them. "She is dancing with the Viceroy."

Of course she was, whirling with him in the waltz like a fairytale princess. And no doubt convincing him to stop the war with just a few soft words and a pretty smile.

"Oh my, won't the mamas be angry. He has distinguished her now—they will all have to extend invitations to their ranchos or be considered rude."

Social interaction was exhausting. He could not bear it. "Then I recommend you find a place in line and dance with him, too."

"Oh, I already have, in the first set. He has made a tiny *faux pas*, you know—the first waltz should have gone to Mama. But I will have the fourth one. Luckily I love dancing much more than my sisters." She executed a step and a twirl, then took his arm once more. "Do you feel better? We could waltz right here. We can still hear the music."

Like an automaton, he bowed to her with the gentlemanly flourish of the hand due a lady, and then swept her into his arms. She was indeed a very good dancer, light as thistledown and so responsive to his touch upon her back and wrist that it seemed she could read his mind. When the waltz ended, they had traversed the length of the gravel walk and found themselves so close to a rose arbor that it seemed natural to walk into it.

"I will lay you odds that either a troop of soldiers or your duenna will appear in less than five minutes," he said.

She laughed, a tinkling sound that nevertheless sounded sincere. "My duenna is dancing with Papa's majordomo, with whom she is desperately in love despite the fact that he is married, and the soldiers are so terrified that something will happen to the Viceroy that they have no powers of observation left for someone as insignificant as I."

"That is their loss, then," he said gallantly. "However, the first eligible suitor to present himself to defend your honor may be right behind us."

She snorted in a most unladylike fashion. "I am glad to hear you sounding better. If you are to fight a duel, at least you will be in good spirits."

"I am not a very good fighter, sadly," he admitted. "Though I have learned to shoot well enough to defend myself, and I can operate the behemoth, which has a cannon in one arm."

"Dios mio!" she exclaimed. "Are you speaking of the monster they call *el Gigante*?"

"How does a gently bred young lady know about that?" he asked in some astonishment, having looked forward to explaining in some detail what the behemoth was.

"You forget our close ties with San Gregorio," she said, tapping him on the arm. "The last time Senor de Aragon was here to visit Papa, they talked of it at length. I heard His Excellency say that he wanted five hundred men from San Luis Obispo de Tolosa to fight in its company when war was declared, right at the front of the host in the place of honor."

"And did your father agree?"

In the silence that fell, Evan heard the music start up again, a polka this time. Isabela's mama would be collecting on what was due her. In the distance, almost under the range of hearing, came the crash and boom of the breakers on the beaches below, and in the gardens, a woman laughed, cut off suddenly as though she had been kissed.

"Papa is a man of honor," Isabela said at last, "and as brave as any general, but he does not believe in war. Not this one, at least."

"Does he discuss these things with you?"

"Of course not," she said soberly. "Everyone thinks I am like *la mariposa*—the butterfly—without a brain to bless myself with. But I listen. I understand. I read, unlike my sisters. And I think—" She glanced down the arbor, with the lanterns swinging rosily at the end of it. No one stood there. "I think that if our glorious Viceroy goes to war with those to the east, many men will die needlessly, including my dear Papa."

"I agree with you," Evan said simply. "Are there others among the rancho families who feel the same?"

"Sí." Her voice dropped to a whisper. "But no one dares say so aloud. It is treason."

"Yet you take this very great risk with me, senorita."

It was difficult to see in the leafy darkness, but her oval face seemed to tilt up, as though she were trying to see his expression, too. "You are a prisoner of war," she whispered. "You cannot be on His Excellency's side."

"In that you are right. Yet I am forced to operate the behemoth in the south, at the water meadows, at his command."

"Building the dam. *Sí.* I know."

"What else do you know?"

Another silence, as though she were struggling with herself. "I know our Viceroy is not really possessed of the Holy Spirit. Or rather—he may be, since he is anointed of God to be our prince, but that is not what is making him so ill that he cannot keep his food down, or sleep when the night is alive with visions."

Evan was silent with the fear that had never quite receded since the previous day.

She looked up, and clutched his sleeve. "You have been summoned to interpret his dreams. You are a doctor. Use the skill you have gained to help him—but be careful."

"Of course I will—"

She leaned in, so close her words were hardly more than a breath beating on his skin. "I was my great-grandmother's favorite. You were right earlier. She taught me a little of herbs, and lore. I do not know much, but I will wager my chance of a wedding that somehow, his doctors are behind his decline. Why, I do not know. But be careful, Evan Douglas."

And before he could ask her anything more, she danced away down the tunnel formed by the rose vines, and disappeared into the lights and the crowd.

*

Well, his grandmother had not brought him up to be a coward. Evan was a scientist, and he knew better than anyone that feeling sorry for himself would not elicit a reciprocal emotion in the hearts of others—

rather, they would simply despise him. So, back to the fiesta he would go, difficult and painful though it might be.

At the table he found Joe with his pretty partner, and did his best to smile. "Wondered where you'd got to," Joe said.

"Isabela took me out for some air and a waltz."

"Careful, or you'll give San Gregorio's heir something to worry about."

"Is he here?"

But Joe only shrugged. "Evan Douglas, may I present Ella Balboa, companion to your friend Mrs. Fremont and a friend of mine for many years."

Evan bowed, while the young lady treated him to a smile of such sweetness that for a moment, he envied Joe. Then reality got the better of him. No matter how lovely her smile, the girl could not change the fact that Joe was a prisoner, too, and despite what Commander de Sola had said about citizenship, he had as much hope of a life with her as Evan had with—

"Gloria speaks of you all the time," Ella confided, inviting him to sit on her other side. "I cannot tell you how wonderful it is for her to see you alive and well when she believed you to be dead."

"It is wonderful for me, too," he managed past a throat swelling with emotion. "Is there any news of our other friends—Alice Chalmers, Ian Hollys, the members of *Swan*'s crew?"

She shook her head. "Not that we had heard before we left, I am sorry to say. But take heart. If the two of you survived the Battle of Resolution and everything that came after it, chances are good that they did, too."

"I hope you are right." As though he had no control over his own faculties, his gaze found Gloria out on the dance floor, enjoying the polka with her husband. "Is she happy?"

Ella's gaze followed his own. "I do not know that happiness comes into it, but they certainly get on well."

"How could she?" came out of his mouth before he could stop himself. "Married. And to—" This time he succeeded in controlling his tongue.

"She did not have much choice, you know. Mother Mary and Sister Clara agreed—a woman cannot travel alone in this country, and her best chance of gaining an audience with His Highness was to accept the captain's offer and then form a party with me as maid and Riley—he's the navigator on the captain's steamboat, the *Colorado Queen*—as escort. We have two others with us, but they are below on the docks, probably getting drunk with the sailors."

"It seems to have worked," Joe said. "Her dance with the Viceroy, I mean, not getting drunk with sailors. She returned after the waltz and told the captain she had an audience tomorrow. She didn't seem as happy as I would have expected, though."

"That was a little worrying," Ella admitted. "Though if I had an audience with the Viceroy I would probably faint dead away and have to be carried out."

"Does he love her?" Evan blurted, then wished he could smack himself—or leave the table before he simply cut out his heart and offered it on a plate for everyone to view.

"The captain?" Ella laughed merrily. "I do not know if he loves anyone—or rather, he loves them too well. There is many a woman along the river waiting for the sound of the ship's whistle." She laughed again, while Evan felt his face turn cold with dismay. "They do not even share a bed at night—well, they do, but she always rolls up a blanket down the middle. Half the time she and I sleep together, depending on whether our rooms have a connecting door and we can maintain the fiction for the others in the party. It would not do to have the men gossiping at this late stage."

Joe's eyebrows rose, and she stuck out her tongue at him. "Never mind looking all scandalized, you."

"So they haven't—you know—that is, there's no danger of—" Joe couldn't quite seem to get the words out, which suited Evan admirably. There were some things he really did not want to know.

Now Ella poked Joe in the stomach, just where the silver chain hung from the bottom-most pair of buttons on his short jacket. "That is none of your nevermind, sir. But I will say that she and I are both pure as lilies." And she laughed again, as though this were a fine joke.

Evan stood, looking this way and that for a way of escape. And then his gaze met that of Gloria, being escorted toward them by her husband. The captain. The scoundrel. Behind them trailed two young dandies, clearly the scions of rancho families determined to make their own impression upon the Viceroy's new favorite.

"Why Evan, I believe this one is yours," she said, her clear blue eyes beseeching him to play along, though he hadn't said a word and in fact, would rather faint and be carried out himself than expose his emotion in a dance with her.

But her hand slipped into his and his arms gathered her in for the second waltz and before he knew it, they were whirling out onto the floor.

"Thank you for the rescue," she said, her hand warm in his own. "It is one thing to dance with the captain, but quite another to put up with those boys. They have been following me about like puppies."

"Apparently their mamas are obliged to extend you invitations to stay, now that the Viceroy has shown you such favor," he told her. Thank goodness for facts, and for having something innocuous to say. "They are likely seeking to initiate the acquaintance."

"Perhaps, but that does not obligate me to dance with them. Goodness, I am a married woman."

"Yes," he said faintly.

"But how glad I am to see you safe, Evan!" She squeezed his right shoulder, where her hand lay, in delight. "I want to hear more, but I understand from your translator that you are under house arrest."

"For now. Until I am called upon by the Viceroy. If he should have a nightmare, I am to interpret it. When my usefulness is ended, I expect I will be shipped back to the water meadows."

"Not if we can help it," Gloria said firmly. "We will come up with a plan. My husband can defend a train from robbers, so I have every confidence he could stop and rob one. We shall steal you and Senor San Gregorio in short order."

"I would not put him or you in such danger. No, Barnaby and I had a plan in support of your efforts. I will simply return and wait for the right moment to carry it out, and escape in the behemoth."

"But if I can convince the Viceroy not to go to war—"

Evan nodded, and twirled her out, then in, in the manner he had seen the Viceroy do. "That would be wonderful. Then I will merely have to mount a rescue, not an attack."

"Oh, Evan." She smiled up at him, her eyes soft. "I cannot believe you pursued me across all those miles of desert, only to miss me by mere moments! How different our lives might have been." The smile faltered, and her gaze came to rest on the button of his collar.

"One must not wish for the might-have-beens," he said as bravely as though his heart was not beating practically out of his chest. "Mrs. Fremont is the belle of the ball, with the Viceroy's regard, a handsome husband, and every prospect for happiness ahead."

"Yes," she agreed slowly, as though the concept were strange to her.

And when the music ended, Senor de la Carrera y Borreaga claimed her hand, and there was nothing left for Evan to do but return to the table. He met Joe and Ella coming out for the next *contredanse*, which left Captain Fremont and his man alone at the table.

Suddenly, Evan could bear no more—and certainly not a tête-à-tête with that scoundrel.

He waylaid Joe on his way past. "I am going up," he said. "I still do not feel quite the thing."

"As you like," Joe said, never one to mind anyone else's business.

"I'll make your excuses to the others," Ella said helpfully, and he smiled at her in gratitude.

Even as recently as this afternoon, he would never have believed that returning to the beautifully furnished prison of his bedroom would provide such inexpressible relief.

19

Rather than dissipating after her waltz with the Viceroy, the tension in Gloria's belly increased to the point that the thought of dessert made her feel ill. Part of it was due to her inability to tell whether the young prince's agreeing to see her on the following day was a triumph or a disaster. Perhaps he simply wanted to arrange lunch. Or a long stay in prison. Or an execution. How long did it take to arrange one of those?

When at last she narrowed her list of partners to the grandees and avoided their sons who sought to monopolize her dance card, she had finally had enough.

"Captain," she said to her husband as he came off the floor with Ella—so strange, she would have imagined that he would have been cutting a much wider swath through the ladies of all ranks in this crowd. "I am exhausted. May we make our farewells?"

"Is that wise? What if the Viceroy wishes to dance with you again?"

"Senor de la Carrera told me just now that His Serene Highness has retired for the evening. I must say I am glad. The poor man looked ready to drop—and he only danced with the ladies of the house after me."

"Must I go too?" Ella looked distressed, and doing her best not to look over her shoulder, where the slender young man who had come with Evan was lurking in the shadows. "Senor Douglas has gone to bed, though it is only eleven, but Joe is still here, and I am not ready to go."

"If he will escort you down to the inn afterward, there is no reason you cannot stay," Gloria said, smiling.

"He cannot, Gloria," her husband reminded her. "He is under house arrest."

Oh, bother. So he was. How could she have forgotten? "Then Riley must do it."

But Riley was nowhere to be found, and Ella looked close to tears. After a parting with Joe that was heartrending in its restraint, she sulked all the way down the gravel walk to the mission, and said not one word as they hailed a conveyance and were driven along the harbor to the inn. Gloria, fretful and exhausted, put every ounce of civility she possessed to the task of not slapping her and bursting into tears.

At least Ella was free to choose upon whom she wished to bestow her affections. Not that Gloria wanted to give them to Evan, or anyone else. But to have the freedom to give them ... oh, never mind. She was not thinking clearly, and could hardly wait to close herself in her room and bury her face in the pillow.

But the captain paid the conveyance driver and followed her up to the room they shared, complete with bolster in the middle of the bed. She had expected him to join his crew in the public room and drink himself into oblivion, not close the door and assist her in removing her boots after she unhooked the tight bodice of her evening gown.

"Thank you," she said, stepping out of the voluminous skirt and draping it over a chair. What were the odds she would live long enough to wear it again?

"Tell me what is on your mind." He pushed the pillows up against the headboard and stretched out on his side of the bed as though he meant to stay awhile.

"Are you not going to join the others?"

"My crew are not embroiled in a political coil up to their necks, and do not need me at present." He patted the quilt, whose bold flowered pattern made a note of color in the lamplight. "I do not spend *all* my time carousing, you may have noticed."

"I did notice." She curled up against the pillows on her own side. "Stanford, I am so afraid."

She had not meant to say that. She meant to sound firm, and confident, and brave. Instead, her voice broke.

He pushed the bolster to the floor with one foot and drew her to his side. "I am, too. Any sane person would be. You really could not tell the Viceroy's meaning? He knew who you were, and what the Ambassador told him you had done, and gave you no hint of what he plans to say or do tomorrow?"

"Not a word." His shoulder was firm, and steadying, and quite comfortable. He was not making fun of her or casting blame. Instead, he was behaving like ... a friend. A confidante. Someone who could be trusted.

And how badly she wanted to trust! To share the burden she had carried alone for so long. She had had friends to help her—in the beginning, at least. But even they had not known how much fear she had carried, how little self-confidence.

"Truly, I fear he has sent for the Ambassador already, to arrange for my execution," she said slowly. "De Aragon certainly hinted at it on our journey here. But my goodness, can a man dance with a woman one day and order her execution the next?"

"A man might not—but who can tell, with princes?"

"I wonder why the Ambassador is not here." It had been bothering her since their arrival. Once her trepidation about meeting him again had lessened, it was only replaced by fear of what he might be up to while no one was watching. "One would think he would be interested in the Viceroy's health, or accompanying him south in order to inspect the troops, or some such."

"That had occurred to me, too. I don't suppose you grilled any of your partners on the matter, did you? I noticed you chose them rather carefully."

"I had hoped no one would notice," she said wryly, and added with a sigh, "I make a very bad spy."

"I disagree. The good ones are pretty—but the best ones are clever. And you qualify on both counts."

"Have you met so many spies?" She poked him, and he laughed. "But a few tidbits did drop between the waltz and the polka. Enough to confirm our guess that not everyone supports this war. Oh, they didn't say it outright," she told him. "But I could read it in the eyes of Santa Cruz and San Carlos Borromeo de Carmelo, and feel the tension in the shoulder and handclasp of San Miguel Arcangel when I danced around the subject."

"Keep your observations close, my dear," he said.

"Oh, I shall, believe me. But I have a feeling the observations of women are not held in high regard in any case."

"Your friend Mr. Douglas made himself scarce earlier than I expected," he said in a change of subject rather abrupt even for him.

"I imagine after being in gaol for weeks, a fiesta would be rather difficult to face, don't you agree? There is too much going on under the surface for a rational person to be entirely comfortable."

"Truer words were never spoken," he murmured. "He appears to be as much in love with you as ever."

And here it was again, rearing its ugly head. She tilted her head to gaze up at him, his shoulder suddenly hard as stone beneath hers. "Let us be clear on one thing at least," she said. "I care about Evan very much. I owe my life to him, for he pulled me off that gun before the missile hit, risking his life to save mine. But I said my vows to you. And while we both know that they were said to further a cause, I for one do not plan to break them."

"Only to release me from them?" The words were said with casual ease, but the tension in that shoulder had not eased in the least.

"We will release each other if that is what we both want," she said awkwardly. "But ... for my part ... if one must be married ... there are many worse persons to be married to."

She wasn't sure what she expected, but a chuckle was not among the possibilities she might have considered. "Do not overwhelm me with the force of your affections, dear," he said.

At least the tension had gone out of his shoulder, making her bold enough to say, "We agreed to be honest with each other. And ... I have never met another man to whom I could countenance marriage, despite my father's best efforts to rope and tie one and drag him to church."

"There must have been a few willing victims. After all, you were the first choice of a prince this evening."

"True ... he did not know about the Meriwether-Astor millions at first, which at least made his choice disinterested."

"A face like yours would interest any man." He sat up to look into her face. "They cannot really all have wanted you for your money."

She lifted a shoulder, clad only in a chemise. "I could not take the chance. My parents' marriage was ... well, if you had been at the Battle of Resolution, you would have seen similarities. And he had the nerve to elevate her practically to sainthood the moment she died, after treating her abominably while she was alive."

If she laid her cheek on his shoulder, would he allow it?

The crisp linen was soft and warm against her skin, and more than merely allowing it, he lifted his arm and put it around her. With a sigh of relief, she settled against him. "This would have been unthinkable for them."

"What—sitting and talking like this?"

With a nod, she said, "I feel as though I am sailing in uncharted waters. I—I do not actually know how to be a wife. Only a comrade at arms. A friend. A traveling companion."

In the silence of the room, he drew a breath, and then it hitched, as though he had thought something that he would not say. "Though I have as little experience as you, I imagine that a wife can be all those things if she wants to." And then— "Do you want to be more?" This time it was he who tilted his head to see her face.

She swallowed. Had her toes been clinging to the edge of a precipice, she could not have felt a greater sense of ... falling? Flying? "I—I think I might."

"But not tonight?"

"I do not think so." She was having a hard time breathing, so intense was his gaze. "But perhaps ... soon."

"When you accomplish your mission?" His voice was low. Soft, yet musical. So unlike his usual tone of command, or sardonic observation. "Because, you know, that could be as soon as tomorrow night."

"Tomorrow night," she repeated in a whisper.

It sounded almost like a promise.

20

Evan was dragged abruptly from sleep by a rough hand on his shoulder. "Senor! Wake at once. You are needed."

He blinked himself awake, only to squint in pain at the light of a lamp in his face. He pushed it away. "What the devil—? Who are you? What do you want?"

By the time he'd swung his legs over the side of the bed and reached for his borrowed pants, he had recognized the familiar face and form.

"Senor de Sola. Am I needed by the Viceroy?"

"*Si*, I am sent to fetch you. He has had a dream, and wishes you to interpret it."

Evan had been having his own dream, a puzzling but exhilarating one that involved blond hair and dark

Californio eyes and delicate fingers caressing the leaves of lemon balm. One could not smell in a dream, he knew that, and yet it seemed as though the scent lingered in his nostrils even now.

"Of course." He shook off the last shreds of sleep and dressed quickly, pulling on his boots not because he thought he would be taken away in chains, but because one simply did not approach a prince in stocking feet.

As they walked quickly along the dark, deserted colonnade and into the guest wing occupied by the Viceroy, he said as calmly as he could, "Commander, if I might make a request?"

"Of course, if it is within my power. What is it?"

"Have you said anything of my abilities as a doctor to those attending His Serene Highness?"

The man glanced at him, puzzled. "Why should I not? Certainly His Highness's councilors and staff wished to know everything about you before you could be permitted to attend him in such an—intimate capacity as this."

Evan's heart sank. Even now he was not certain that it mattered if they knew he was a doctor, but Isabela had spoken so seriously... "I see."

"You are not here in that capacity in any case. You are here because of what you did for me."

There was nothing for it but to hope that his medical skill or lack thereof would not matter. He was an interpreter of dreams and a prisoner to boot.

A guard at the door ushered them through, and Evan walked down a flagged corridor to the Viceroy's bedchamber, where another guard stood at attention, and they were admitted by a gentleman as fully dressed as they. Perhaps these men slept only in the daylight hours.

A fire burned briskly in a raised hearth shaped like a beehive, and in a comfortably upholstered chair next to it sat the Viceroy in a rich burgundy velvet dressing gown, a tiny glass of some dark liquid at his elbow. A man in a black linen jacket, wearing augmented spectacles that allowed him to see in very fine detail, leaned over him, pressing his forehead and chest as if he were feeling for fever.

The man, clearly one of the doctors, tilted up his eyepiece and stood to one side with a disapproving frown as the commander approached with Evan. They bowed deeply, and de Sola said, "Here is the interpreter of dreams, Your Serene Highness."

The young man glanced at Evan with infinite weariness, the hollows under his eyes even more apparent in the gentle lamplight, then at his companions. "Leave us. Commander, you may remain."

The man at the door stirred, and the doctor straightened in protest. "But sir, we cannot leave you alone with this—"

"I will not be alone. Are you saying the commander of my military garrison is not capable of his duty?"

De Sola, hands clasped behind his back, did not move, but his face became so forbidding that the doctor wilted. "*Si,* Your Serene Highness. We will be waiting outside should you need us." He indicated the glass of liquid. "Do not neglect your tonic."

The Viceroy ignored him. It was not until the door was firmly closed that he indicated the chairs that had been set facing his, comfortably close to the crackling fire. "Thank you for coming at this hour."

"We are at Your Serene Highness's service," de Sola said gently. "We will help in any way we can."

"I wish I did not have to ask for help," the young man said, rather plaintively, Evan thought. "A prince should ask assistance only from a king—or from God."

"A prince may certainly ask, and receive," Evan said, "especially when the Lord may send human hands and hearts for the purpose."

A faint smile. "You may be right. Tell me, what is the nature of your relationship with Senora Fremont?"

Evan blinked at this sudden swerve from the celestial to the secular. "Why—why, we are friends. We came to the Texican Territories on the same ship. Of course, she was not married then."

"She said she is but newly married." His gaze drifted away. "She is very beautiful."

"She is," Evan said, trying to imagine what he could mean by such impertinent remarks. "As well as clever, and brave, and good."

The Viceroy nodded. "Well said."

"To say nothing of a crack shot. She knows more about weapons and arms than any man I ever met."

"Her father trained her well."

"You knew her father, I understand," Evan said cautiously. "He passed away recently."

"I met him once. Her father and mine were as alike as—what is the expression?" He glanced at de Sola.

FIELDS OF IRON

"Two kernels on a cob?" the commander suggested.

"*Si*, indeed." The Viceroy seemed to sink into himself again, as though contemplating a view he did not favor much.

Evan plucked up his courage. Talking about Gloria was not safe, and prisoner or not, he had a service to offer. The sooner he offered it, the sooner he could go back to sleep.

"Sir, if I may ask about your dream ... is it one that has been recurring, or was it of an original nature?"

"Ah yes. The dream." The prince straightened in his chair and wrapped his robe more tightly around himself. "Parts of it I have dreamed before, and parts of it ... perhaps a prince may dream of golden hair and blue eyes as freely as other men?"

"Perhaps he may. He would not be alone." Evan smiled at him, but the Viceroy did not smile back.

"I have seen her before, you know. In dreams."

"As have I," the commander said.

"That was Gloria?" Evan exclaimed, turning to him. "You did not say so."

"I did not know it—until the moment I stepped into the courtyard here and saw her in the receiving line. I must say, she was dressed much more suitably tonight than she was in my dream—and she was not painted."

"Sir!" the Viceroy exclaimed. "You malign the lady!"

"I humbly beg your pardon, sir, but in my dream, she was a witch. She wore white—a petticoat and chemise—and about the waist a leather corselet. And boots. And a man's bowler hat topped by lenses much as your doctor wore. Most unsuitable and outlandish."

"And what was she doing?" the Viceroy asked, his indignation lightening into interest.

"She was looking for something you had lost, sir, as was I, and when neither of us could find it in the road under the light of the moon, she turned into a dragon and incinerated me."

The Viceroy frowned at this conclusion, which he clearly had not expected, and turned to Evan. "This is the dream which I am told you interpreted?" At Evan's nod, he frowned. "Let me tell you mine, though I hardly know where to begin."

"Start with how you felt," Evan suggested.

The Viceroy gazed into the flames. "Fear? No, not that. I have nothing to fear. Confusion, perhaps. I was lost—in a castle." Relief at having remembered something clearly smoothed the frown from his brow. "I wandered down corridor after corridor, looking for the door."

"There were no doors?"

"Yes—to rooms that had no exit. To staircases, which I took."

"Up or down?"

He thought for a moment. "Up. But instead of the rooms becoming lighter, they became darker, with fewer windows. Until at last I walked into one that had a door on the other side. Somehow I knew that this at last was the way out—though how it could be, when it was at the top of the castle, I did not know."

"Did you open it?"

Commander de Sola sat silently, his gaze moving from one face to the other. Perhaps he was remembering his own dreams. Or perhaps he too had fallen under something like a spell, listening to a story that seemed to have no point, as dreams often seemed.

Though Evan already suspected it did have a point.

"I crossed the room, my steps quickening in anticipation, when I noticed that a picture hung on one wall. A still life of an enormous vase of flowers."

"What kinds?"

"Roses, for one. Yellow roses. Hundreds of them, it seemed, and then I realized that they were not still at all. They were multiplying in the frame, and then flowing outside it, and until the very walls of the room were blooming in yellow roses, in dahlias, in rosemary. It was then that some part of me remarked on the fact that I could see color in the dream. I do not remember ever having done that before."

Evan nodded thoughtfully. "It is said to be the sign of an intelligent and creative mind."

The Viceroy lifted a brow. "Indeed. And what significance can you attach to the flowers? For I cannot ever remember such a painting, or even such flowers in the palace in San Francisco de Asis. My mother was no gardener."

Evan remembered talking with his cousin Maggie at Gwynn Place about one of her favorite subjects, after the events that had preceded her discovery of her real parents, and that her beloved poultryman on the estate was in reality her grandfather. The two of them had walked the paths in Lady Flora's garden while Maggie had picked a stem here, a blossom there, and told him a little of the language of flowers.

"There are those who say that while red roses stand for love, and white for innocence, the yellow ones stand for jealousy."

"Jealousy," the prince repeated. "There were many, many yellow roses, growing and melting and accumulating in the corners of the room. If what you say is true, I do not like that at all."

"It is also thought that the dahlia stands for betrayal—though some say travel or a journey—and rosemary, of course, means remembrance. All of which leads me to believe that your sleeping mind is locked in a struggle with a truth that your waking mind cannot bring itself to grapple with."

"That someone harbors jealousy against me, and plans a betrayal?" A wry smile touched his mouth. "This should not surprise any prince—and indeed does not. But I have not told you what happened next."

He glanced at his glass of tonic, then looked away with a frown. Evan wanted to ask if he knew what was in it, then decided not to draw the subject away from dreams. Those he was equipped to deal with. Reality could come when it would.

"The flowers dribbled and flowed out of the painting's frame and across the walls—and then, as though they were made of some acid, they melted the plaster and revealed the structure beneath."

"Brick?" Evan guessed. "Stone?" One made by man, one by nature—either might add a little to the interpretation forming in his mind.

"Neither," the Viceroy said, his voice low. "For as the flowers melted and ate away at the walls, more and more was revealed, until finally I realized the castle was made neither of brick nor of stone." He looked directly into Evan's eyes. "It was made of bone. Or bones—thousands of them. I was trying to find my way out of a castle built of dead men's bones."

Evan felt his jaw slacken a little—knew the prince's horror was reflected in his own gaze. "And then?" he whispered.

"And then I woke, calling for I know not whom." Visibly, he attempted control of himself. "For you, perhaps."

Evan released a long breath. "I can understand why. I should have done the same—though I confess I have no one to call for. My mother died when I was very small, and the grandmother who raised me did not hold with running to comfort those who suffered from nightmares. She said facing my fears would enable me to overcome them."

"And did it?"

With a rueful smile, Evan shook his head. "Even yet my blood runs cold at the thought of dark tunnels, or of being underground."

The commander nodded, as though Evan might not be alone in his fears.

"But what can you tell me of this dream?" the Viceroy asked. "For I can assure you that the palace in which I grew up is made of solid stone, with not a bone to be found outside the kitchens."

"But you live in a kind of palace that is not constructed of stone, and travels with you every moment,"

Evan told him. "A palace made of the regard of your people, of the soul of your kingdom. Is that not so?"

"Ye-e-es," the young man allowed. "Though I have not been taught to think of it in such a way."

"And yet, far from the reality of daylight, your mind acknowledges that your kingdom has been won by the sacrifice of men's lives."

"True. Though this thought does not horrify me as did those walls of bone, keeping me from escaping."

"Perhaps your sleeping mind anticipates the future," Evan suggested gently. "Could you be trapped in a façade of beauty that yet harbors a deadly jealousy? Turn and wander as you might, you cannot escape it. And under it all is the prospect of more death—more bones upon which to build a larger kingdom. A bigger palace. And deep down, that is the prospect which horrifies you."

The young man frowned, his chin dropping to his chest as he considered pattern in the thick rug under their feet. "I do not like this interpretation," he muttered.

"The truth was a shock to me, too, sir," the commander finally ventured to say, in a low voice.

"But how did you know it was the truth, what he told you? What *did* he tell you?" the prince demanded. "What is it that I have lost?"

The commander glanced at Evan. "I knew ... because it was the truth in my heart," he said simply. He pressed a hand to his chest. "Some weight I had not known was there was lifted as my waking mind understood what my sleeping mind had been trying to tell me. In my dream, both I and this woman—even now I find it difficult to say it was Senora Fremont—were looking for what you had lost in order to return it to you. And what you have lost..."

He took a breath, and Evan realized he was gazing at a very brave man. Perhaps one of the bravest he had ever known.

"What you have lost, sir, is your power."

"I beg your pardon?" The Viceroy had clearly not been expecting this. "I have done no such thing. Why, with a single word I could have you executed at dawn, and there is no one save God who could refuse me."

The commander did not flinch. "I have no doubt of that, sir. But can you say the same of every person in the Royal Kingdom? Can you command every soldier's allegiance ... or does that power belong to another?"

Oh, this young man was not stupid. Evan watched as one conclusion after another tumbled through his mind, as possibility connected with supposition, as he walked through the hallways of fact and memory just as he had done in his dream.

Only this time, was there a way out?

After long moments, in which the only sounds were of men breathing and the fire popping and crackling, the Viceroy seemed to journey back as from a long distance. He gazed at Evan, then at the commander. "If I did not know better, I would say that the two of you are colluding together in sedition and treason."

Evan schooled himself not to flinch, following de Sola's excellent example. "I am glad you know better, then, sir."

Unbidden, a smile touched the young man's lips. "I have asked for an interpretation, and you have given me one. The fact that it can be linked to a dream of a commander of my own garrison is strange, to be sure. And perhaps, miraculous."

"It could be the God of Heaven moving you, sir," de Sola said quietly, "or it could simply be the realization of two rational men that something is amiss in your kingdom, and must be dealt with."

"You know that the people say I am touched by God himself? That I see visions and have revelations sent by Him?"

"I do, sir."

"The question I might ask, though," Evan put in, "is how long have these visions been going on? Your entire life?"

The Viceroy shook his head, and ran a hand through his curly mop. "No. Only since I inherited the throne and was anointed. More than one of my ministers and councilors believe this is a sign from God that I am the true heir."

"There has been some doubt?" Evan asked, surprised.

"No indeed. Though before my father acceded in 1869, there was quite a to-do in Holy Mother Spain about who was the legitimate heir. His success and my heavenly favor have since laid the last of those doubts to rest among the oldest in church and state."

"Heavenly favor ... or a more prosaic explanation?" Evan reached over and lifted the little glass filled with dark green liquid. He sniffed it, smelling the crisp scent of lemon at the top, the heady golden wine they had served at the fiesta, and under it something else. Something musky and dark and rotten that he could not identify. "Who makes this for you?"

"My doctors. They compile it themselves. You are not saying it has something to do with my visions, are you? That is mad. It is to help me sleep."

"I am simply saying that a healthy young man has no need of medicines and tinctures, and sleep comes as a result of an active life."

"I need it to feel better."

"Did you feel poorly before? You have been on the throne less than a year—what was your condition then?"

"You speak like a doctor yourself."

Evan's stomach plunged, yet he could not stop now. "I am a scientist specializing in the mind. A tincture that causes vivid dreams and saps the health of a young man is of great interest to me ... if indeed that is what it does. If you would allow me to advise you, sir, I would ask you to refuse it. Pour it away. To be honest, I should like to take this away and discover its ingredients."

"Have you a laboratory here?" The prince looked amused.

"I can find an apothecary's laboratory, with your permission, sir," de Sola said. "It may be that it is indeed necessary for your health. But I see for myself the possibility exists that there may be those close to you who do not wish the best for you."

At this reminder, the young man sank once more into gloom. "I do not wish to think of that. Do as you like. Let us turn instead to happier topics. As a friend of Senora Fremont, do you know how long she and her husband plan to stay here in San Luis Obispo de Tolosa?"

"She is here for only one reason, sir, and that is to express her misgivings about the weapons sold to you by her father."

"To my knowledge, they are to be used in exactly the manner for which they were designed."

"True, but need they be?" Evan persisted. "Could their use be part of the expansion of the castle of bones? So that instead of lush farmlands and a loving people, you are left with fields of iron and castles of bone—with thousands of lives lost?"

"I said I did not wish to discuss this," he said crossly, shifting in his chair.

"Very well," Evan said in his most soothing tones. "I believe Mrs. Fremont will state her case, and then depending upon her success, will either return to Philadelphia or stay to assist you in whatever manner she can."

"She cannot go to Philadelphia." The young prince's brow furrowed. "I wish her to stay."

Evan felt that now was not the time to remind him that she was a free citizen of the Fifteen Colonies, and as long as the trains were running, she could board any one of them whenever she wanted to.

"She is certainly an ornament at the fiesta," the commander ventured. "And is it true that before she was lost in the Rio de Sangre Colorado, Ambassador de Aragon was bringing her to you in connection with these very weapons?"

"Yes, he was," the Viceroy said absently. "He has remained in San Francisco de Asis to attend to matters of state while I am on progress. I have trusted him ..." He seemed to shake himself. "Tell me, does Senora Fremont seem happy in her marriage?"

Evan blinked, a little taken aback. "That is hardly my affair, sir, though a woman of such strong convictions and moral fiber would hardly choose a man with whom she could not be happy."

"Yet de Aragon would have brought her to me a month ago had she not been lost to the river. Had they been known to one another before?"

Evan began to perspire. "Sir, I am hardly equipped to comment on the lady's attachments. I only met her a week or two before that, when we landed in Philadelphia from England."

"You must know something. Speak, and I will have you released from your imprisonment. You and your translator may leave here as free men if you do me this small, simple service."

"Sir—" Commander de Sola sat up straight. "This is the only man in the country capable of operating *el Gigante.* His services are urgently needed in the water meadows."

"Then find someone else to do it, or pay him a wage for his services," the Viceroy snapped. "Now, Senor Douglas. There is something on the tip of your tongue and I wish to hear it."

Betray Gloria's most private concerns and become a free man? Or keep silent and return to gaol, possibly for the rest of his life—to say nothing of Joe's life?

And of what significance was it, really, the little tidbit that Ella had let drop? How much of a secret could it be if she had no fear of taking all and sundry into her confidence? Perhaps it was not a secret at all. Many couples in London society lived that way, and no one seemed to think it of any consequence.

"I—I do not know much of her marriage at all," he said awkwardly, his heart beating as though it would gallop out of his chest. "We were only reunited this evening, where there was not much time for intimate conversation. But her maid let slip that her—that is, that she and Mr. Fremont do not—I mean, that—"

"The marriage has not been consummated?" the Viceroy finished, his face shedding its gloom and becoming animated.

Dash it all. This really was most uncomfortable. And society couples notwithstanding, he was betraying Gloria in a most intimate manner by talking about her behind her back.

"I do not think so," he mumbled, sinking into his chair in shame. "But I have not been brought up to talk of such things."

"Ah, but in the Royal Kingdom, such things are the currency of life," the commander said in an attempt to be reassuring. "You have paid a small price indeed for your freedom."

Perhaps he had. But Evan did not think so.

Nor did he feel much like a free man as they rose and took their leave.

FIELDS OF IRON

21

Despite the fact that she wore a secondhand dress, Gloria sailed into the de la Carrera y Borreaga hacienda as though she were a queen. Her hair was soft and still held its curl from the fiesta the night before, and was twisted and pinned up into the most flattering chignon of which Ella was capable, with a festive little pouf of ribbons tucked into it that matched the trim on her gown. She wore her wedding ring on her left hand, and her mother's tawny topaz on her right, none the worse for wear for having spent weeks sewn up inside her corset.

With the captain waiting outside in the courtyard, she was shown into what could have passed for a morning room in any house in England, save for the fact that it looked westward, out to sea. The Viceroy sat unattended in a wingback chair near a leaping fire, though it was not cold.

She sank into a curtsey and bowed her head.

"Senora Fremont. Please rise and join me. Would you care for tea?"

A pretty Sèvres tea service sat on a low table. "Thank you, sir. May I pour for you?"

He smiled, and she pretended she had not seen the dark circles under his eyes, nor the cheeks that seemed to have hollowed out another fraction since they had danced together the evening before. When she handed him his tea, prepared the way she liked hers—with milk, not lemon—the cup rattled just a little as he took it from her.

Ella had said the burden of prophecy might be too much for him. Gloria had an uncomfortable feeling she might be right.

"Are you well, sir? Did you sleep well?"

He took a sip of his tea and put the cup and saucer aside. "I cannot say so. I was obliged to send for your English friend, Senor Douglas, to interpret a dream."

She hid her reaction behind her own cup, and said merely, "I hope he was able to help."

"I do not know. He gave an interpretation, but I do not believe it can be the truth."

"That is the way of dreams, is it not? Though I understand that Mr. Douglas is highly regarded in scientific circles on the subject."

"Has he interpreted any of yours?"

FIELDS OF IRON

Gloria shook her head, the three dangling curls at the back of her chignon tickling her neck. "We have not known one another long enough to discuss our dreams—our conversations have been more along the line of 'You've assembled that gun incorrectly' and 'Pass the stew' and 'Will we ever see home again?'"

The corner of his mouth lifted in a smile. "He thinks very highly of you. As do I."

Heat scalded her cheeks. "That is very kind of you, sir." But he had much less evidence on which to base an opinion than did Evan. The latter had saved her life, and she had saved his.

"As you have come all this way to speak with me, perhaps you ought to begin."

Gloria set her cup aside and took a breath to steady her nerves. "Thank you for your willingness to hear me, sir. As His Excellency the Ambassador will have told you, the train bearing your purchases was set upon by air pirates near the town of Resolution, and the mechanicals stolen. But even if they had not been, I would still have journeyed here after my father's death to beg you not to put them into use."

She lifted her gaze to find his upon her, steady and waiting for her to go on.

"It is the ambassador's belief that the lands east of the mountains, the Rio de Sangre Colorado valley and the Texican Territories, are somehow rich with gold. But sir, it is a fact that no gold has been found there."

"A fact according to whom? For stories have been handed down for generations in our families telling of rich deposits in the river caves. Of treasures left behind when families were forced to move farther west by flood and attack."

"Believe me, sir, there is nothing in those caves but the villages of the ancient ones. They are sandstone. My knowledge of geology is sparse, but even I know that gold is not formed in sandstone."

"It was carried there, of course, by our forefathers."

"Why should they do that?"

"To keep it safe from robbers."

"They have more concern for gold than for the persons of the women in their own country? No one keeps them safe from robbers." Gloria struggled to calm a sudden burst of nervous energy that came perilously close to temper. "Do forgive me, sir."

"Women must be kept safe and protected by their own families."

"I know. Except for women like me, who have a legitimate reason to journey so far—we are reduced to—" She stopped. "But I am wasting Your Serene Highness's time. The point is, it is my belief as the president of a company that trades in both the Royal Kingdom and the Texican Territory that your people would find more prosperity in opening your borders to trade and the pursuit of their gold through business than they would in declaring war in an attempt to take it by force, if it really exists."

"Go on."

Could he really be listening? Was there truly hope, after all that she and her friends had been through? Gloria fortified herself with another sip of tea.

"I inherited the Meriwether-Astor Munitions Works and all its subsidiaries when my father died. I propose that we work together not by importing mechanicals of war, but machines for agriculture, for construction, and for exploration. We might form partnerships among the Texicans and enjoy mutual profit—and we might also find ways to see to the care of those who are less fortunate, offering them a means of making their living off the rancho."

"In other words, you would have us change our entire culture in order to make money?"

Oh, dear. That was not what she meant at all. She must make him understand. "By no means, sir. I simply suggest that there are ways of accumulating gold that do not involve declaring war on others and putting innocent lives at risk. And I believe there may be those among the rancho owners who share this desire for peace. They would certainly support you should you decide to change the direction in which you steer the kingdom's future."

She could say no more without being accused of sedition. But surely he must see that people who wanted peace were no threat to him?

"You state your case eloquently," he said.

A trickle of relief ran through her. Perhaps she would not be tossed into gaol just yet. "I can only say what is in my heart." She gave him a soft smile, and did her best to look feminine and unthreatening.

"A heart that is brave, and loyal, and good."

"Sir..." She blushed and bowed her head.

"So says your friend, Senor Douglas. He also says you are a crack shot."

With a smile, she said, "He possesses the same qualities, and means Your Highness and your kingdom no harm."

"Tell me this, Senora Fremont ... how did you reach San Luis Obispo de Tolosa when my roads and trains are so dangerous to a lady traveling alone? What means did you employ to ensure your safety so that you could reach your objective and we could have this audience here today?"

She gazed at him. What on earth ...? "I came in the company of my husband, my maid, and an escort of my husband's crew," she said at last. "Is there another way I should have come?" She restrained herself from mentioning the silly prejudice against airships, which would have made the journey much more comfortable, to say nothing of short.

"No. But by your own admission, your marriage is in its infancy. Could it be that it is a marriage of convenience only, formed between two people with a common goal? What is the captain's stake in this?"

Now she hardly knew where to look. "Sir ... my goodness ... that is very ... you cannot expect me to ..."

How had he known?

"You have not consummated your marriage, have you, Senora Fremont?"

"Good heavens!" Gloria stood—turned—remembered she could not leave the royal presence without permission—and sank again on to the little sofa. Or rather,

her knees gave out and it was lucky it was there. "That is most impertinent!"

"You are even more beautiful when your color is high," he said, apropos of nothing.

"Sir, I must insist—I request your permission to withdraw."

"I do not give it. I am the only one who may insist."

"Then you need a lesson or two in propriety," she said crisply. The nerve! "I trust you are not making an inappropriate suggestion to me? I must confess I had thought better of you than that."

She thought he might turn her out of the room, or order the execution with which his wretched Ambassador had threatened her. But instead, he grinned, like a small boy who had been irritating on purpose, to stimulate a reaction.

"Heaven forfend," he said. "No, I am making the most appropriate suggestion possible. I do not know how you convinced the good captain to make your mission his own, but let us come to an agreement here and now. I will stop all preparations for this war and send all my troops back to their homes ... if you will allow me to have your marriage annulled."

She stared at him, her mouth going slack and her eyes widening with shock. She could not have heard him correctly. One did not simply wave one's hand and make such momentous changes in the lives of near strangers. Even kings and princes did not have that power over citizens of other nations.

And yet ... was this not everything she had dreamed of? To stop the war, to save countless lives, including those of her friends along the river, who even now were counting on her to succeed? And as for her marriage ... was not the dissolution of something that had barely begun a small price to pay?

Her husband understood the terms under which they had agreed to marry. She did not know how the Viceroy had come by his information, but it did not matter. Stanford did not love her. They had barely even become friends. And if at times she wished she had not been quite so firm about the bolster down the middle of the bed, if her blood had rushed in her veins just a little at the thought of what might have come to pass this very evening ... well, the two of them would recover, in time.

The consequences were simply too important for one woman and one man to put their own wishes and needs before those of others far greater. Before those of countries whose stability and peace depended on them.

"And ... if I do?" she finally managed past a constriction in her throat that felt very much like tears. "What possible benefit could there be in my once again being unmarried? I shall still have to travel, and in greater danger than ever."

He shook his head. "No, my dearest lady. You would not be unmarried for long."

He rose, and extended a hand. Wordlessly, she rose, wondering what on earth he meant. Was their interview concluded?

He clasped both her cold hands in his own, which were equally cold.

"Gloria Meriwether-Astor," he said gently, his dark eyes intent upon her face, "I have never met anyone like you. You are not only beautiful, you are brave and compassionate, to say nothing of clever, and a visionary in business. I am making you the offer of my hand. Once you are a free woman—which will take no more than three days, I promise you—will you honor me and all my people by becoming my wife, and Vicereine of the Royal Kingdom of Spain and the Californias?"

Gloria stared at him. Gulped. Opened her mouth, then—

"Oh, dear," she said.

Epilogue

Dearest Mother,

Find Tia Clara at once and brace yourselves for the happiest of news—Honoria is alive! I have seen her—touched her—even danced with her. She is posing as a man, as translator to Evan Douglas, the friend of Gloria whom she thought was dead. Forgive my grammar—time is short and I must get this to the padre or it will miss the mission mail packet.

I do not know when we will see your faces again. I only know that now that I have found her, only God may separate us. She and Evan are both prisoners, though there has been talk of giving her citizenship papers from San Gregorio. If I have to become a camp laundress at the garrison, I will do it, if only I may be near her. Our sister Gloria meets with the Viceroy this very morning. I pray that she is successful, for the burden of prophecy lies heavy on him.

Honoria sends her dearest love to you and Tia Clara, and covers your faces in kisses. I will write again the moment I have news. May God bring us all safely together on the banks of the river.

*Ever your loving
Ella Maria*

THE END

A Note From Shelley

Dear reader,

I hope you enjoy reading the adventures of Gloria, Lady Claire, and the gang in the Magnificent Devices world as much as I enjoy writing them. It is your support and enthusiasm that is like the steam in an airship's boiler, keeping the entire enterprise afloat and ready for the next adventure.

You might leave a review on your favorite retailer's site to tell others about the books. And you can find print and electronic editions of the entire series online, as well as audiobooks. Do come visit my website, www.shelleyadina.com, where you can sign up for my newsletter and be the first to know of new releases and special promotions.

And now, for an excerpt from *Fields of Gold*, the final book in Gloria's trilogy—indeed, the final book in this twelve-volume segment of the Magnificent Devices series—I invite you to turn the page ...

Excerpt

FIELDS OF GOLD
BY SHELLEY ADINA
© 2017

SHELLEY ADINA

1

Somewhere in the Wild West
March 1895

It was one thing to be afraid for yourself—that cold, paralyzing fear that paradoxically made your innards turn to liquid instead of a solid block of ice. It was quite another thing to be afraid for someone you loved—in a massive, towering cloud of fear that blotted out even the memory of sunshine.

Alice, Lady Hollys, crouched in the dirt next to the prone form of her husband. He lay beneath a stand of ironwood trees in an arroyo that fed runoff into the mighty Rio de Sangre Colorado de Christo. "Ian," she whispered through dry lips. "Ian, hang on. I'm going for help, but you have to wake up, and press this handkerchief against the wound."

His eyelids fluttered open and tears of relief sprang into her eyes.

"What ... happened?"

"That dadblamed Prussian she-wolf shot you." And if it was the last thing she did on this earth, Alice was going to return the favor. In spades. Lots of spades. The kind you dug a grave with, and that was a promise.

Ian turned his head weakly to the side, and frowned. "Where ... are they?"

"Back on the steamboat and already a mile upriver, no doubt. There's a Texican Ranger airship in a mooring pattern overhead, and the witches vanished like water on a griddle."

"What's a griddle?"

Alice's grim face contorted in pain that radiated from deep inside. "Oh, my darling," she said brokenly. "This is no time for jokes. She might have been aiming for the heart, but you moved at the last second and she got you right below the collarbone. Heaven only knows where the bullet is, but I have to get you to a doctor, and our only hope is that ship."

"Santa Fe." His dear gray eyes searched hers. "You'll be ... recognized."

"I don't care," she told him gently. "If I'm lucky, it'll happen after I get you into the hospital, and not before. Dearest, I hate to ask this of you, but you must stand and try to walk. We need to signal them, and then find some open ground so they can lower a basket."

"I'll try."

That was her man. Not a word of complaint, not a moan. Simply determination—and a harshly indrawn breath that told her just what it cost him to do as she asked.

But the arroyo that had made such a superb hiding place for the reconnaissance party—intent on destroying the dam the Californios were building across the river—was a disaster for two people needing help. Alice searched frantically from side to side, looking for a place clear enough for the airship's crew to see them, and large enough for them to let its basket down and get Ian into it safely. But these canyons had long been used for concealment, not rescue. Half a mile from the river, it became obvious that Ian's strength was at an end, and she was going to have to leave him and attract their attention alone.

She made him as comfortable as possible with his back against a red boulder. "I'll be back as soon as I can. You'll see the ship lose altitude, and then you'll see me, I promise."

"Be … careful."

She kissed him and rose. But before she could choose a path to higher ground so that she could get a better view of their options, a voice hailed them from the direction of the river. In a moment, two of the witches that had deserted them came pelting into sight, with something that looked suspiciously like a door suspended between them.

"Alice!" Betsy Trelawney called when she was within earshot. "Where is he? Is he all right?"

Alice's grip tightened on her lightning pistol, and in a moment, when she recognized Gretchen the she-wolf in the rear, she pulled it out and thumbed on the ignition switch. The pistol began to hum in a cheerful treble.

"Don't shoot!" Gretchen shouted, skidding to a halt. This jerked the door out of Betsy's hands, and Gretchen flipped it up to crouch behind it, leaving poor Betsy standing in the clear. "We mean you no harm. We went back to the steamboat to get something to carry him with."

Alice lost her tenuous grip on her temper. A bolt of lightning sizzled past Betsy, who threw herself to the ground with a scream, and fried the top off a pinon pine where Gretchen's head had just been.

"Alice!" Betsy shrieked as smoke curled up and the air filled with the scent of hot resin. "We're trying to help you!"

"The only thing that will help me is the sight of her dead body," Alice snapped. "Get out from behind that door, you yellow-bellied sapsucker." She cast a glance upward, but the Ranger ship was nowhere to be seen. Were they circling around for another pass? Or had this ridiculous delay cost her Ian's only chance at getting to a doctor?

"Forgive me," came from behind the door. "I lost my temper. I intended to shoot wide, but he moved."

"Liar!" Alice's voice was hoarse with fear and dust and tears. "You aimed at his heart, you filthy toad. Now, stand up and take what's coming to you."

Betsy scrambled to her feet and leaped back into Alice's line of fire, her hands extended in a plea. "Alice—Alice—this is no time for revenge if we hope to get your husband to Sister Clara."

"What is a cook going to do for him?" Tears of fear and frustration leaked from Alice's eyes, which did nothing for her temper. "I need to get him to Santa Fe, and now the Ranger ship is gone!"

"The others are causing a distraction," came from behind the door.

"What?" Alice's trigger finger jerked, and the top left corner of the door blew off. Blue tendrils of light explored each panel, dancing and sizzling. With a shriek, Gretchen shoved it over and leaped away from it.

Finding nothing to ease its appetite in the wood, which bore neither knob nor hinges, the lightning attacked a rock. It exploded, and a chunk of it struck the other woman, knocking her to the ground.

Alice smiled the smile with which air pirates from Santa Fe to the Canadas had become all too familiar. She buffed the flared barrel of the pistol with her sleeve and deactivated it.

"Dadgummit, Alice, as I was saying," Betsy went on furiously, "Sister Clara and May Lin between them do our doctoring. They've pulled out plenty of bullets. Now stop this nonsense and take us to your husband."

"I'll take you." Alice jerked her chin at the moaning Gretchen. "She stays out of range or I'll shoot a bigger boulder."

Gretchen was no fool. She pulled herself out of the way as Alice and Betsy picked up the door and jogged back to where Ian lay. Her heart ached at the fresh blood that oozed from the wound as they laid him on the door. He was heavy, but the strength of desperation and love seemed to fill her muscles, enabling her to cover the half-mile to the river at something approaching a fast shamble.

The boat and crew were waiting on watch, as though every witch aboard was anxious to rectify the mistake their sister had committed.

"You get him home," Gretchen told the man at the wheel. "I'll join the distraction party and make sure you aren't followed."

Which suited Alice right down to the ground. Maybe the Rangers would get a good shot at her.

The witch had barely leaped to the rocks when a crewman dragged the gangplank in and they were on their way. The walls of the canyons slid past faster than anyone could walk, echoing the chug of the steam engines back to them, but still it was not fast enough for Alice. She crouched next to Ian on the deck—for the door was too wide to carry him into the main saloon from which it had come—and held his hand in both of hers, trying to smile reassuringly when all she wanted to do was weep.

Or shoot something.

A cloud passed over the sun, and instinctively she looked up. "There they are!"

"So much for a distraction," Betsy said anxiously. "What happened?"

But there was no answer to this. Then Alice realized something else. "Are they—? Yes, they are. They're following us."

Betsy scrambled to her feet. "They'll discover the village. I must tell Jack. He cannot take us home yet."

"He better dadblamed well take us or I'll shoot him myself!"

Betsy squeezed her shoulder, no doubt feeling the tremors that Alice couldn't control, as though she'd been soaked and now huddled in the cold. "We must protect the village. Jack knows a thing or two about the river. It will be all right."

"But there's no *time*. And what if they can help—"

But Betsy had already released her and gone forward, and in a moment, the pitch of the engine changed, the great brass wheels in the stern digging into the water and increasing their speed against the powerful current. Now even a steam landau running wide open could not match them as the rocks and water slid by at a hectic pace.

Alice sagged onto the deck, her anxious gaze on Ian, not the Ranger ship. She should have stuck to her guns, and flagged the Rangers down when she had the chance. What had she been thinking—trusting the witches when other than Betsy, she had no reason to? Ian's beloved face blurred in her vision.

And then a shadow passed over them again, and the sun went out. With a gasp, she wiped her eyes with the heel of her hand and looked up.

Her mouth fell open.

The steamboat slid under an arch of red rock so massive that it was dwarfed to the size of a child's toy. On the far side, light played on the water of the main artery of the river, but as they passed through the opening of this smaller tributary, she felt the engines slow and echo from a great distance.

Betsy jumped down the steps from the wheelhouse. "Jack is going to bide here until they get tired of looking for us."

FIELDS OF IRON

"What is this place?" Her fear backed off just a fraction as she stared up ... and up ... to the ceiling of the natural chamber, where ripples of light seemed to dance and play.

"One of our little secrets." Betsy's lips, painted black with flowers at the corners, tilted up. "One of the very few we let the boatmen in on."

An eternity passed in which Ian's breathing became increasingly labored, and Alice's fear stampeded back in to seize up her lungs and burn the edges of her temper. Finally she could bear it no longer. She stomped up the iron stairs, thumbing on the lightning pistol as the filigree treads rang under her boots.

"Get this boat back to the village now," she rasped, "or I'll put a hole through you and do it myself."

The man who must be Jack turned from the wheel to face her. His eyes widened at the sight of the pistol. "What does that do?"

"You won't survive the answer," she snapped. "Get this tub moving."

"But the Rangers—"

"I don't care about the village, or the Rangers. All I care about is getting that bullet out of my husband before it's too late. *Now move!*"

Watching her as though she were a she-bear and he stood between her and her cub, Jack found the acceleration levers by feel alone. In a moment the pitch of the engines changed and they began to make way across the lake, heading for the bright daylight glow of the arch on the far side.

When they emerged, the skies were empty.

But Alice did not leave the wheelhouse. Instead, she kept the humming pistol aimed at the captain's left ear, her face grim. Her hand did not shake. But her heart was pounding in her chest, her legs quivering from more than the vibrating deck, and pride and fierce love were the only things holding her upright.

*

Watch for Fields of Gold, coming in early spring 2017!

About the Author

Shelley Adina is the author of 24 novels published by Harlequin, Warner, and Hachette, and a dozen more published by Moonshell Books, Inc., her own independent press. She writes steampunk and contemporary romance as Shelley Adina, and as Adina Senft, writes Amish women's fiction. She holds an MFA in Writing Popular Fiction from Seton Hill University in Pennsylvania, where she teaches as adjunct faculty. She won RWA's RITA Award® in 2005, and was a finalist in 2006. When she's not writing, Shelley is usually quilting, sewing historical costumes, or hanging out in the garden with her flock of rescued chickens.

SHELLEY ADINA

Also by Shelley Adina

STEAMPUNK

The Magnificent Devices series:
Lady of Devices
Her Own Devices
Magnificent Devices
Brilliant Devices
A Lady of Resources
A Lady of Spirit
A Lady of Integrity
A Gentleman of Means
Devices Brightly Shining (Christmas novella)
Fields of Air
Fields of Iron
Fields of Gold

ROMANCE

Moonshell Bay: The Men of CLEU
Call For Me
Dream of Me
Reach For Me

FIELDS OF IRON

Also in the Moonshell Bay series
Caught You Looking
Caught You Listening
Caught You Hiding

The Wedding Scandal
(a Four Weddings and a Fiasco novella)

PARANORMAL

Immortal Faith

YOUNG ADULT

The Glory Prep series:
Glory Prep
The Fruit of My Lipstick
Be Strong and Curvaceous
Who Made You a Princess?
Tidings of Great Boys
The Chic Shall Inherit the Earth

Printed in Poland
by Amazon Fulfillment
Poland Sp. z o.o., Wrocław